Luc leaned
swirling depth~~s of his emerald green eyes~~.

"Luc, kiss me," Linsey whispered. "Please?"

With a moan he complied, lowering his head to hers. He softly touched his lips to hers, tasting, sampling.

Linsey responded eagerly, urging him to deepen the kiss, but his teasing continued until she was nearly mindless, wanting more than the light kisses he was offering.

His lips left her mouth, gently moving to her neck and making a trail up her cheek, over her nose then back to her lips. He raised his head, his burning eyes meeting hers.

"If I make you mine, my angel, I may not be able to let you go in the spring." His voice was husky with his rapidly rising passion.

"Spring is far away," she replied in a whisper, "and I may not want to go. . . ."

HEARTFIRE ROMANCES

SWEET TEXAS NIGHTS   (2610, $3.75)
by Vivian Vaughan
Meg Britton grew up on the railroads, working proudly at her father's side. Nothing was going to stop them from setting the rails clear to Silver Creek, Texas—certainly not some crazy prospector. As Meg set out to confront the old coot, she planned her strategy with cool precision. But soon she was speechless with shock. For instead of a harmless geezer, she found a boldly handsome stranger whose determination matched her own.

CAPTIVE DESIRE   (2612, $3.75)
by Jane Archer
Victoria Malone fancied herself a great adventuress, but being kidnapped was too much excitement for even Victoria! Especially when her arrogant kidnapper thought she was part of Red Duke's outlaw gang. Trying to convince the overbearing, handsome stranger that she had been an innocent bystander when the stagecoach was robbed, proved futile. But when he thought he could maker her confess by crushing her to his warm, broad chest, by caressing her with his strong, capable hands, Victoria was willing to admit to anything. . . .

LAWLESS ECSTASY   (2613, $3.75)
by Susan Sackett
Abra Beaumont could spot a thief a mile away. After all, her father was once one of the best. But he'd been on the right side of the law for years now, and she wasn't about to let a man like Dash Thorne lead him astray with some wild plan for stealing the Tear of Allah, the world's most fabulous ruby. Dash was just the sort of man she most distrusted—sophisticated, handsome, and altogether too sure of his considerable charm. Abra shivered at the devilish gleam in his blue eyes and swore he would need more than smooth kisses and skilled caresses to rob her of her virtue . . . and much more than sweet promises to steal her heart!

Available wherever paperbacks are sold, or order direct from the Publisher. Send cover price plus 50¢ per copy for mailing and handling to Zebra Books, Dept. 3133, 475 Park Avenue South, New York, N.Y. 10016. Residents of New York, New Jersey and Pennsylvania must include sales tax. DO NOT SEND CASH.

AUTUMN ECSTASY

PAMELA K. FORREST

ZEBRA BOOKS
KENSINGTON PUBLISHING CORP.

ZEBRA BOOKS

are published by

Kensington Publishing Corp.
475 Park Avenue South
New York, NY 10016

First printing: September, 1990

Printed in the United States of America

To Bill with love
and
to Bob who isn't able to count footsteps,
but knows the true meaning of friendship . . .
thank you.

Chapter One

Ohio River Valley
Fall—1784

The softly gurgling water followed a gently meandering course, its calm journey a reminder of lazy summer days just past. A patchwork of color wove a tapestry in hues of red and gold through the trees. The leaves, their glorious shades fading and turning brown, rustled in a cool breeze that hinted of rapidly approaching winter.

Linsey MacAdams leaned against the rough bark of one of the giant trees lining the riverbank. Her gaze followed the path of a leaf as it relinquished its hold on life and aimlessly drifted down to the water below. Landing without sound, it twirled and swirled with the current, beginning its journey to a new destination. She envied the leaf its freedom and wondered, given the same opportunity, if she would have the courage to fling herself on the mercy of the murky river.

"Girlie? Where's Zeke's purty girlie?"

The tranquility of the moment was harshly shattered by the strident whine of a male voice that sent terror rippling down her spine. Watching him approach, she knew it was useless to fight the rope that tightly bound her wrists in front of her. Nonetheless Linsey struggled to avoid the dirt-encrusted fingers reaching toward her tangled auburn hair.

"Purty, purty," he chanted incessantly, wrapping the silken curls around his hand and watching them cascade like a russet waterfall through his stubby fingers.

Above the filthy gag they had put in her mouth, her emerald eyes glared at him with loathing. She felt the nausea burning in her throat as his hand left her hair to stroke her face.

"Soft girlie, soft purty," he muttered, tracing the slope of her cheek.

The overwhelming odor of his unwashed body left the taste of bile on her tongue. Trying to avoid him, attempting to free herself from his repulsive touch, Linsey fought the chafing rope, twisting and turning in its limited boundaries. Her long skirt entwined around her legs, making escape impossible. She recoiled from his encroaching hand, lost the support of the tree and sprawled faceup on the hard ground.

He took advantage of her helplessness, easily holding her down. His hand created its own trail, caressing her cheek and neck, hesitating momentarily before lowering to the feminine swell of her breasts. As his fingers closed over the mound, he whispered with a sigh, "Purty girlie, purty girlie."

The rancid smell of his breath clogged her throat; terror clouded her eyes when she realized that this time there would be no reprieve. The other trapper would not return in time to stop him.

Each night after setting up camp beside the river, the trapper named Jeb went to hunt the wild game for their evening meal. Left alone with this trapper, Linsey would try to ignore him as he sat beside her, hands dangling between bent knees, his eyes watching her every move. As if the passing of time had given him courage, one night he had hesitantly touched her hair. Stroking its softness, fascinated by its fiery color, he had been content as he repeated his chant of pretty, pretty. Usually it was long after Jeb left camp before this trapper found the courage to touch her. Tonight he had not waited, but had come to her almost as soon as Jeb was out of sight.

He painfully kneaded her breast with one hand while the other stroked the growing rigidity at his crotch. Spittle drooled down his chin and into his scraggly yellow beard. The frequently vacant look in his watery blue eyes was replaced by one of intense concentration as he began to unbutton the front of her dress.

"Purty girlie, purty girlie," he chanted endlessly, laboriously working open the first button.

With terror-wrought strength Linsey twisted away, mindless of her long hair tangled in the debris on the ground. Maybe if he couldn't unbutton her dress, he would stop, she thought. Maybe if she fought long enough, Jeb would return. She tried to pull the gag from her mouth hoping her screams for help would bring Jeb back to camp. She cursed the skirt that held her legs immobile.

"Holt still, girlie," he whined. He pulled her hands to the center of her chest, his wiry strength easily keeping them in place and holding her to the ground. Feverishly, he worked open several more buttons. Frustrated, when the last few would not cooperate with his clumsy fingers, he pulled until they popped from the dress and rolled to the dirt.

Linsey trembled with revulsion as he opened her

9

dress, licking his lips at the sight of her chemise-covered breasts. Horrified, she felt a finger trace the pink tip visible through the thin cotton. She screamed at his touch, the sound only a muffled groan.

"Purty, purty," Zeke crooned.

His foul breath assailed her nose, and spit beaded on his beard. Linsey moaned at the pain lancing through her as he cruelly squeezed the tender flesh. Tears of agony traced silent silver paths down her cheeks. Powerless to stop him, terrified by her own helplessness, she twisted on the leaf-covered ground, trying to bring both her arms and legs up to cover her chest.

No longer using a hand to hold her down, Zeke grabbed both breasts, kneading them, unconscious and uncaring of the pain his strong grasp was causing. As her skirt gave slightly, Linsey brought her legs up, kicking and twisting at the same time, catching him firmly in the stomach. The breath swooshed loudly from his chest as he rolled away.

Linsey was amazed by the agility of the normally slow-moving Zeke. He quickly stood and returned to her, dropping astride her hips.

"Ya hurt Zeke, girlie," he groaned, rubbing his stomach. "Ma ain't gonna be happy at you. Ma sez nobody's gonna hurt her baby boy."

The heaving of her chest as she tried to breathe brought his attention back to her breasts. With a sudden jerk, he ripped the lacy chemise to her waist, baring her creamy flesh. Linsey screamed.

"Zeke, leave 'er be," the quiet voice of command called over her shoulder. "Ya know Ma don't hold with forcing no women."

"But Jebby," Zeke whined, "ya done promised Zeke he could have a woman."

"This'n ain't for you," Jeb replied with gentle patience. "I done tolt you, this here gal is gonna bring us lots of money when we sell 'er downriver." Jeb dropped the rabbits hanging from his belt and walked over to his brother. He pulled Zeke off the trembling girl and smiled maliciously into her terrified eyes.

"Ain't she 'bout the purtiest little ole gal you done ever seed, Jebby?"

"Shet up, Zeke, and start gatherin' firewood like I tolt you to do afore I left camp."

Reluctant to leave the girl, Zeke continued staring at her, rubbing his crotch. "She's so soft, Jebby, just like that there puppy Ma gived me. I sure do like all that there red har of her'n."

"After we'ns sell 'er there'll be 'nough money for all the likker and white women ya want, Zeke."

"Hit just won't be the same, Jebby," he grumbled. Turning, he walked away, shoulders drooped, feet shuffling through the thick carpet of leaves and hands thrust deeply in his pockets. "I ain't never had me no white woman what's got red har, and she sure is purty."

Tears ran freely down Linsey's cheeks as she tried desperately to cover her bare breasts with her tied hands. Jeb's success in quickly finding the rabbits and returning to camp had saved her. But what about the next time? Some nights he was gone for hours. How could she defend herself from another attack by Zeke? Another attack that was sure to happen within the next few days.

"Saved you this time, girlie," Jeb said, an evil smile crossing his face. "Wouldn't stop him 'cept old Zeke there is just a mite bit tetched, and once he gets started with a woman he don't stop till she's daid."

Linsey attempted to wrap her cape around her shoulders, but her tied hands and trembling body made it an almost impossible task. Jeb watched her feeble efforts, enjoying her humiliation and offering no help.

"Yep," he continued, "old Zeke just keeps stickin' it to 'em till they's daid. He don't even stop then lessin' I pulls him off. I let him have the first woman we stole. Got most of the way to a tradin' post, and I thought to let him celebrate a little." He shook his head as if in irritation, but the evil smile spoke loudly of remembered pleasures. "A daid woman don't bring me no money. Had to go most of the way back to a big settlement afore we found 'nother one, and she tweren't nothin' more than a squaw. So's I gotta keep you away from him. But you give me any trouble, and I'll just tell ole Zeke to have his fun with ya."

He stared at the tangled mass of waist-length red hair, its color only slightly dulled by weeks of neglect. "Ole Zeke's right though, you sure is a purty thing. Wouldn't mind havin' ya for myself." His voice lowered to a whisper. "Might just find somethin' for him to do next settlement we comes to. Then you and me can has us a good time. I'll show you how a real man does it."

Linsey's eyes widened with the new threat. Until now she had not worried that Jeb would attack her since he ignored her most of the time. Seeing her partially nude body had aroused his interest. With fingers shaking convulsively, and hindered by the rope, she fought to work the buttons through their holes. She closed the dress to beneath her chin and pulled the hooded cape securely around her shoulders, hiding the gaping holes.

Jeb's eyes never left her, watching her struggles with an almost sadistic enjoyment. When she was covered, he turned, picked up the rabbits and walked toward the river. As he knelt, he spoke loudly enough for his voice to carry over the sound of the bubbling water.

"Zeke really loved that pup Ma gave him. Tweren't nothin' but a cur-dawg Ma got from a neighbor."

He raised his head, and a smirk tilted the corners of his mouth. With a sure movement of the knife, he gutted the carcass in his hands. "One day Zeke hugged it to death. Cried for near on to a week when we buried it out back of the house."

She turned her face away from him, trying to hide the repugnance she felt, not only from his words, but because of the hint of sadistic pleasure she had seen on his face when he disemboweled the rabbit. Useless tears coursed silently down her cheeks to be caught by the dirty scrap of material they had used as a gag. Now that Jeb was back in camp, she knew she was allowed to remove it. Her fingers picked at the knot behind her head, a tattered fingernail catching in the material and tearing to the quick. The pain was a small one when compared to the constant agony her life had become since she had been kidnapped by Zeke and Jeb.

Linsey had found that escape from her captors was impossible, and as the days flowed into weeks, her hopes of returning to Philadelphia dwindled with each passing mile.

Holding the cape tightly around her as if it were capable of providing protection, she rested her head against the tree. Absently rubbing her aching jaw, she tried to remember how many days it had been since they had stopped her stepmother's carriage, first killing Elizabeth and then taking Linsey captive. Her mind flickered away from the picture of Elizabeth's broken body flung carelessly onto the seat of her new carriage, while bright red blood trickled from her mouth onto the rich leather. Linsey had not wanted to accept Elizabeth's death but knew it was the only reason she had been left behind. Jeb and Zeke wanted women to auc-

13

tion off to the longhunters. Elizabeth, with her sparkling blue eyes, tiny, perfectly formed body and golden blond hair, would have brought a big price.

Linsey blinked away her tears as she vividly remembered that day and Elizabeth's excitement over the carriage that had been delivered only two hours earlier. She could still hear Elizabeth's voice as she pleaded with Linsey to take a ride with her.

"Please, Linny?" Elizabeth's deep blue eyes glittered with excitement, and dimples peeked enticingly from the corners of her mouth. "Just a short ride; we won't go through town, just out to the country and back."

"Elizabeth, I'm not dressed for a ride," Linsey replied, pointing out the cotton day dress and house slippers she was wearing. "Besides, in another hour or so it will be dark."

"Oh, please?" Elizabeth pleaded. "I promise no one will see you."

Since her father's death, Linsey had become very protective of Elizabeth and found she could not refuse her tiny, pretty stepmother's slightest request. Smiling her reluctant agreement, Linsey returned to her room to change her shoes and pick up her serviceable wool cape. Innocently, she stepped outside to the new carriage—and certain death for Elizabeth.

True to her word, Elizabeth directed the matched pair of bays away from town, following the winding, tree-lined road into the country. The well-sprung carriage handled well, its heavily padded seats cushioning the larger jolts. The wind tore at their hair, pulling it free from its pins until gold strands mingled with auburn, making them appear to be a dancing wave of fire.

Giggling like a mischievous child, Elizabeth pulled to the side of the road, insisting that Linsey take a turn driving the carriage. As they were trading places, Jeb and Zeke appeared from behind the trees. Each man grabbed a woman, his filthy hand over her mouth so that she could not scream and possibly alert a nearby traveler. Linsey and Elizabeth were both small women, but they fought with all their strength. It was fate that Linsey looked toward her stepmother at the instant Zeke's handling became fatally rough. A sound like the snapping of a twig filled the air, and suddenly for Elizabeth the fight was finished. Her head hung at an odd angle from her slender neck, her eyes staring sightlessly at the azure sky.

Linsey struggled even harder to escape her captor and go to the aid of Elizabeth. She refused to accept what her rational mind told her was true. A well-aimed blow turned the nightmare scene to darkness as she sank unconscious to the ground.

Linsey cursed the unfairness of life. Only six years older than her own nineteen, Elizabeth was much too young to have been married, widowed and now dead. She should have gotten married again, to a man much younger than her first husband. She should have had the joy of children, the knowledge of being loved and adored by her family.

Forgetting, if only for the moment, that she was heading farther and farther into the wilderness, Linsey mourned the death of the woman who had been not only her stepmother but a dear friend as well.

Laying on the ground where they had left her, Linsey watched the dappled colors of the autumn leaves above her head. A chorus of sounds played soothingly around her: the bubbling of the water as it danced against the bank, the wind rustling through the leaves, a whippoorwill's plaintive call. Her thoughts were anything but peaceful, and her agitation grew when she

15

once more tried to recount the number of days they had traveled. Linsey soon realized that each day had blended into the next until she was no longer certain of the number. They had walked for several days before reaching the river and the poor excuse for a boat. Jeb seemed in no hurry to arrive at his destination, letting the dilapidated flatboat drift with the current.

At the beginning, they had passed several settlements, and Linsey had hoped to attract attention. Jeb prevented her by throwing a rotting fur over her and warning her against making any noise. Her fear of him had been too great, and she cursed her own meekness at cowering before his threats.

Linsey's thoughts returned to the present when Zeke entered the camp with an armload of firewood. Not wanting to attract the attention of any roving Indians, he quickly made a smokeless fire. The Shawnee normally stayed on the other side of the river, but Jeb took no chances. He used the fire only long enough to cook their meager dinner.

When the rabbits were cooking, Jeb turned once more to his captive. "Time for us to take a little walk, girlie." He grinned behind blackened and broken teeth as he untied her.

Linsey climbed clumsily to her feet, rubbing gently at the raw skin of her wrists. She turned her back on his leering face and headed away from the river. At the beginning she had thought she would die of embarrassment when she discovered he would not allow her the privacy of even a few minutes alone. She knew he would just sneer if she asked him to leave her. She had tried, at first, but begging and pleading seemed to increase his feeling of power. Now, after weeks of having his sharp eyes on her, she simply turned her back and did what was necessary.

"That's far 'nough." Jeb smirked as he watched the blush crawl up the side of her neck. He leaned against the nearest tree, spitting a stream of tobacco into the dirt at his feet, and licked at the juice on his lips. "Ya know what we comed out here for, so get to hit."

Keeping her back to him, she used her cape as a shield from his prying eyes. Since the evening of the carriage ride, she had lived a nightmare. This was only another part.

Linsey quickly readjusted her clothing and walked back to camp. Kneeling at the edge of the river, she cupped the water in her hands and splashed it on her face and neck.

Letting the cool water flow soothingly around her battered wrists, she looked past the river to the far side. By rights of an oft broken treaty, it belonged solely to the Shawnee. If she could swim, she'd go to their side and throw herself on their mercy. Even facing the hostile savage known for his hate of the white race was preferable to facing the fate planned for her by Jeb. A quick death by one of their arrows would be a blessing in comparison to being sold to a trapper somewhere downriver.

"That's 'nough, girlie," Jeb called from the fire, his leering eyes never leaving her back. "If'n ya wants your supper, ya'd better get your purty butt over here."

Sighing at the if's and maybe's that now filled her life, Linsey took a last longing look at the far bank.

"Six of one, two three's of another." She murmured the phrase so often used by her father, her voice sounding rusty from disuse. Rising from her knees, she walked back to the campfire.

She accepted the plate and cup Jeb handed her. She was far past being revolted by their eating habits or by

17

the fact that the meat they gave her to eat was half raw. Even the grunting, slurping sounds made by Zeke no longer affected her.

Sitting on the hard, cold ground with the plate balanced on her lap, Linsey wondered if she had ever really sat at a table with sparkling crystal and polished silver. Had she worn gowns of fine silk and delicate lace? Was the past only a dream, a means to escape the reality of the present? Or was this a dream, a nightmare, never to be broken by the dawn of a new day. Wanting to cry, knowing tears were useless, she ate the undercooked meat to stave off her hunger for the past.

While Linsey nibbled on the rabbit, she watched the men begin to settle the camp for the night. The ritual had been established the first night on the trail and never varied. Jeb hunted, cleaned and cooked the meal. Zeke gathered firewood, built the fire and then, after the meal, cleaned the metal plates and cups they used.

She watched Zeke wipe the plates and cups with the tail of his buckskin shirt. The first time she had seen him clean up, she had been so repulsed she had not eaten for two days. Now it was simply another of the many things she accepted. The cups and plates that had been nearly new at the beginning of their journey were now dull and battered, and at each meal she tried not to think about how truly dirty they were.

As Zeke cleaned up, Jeb kicked dirt over the fire and checked that the flatboat was secured for the night. Once more her wrists were retied. Jeb used a long rope at night. He tied one end to his own wrist, and she had discovered the slightest tug on it would wake him.

Linsey settled as far away from Jeb as the rope would allow. She wrapped her cape around her and with a grimace of distaste pulled the tattered fur over her. Jeb and Zeke each used new wool blankets that were beginning to show signs of wear.

Diamond bright stars played hide and seek behind fluffy moonlit clouds as the night sky darkened. Loud snores from Zeke's side of camp echoed reassuringly to Linsey. She wiggled, trying to find a little softness somewhere, but as she had discovered every night since the beginning of her nightmare journey, the ground was unrelenting in its hardness. She counted the stars she could see peeking through the clouds and the overhanging trees, hoping to clear her mind of thought until sleep could envelop her in its blessed oblivion.

"We'uns should pass Big Jim's tradin' post sometime tomorrow," Jeb said quietly. "If'n there be 'nough trappers around, I may just decide to holt me a little sale." He snickered as if sensing the fear that threatened to consume her.

"I'm still willing to pay you if you'll return me to Philadelphia," Linsey replied, trying to hide the quiver in her voice. It was an offer she made daily—and he ignored.

"I done tolt ya, girl, I ain't gonna take ya back," Jeb snarled.

"I don't understand why you continue to refuse," Linsey said. "I'm willing to pay you considerably more than you'll make if you auction me off somewhere."

"Shet up, girl. I ain't takin' ya back!"

"Why?" she whispered, her voice laced with ill-concealed desperation.

Jeb snorted, "Sure you'd pay me! And afore I could get out of town your Pa'd come a'lookin' for me. May not make me as much with the hunters, but I'll be alive to spend it.

"Sure is gonna be one mighty happy trapper this winter," he taunted softly. " 'Course hits gonna cost 'im a mite, but I figure how he'll think hits worth hit once he gets hisself atween your legs."

His snickering laugh made her cringe. "Yep, I reckon just 'bout any of them trappers would be mighty pleased to winter with ya. Gits a mite bit cold 'round here during the winter, and you're 'nough to warm any man's feet. 'Course hit ain't my feet I'd want ya to warm. No siree, my feet wouldn't even know they's cold if'n I had ya on a long winter night."

Linsey bit her bottom lip to stop the tears rimming her eyes from rolling down her face. She would not give him the satisfaction of knowing her terror. To spend the winter alone at the mercy of a stranger, knowing he could, and probably would, use her in any manner he saw fit! To be sold, given no choice, to lose her freedom!

A rustling of leaves followed by a contented sigh told her Jeb had settled himself for the night. "Don't reckon I mind if'n theys nobody at Big Jim's tomorrow. That'll give me a time to have ya for myself."

Linsey was unaware of the cool breeze playing across her face and teasing the hair around her nape. Tomorrow. It would bring escape from one situation and send her into something that could be far worse. She wondered which was worse; to be sold to an unknown trapper or to be used repeatedly by Jeb. Neither situation was one she would willingly chose for herself, and yet one of them would be fact by the next evening. Linsey tossed and turned, trying to escape her thoughts.

"Lay still, girlie, or we just might see if'n we can do it without waking Zeke. Reckon if'n I put the gag back in your mouth, it'd keep ya quiet like."

Linsey froze, afraid to move a muscle for fear Jeb would make good his threat. Night passed slowly, Jeb's snores soon mingled with the sounds of the night creatures, reassuring her that he slept. She drifted in and out of sleep—praying desperately that tomorrow would not come, certain it would be easier to face death than the new day.

The feeling of being watched woke Linsey from a restless sleep the next morning. Zeke hunkered down beside her and reached for a tendril of hair peeking from beneath the fur.

"Purty, purty," he mumbled softly, wrapping it around his hand.

"Zeke, leave 'er be," Jeb called patiently. "Come eat so ya can get things loaded in the boat. We's got 'portant things to do today."

"Please, Jebby?" Zeke whined as he unwrapped her hair from his hand. "Zeke'll be real careful. Just one time?"

Jeb patted his brother on the back and lightly pushed him toward the fire. Not once in all the weeks of travel had Linsey seen Jeb lose patience with his brother, always treating Zeke with a parental gentleness.

"Not this un, Zeke," he said quietly. "But I promise ya we'll find ya one even better after we's sold her."

"Hit just won't be the same, Jebby," Zeke grumbled, sadly shaking his head as he walked away. "Hit just won't be the same."

Their breakfast consisted of warmed-up, left-over rabbit and weak coffee. After the meal, Jeb pushed Linsey to the boat. She settled into the spot in a corner that had become hers. Jeb tied both her wrists and ankles this time and replaced the gag.

They slid leisurely away from the bank and into the current, letting the flow of the water send them downstream. Using a long pole, Jeb would occasionally push

21

away from the bank when the boat floated from the center of the river.

Zeke sat at the front, his loaded rifle across his lap, a piece of wood and a pocketknife held lightly in his hands. Linsey had discovered that Zeke, so clumsy and inept in doing the simplest tasks, took on an amazingly natural grace and dexterity with a pocketknife. She had spent many days of travel watching as he carved small animals in minute detail. A tiny squirrel clutching an acorn between its paws or a mountain cat poised delicately, ready to spring on its prey, each was carved with the accuracy and care of the finest craftsman.

A small pouch, containing his most prized carvings, was tied by a rope at his waist. When he wasn't involved in making the creatures, Zeke would open it and spend hours happily talking to and playing with them.

Linsey had spent hours staring at the pouch, trying to decide from what it had been made. It had no seams; the draw string was woven through holes punched in the top. One day, in horrified revulsion, she watched as Zeke held it upside down and played with the tip on the bottom. That was the day she knew without a doubt that the pouch was a woman's breast.

This morning Linsey's terror of what the day would bring would not allow her to appreciate his artistry or the shadowed beauty of her surroundings. Even her usual disgust at the sight of the pouch was missing. Leaning her head against the rough wood of the boat, she closed her eyes. Nothing or no one would help her. Her life, her very existence, was in the hands of two worthless men: one with the wily cunning of a fox, one lacking the basic intelligence of most of God's creatures.

She had even given up praying.

* * *

The lack of sleep the night before combined with the sun flickering through the trees and the quiet lapping of the water against the sides of the boat lulled her. When Jeb nudged her with his foot, she was startled to discover she had fallen asleep, hours had passed and they were entering the boundaries of a small settlement.

Two small log cabins sat to each side of a larger one. They were connected by a dogtrot and were surrounded by a log stockade whose massive gates stood open. The trees had been cleared away from the cabins, allowing the men inside an unimpeded view of anyone approaching by foot or water. Several longboats and canoes were pushed up on shore or tied to trees a short distance away.

"Looks like we'ns might have us a sale after all, girlie." A pleased smirk rode his thin lips as Jeb picked up the long pole from the bottom of the boat and pushed toward the bank. "Yes siree, I'd say there's a might good number of trappers a gettin' ready for winter." He turned from his study of the settlement to give her a malignant grin. "I'ma thinkin' they's gonna be plum tickled with my offeren."

His chuckle grated down Linsey's back, his words strengthening her ever present terror. Always having loved life and finding joy in her surroundings, she felt no guilt in now wishing for death.

Jeb jumped from the boat and tied it to the nearest tree. "Stay here till I get back, Zeke. I'm gonna make certain there's 'nough buyers for our goods." He smiled evilly at Linsey before turning to walk away.

"But Jebby, I wants to go too!" Zeke called in a woebegone voice.

"Ya gots to guard her. They'll be plentiful time for ya later."

23

Linsey watched him walk out of sight. Zeke grumbled like a small child denied a special treat, pouting and giving her accusing looks. She scanned the trees in the distance and wondered if she could somehow escape, losing herself in their concealing cover.

If only her hands and feet weren't tied. If only she could get a knife to release herself. Linsey leaned her head back, staring at the overhanging trees. If only she had never taken that ride with Elizabeth!

Might as well wish for the moon, she thought. With Zeke standing guard it would be as easy to grow wings and fly away as it would be to untie the ropes and run to the trees. Zeke might be "a little tetched" as Jeb called it, but even he would question her request for a knife!

Jeb returned quickly, a grin splitting his face from ear to ear. "Welp, girlie, looks like we's gonna have a sale!"

He climbed back into the boat, untied her ankles but left the rope on her wrists and the gag in her mouth. With a yank he pulled her to her feet. "Won't do no good to try and run. Ole Zeke here is a mighty good shot, and he'll have his gun real handy like." He watched as the last dwindling hope faded from her eyes. " 'Course he won't kill ya. Ya wouldn't bring us no money thata way. No siree, Zeke'll just aim for one of your legs to slow ya down a mite. Them trappers ain't gonna care 'bout your legs none, only what's atween 'em!"

He chuckled at his own crude wit as he pushed her from the boat. Keeping a firm hold on her arm, he led her toward the largest of the cabins.

Several men were sitting on the porch while others were milling around in front of it. Their conversations halted slowly as one by one they saw Linsey and Jeb approach. Zeke followed a few steps behind them, his rifle cradled in his arms.

Jeb pulled her to a tree stump the size of a table and lifted her onto it. Turning, he bowed theatrically to his audience and pointed toward her.

"Welp, gents, din't I promise ya a special treat?"

The dirt and grime of weeks of travel could not hide the natural beauty Linsey possessed. Accustomed to women aged beyond their years by the hardships of life on the frontier or the women of the various Indian tribes, few of the men had ever glimpsed such rare beauty. Speechless, they stared at her with longing.

Hunters by choice, each man would spend the long winter in his secluded cabin running traplines. In the spring they would bring the furs to the trading posts, selling them or trading them for supplies. Some of the men turned to farming during the summer to raise the food they needed.

A few had families waiting for their return, but most of the men were single, living for a short time in one place before moving on. It was a lonely life, sometimes isolated for months at a time. All of them, even the ones with wives waiting for their return, nurtured the thought of owning such a woman and spending the long, cold winter discovering her charms.

Linsey stood on the stump, the cape around her shoulders, her eyes focused on the thin stream of smoke coming from the chimney of the largest cabin. She followed its wispy trail as it merged with the gray sky, knowing it was impossible for her to follow it but wishing just the same.

"Ever seed anything this purty?" Jeb asked as he pulled the hood from her hair, causing fiery streams of red and gold to ruffle around her.

As a group, the men sighed, each wanting to run his

25

fingers through the glorious mane's promise of warmth and feel it tangled around his body.

Jeb's movement startled Linsey, bringing her back from her futile thoughts of escape. Her green eyes wandered from one man to another, desperate to find in one the hope of rescue. Each of them looked identical to the others, different only in age. From one who could be no more than fourteen to one whose age could have been anywhere under one hundred, each was dressed in baggy buckskins, stiff with dirt, stained with the dried blood of their trade. Except for the very young trapper whose face was smooth, all wore beards of various lengths. In their eyes, Linsey saw only one thing—lust.

"Sure would cherish gettin' me a handful a her," the youngest trapper said loudly to the man standing next to him. He gestured obscenely with his hands, drawing a laugh from the crowd.

"Ya wouldn't be a'knowin' what to do with prime goods like her, boy," another man called.

"Doin' is learnin'," he replied good-naturedly. "What I don't know now I'd sure be a'knowin' once winter was done."

"She'd be better off with me," one of the older trappers commented. "I'd break 'er in real gentle-like."

"Ya'd be daid come spring, Sam!"

Sam leaned against the rail of the porch, spit a stream of tobacco juice on the ground and rubbed his crotch. "Yep, mayhaps, but I'd be happy daid."

The good-natured ribaldry continued for some time, and a fiery blush spread across Linsey's face at the comments. The trappers boasted about what they would like to do to her, inciting each other on to even greater obscenities. Occasionally Jeb would throw in a word or two to spur them on.

Linsey watched as another trapper came out of the cabin, limped to the porch steps and leaned negligently against a post. His buckskins were as baggy and as dirty as any, and his gray beard hung down to his chest. When he removed his cap, she gasped at the still red, angry-looking scar that circled the top of his head where hair should have been. His face was a mass of unnatural wrinkles, as if the skin had lost its anchoring and had slipped downward. His brows hung so far over his eyes, she wondered if they hampered his vision . . . until she met the blazing clarity of his eyes.

He did not join in with the other trappers, and no smile crossed his face at the coarse comments falling around him. Watching closely, Linsey realized the other trappers were carefully ignoring him, sending quick leery glances in his direction that never invited his participation. His expression was not one of lust, as the others were, but rather another emotion, one she could only describe to herself as hatred. He had no reason to hate her, but his gaze never left hers. He didn't appear to be interested in her the way the others were, and yet. . . . Linsey shivered at the thought of being owned by him.

When the old man's bitter, burning gaze did not waver, Linsey lifted her chin in determination, her eyes never flinching from his. He nodded his head once as if he saw her show of spirit and approved.

"I'll be a'sellin' 'er to the man what pays me the most," Jeb called loudly, bringing Linsey's attention back to the men surrounding her.

"Show us more," the young trapper called. "Ain't buying no pig in a poke. Might be she's ugly from the neck down."

When the others joined in agreement, Jeb tugged lightly on the cape, and it slithered from her shoulders

27

to land in a mound at her feet. Untying Linsey's wrists, he pulled them behind her back and tightly retied them. His eyes briefly met hers, and he read the intensity of her hatred flaring in them.

"Good thing for me ya ain't got no knife," he taunted. "I'd say right now ya'd gut me with no nary-a-mind."

Giving his audience a big grin, Jeb jerked on the neckline of her dress, ripping it and her tattered chemise to her waist.

The vulgar comments escalated in their crudity as the trappers stared at the firmly upthrust breasts bared to their view. Linsey tried to use her hair as a shield from their devouring gazes, but Jeb easily swept it back over her shoulders.

The trappers surged forward, each wanting to be the first to touch the creamy, tempting flesh. Linsey backed away from their reaching hands only to be stopped by Jeb, who was standing behind her.

"Now gents, no touchin' the goods." He smirked, stepping up beside her and running his hands down her body. He brutally squeezed a chill-puckered nipple, grinning at her moan of pain. "She feels mighty fine, but ya gotta pay for hit afore ya touch hit."

"Is she virgin?" the trapper named Sam called. "Got me a mighty thirst for bustin' 'em open."

"Wal now, cain't be a'sayin' for certain. Only knows me and my brother Zeke ain't touched her."

"Let's find out!"

"Now ya know I cain't be a'lettin' ya do that. It'd be for certain she warn't then."

Mouths watering and eyes glistening with lust, the men began bidding. Jeb kept a wary eye on the old man on the porch. Most of the trappers were nameless drifters, but the old man was well known, as was his reputation. He was not a person to cross—if you wanted to live to see another day.

Jeb continued running his free hand over Linsey, squeezing viciously. The feel of her soft skin beneath his hand brought a burning need to his loins. He pulled her against him, rubbing his hardness against her bottom.

Through her skirt Linsey could feel the thrusting of a foreign rigidity. The humiliation of his abuse was worse than any nightmare. Never had she imagined being stripped and molested in front of a group of men while they bid on her. Jeb seemed to delight in causing her as much pain as possible as he repeatedly squeezed her breasts, laughing softly each time she moaned. Linsey closed her eyes; her determination faltered. She was too horrified to cry as utter hopelessness encased her in a delusion of safety and her mind slipped closer to the edge of insanity.

"Seems to me ya oughter sell 'er to all of us," suggested one of the trappers, realizing his wife would never allow him to buy Linsey and he'd never have a chance to touch that soft, creamy flesh.

Jeb stiffened. If he sold her to someone different each time, then he'd have plenty of opportunity to have her himself. After seeing her stripped to the waist and feeling her soft skin, he knew the whores of the nearest settlement would not satisfy the growing urge he felt. Someday she would no longer be beautiful. He'd use her until her looks were gone. There'd be time to sell her then. There was always a trapper willing to pay for a white woman, even if she was a little worse for wear.

"That there surely is a good idee," he mumbled. "Make me all kinds of money if'n I sold ya for an hour or two to each of 'em."

Linsey snapped out of her protective trance as if

29

she'd been slapped. Her eyes widened, and she began to shake her head. No! she screamed silently. He wouldn't . . . couldn't. . . . Even as she denied it, her frantic gaze met his, and she knew he would. The thought of existing as Jeb suggested was more than she could endure. Quietly Linsey promised herself that before the first man could touch her she would find a way to end her life.

" 'Course I'd have to keep ya away from Zeke. I guess if'n ya din't behave yourself, I'd just let him have ya a time or two."

Her decision gave Linsey the strength to ignore Jeb's threats. She proudly raised her head, and just as a queen surveys her subjects, Linsey looked at the faces beneath her. She saw that they liked the idea almost as much as buying her solely for themselves. Buying her for an hour or so would not cost as much and would give each of them a chance with her that they otherwise would not have.

The old trapper moved from his place on the porch and headed back into the cabin. He quickly returned, his pack firmly on his back and his rifle cradled in his arms. Covering the ugly scar on his head with his cap, he elbowed his way through the men until he was standing at the tree stump.

"I'ma buyin' 'er," he said quietly, but firmly enough for everyone to hear.

Jeb saw his visions of great wealth fade away. "Now wait here just a damn minute—"

"I left two dollars inside with Big Jim." As the old man bent and picked up Linsey's cape, his eyes never left Jeb's

"Two dollars!" Jeb smirked. "Ya think I'ma gonna let ya take her for two dollars when I ken make me lots more'n that?"

"Ya ain't got no choice." He turned so that the rifle, still cradled in his arms, pointed directly at Jeb. "Ya ain't got no way a stoppin' me." He patted the gun with his free hand. "Molly here speaks with a loud voice. Now untie the girl."

Keeping a wary eye on the rifle, Jeb untied Linsey, his mind working feverishly. Reputation or not, somehow he had to prevent the old man from stealing her away.

"Down here, girl," the trapper said quietly, offering her no help as she jumped from the stump and reached for the cape he held out. "Turn around."

She drew the cape around her shoulders, grateful for its concealing thickness, and turned her back. Kaleb deftly untied the gag with his free hand. He pulled it from her mouth and looked at the filthy, dirty scrap of material. His eyes spoke volumes as he wadded it up and threw it into Jeb's face.

Free of the ropes and gag, Linsey stepped behind him, careful not to get between Jeb and the gun. The idea of belonging to the old man no longer seemed repulsive. Almost anything had to be better than Jeb's idea of selling her to all of the men. Perhaps this man would take her back to Philadelphia; maybe he was her salvation.

The other trappers backed away from the old man. They would let Jeb fight his own battles. They, too, knew his reputation and would wait for the outcome. The girl was not worth dying for.

The trapper turned his back to Jeb and Zeke and pushed Linsey toward the river. They had taken only a few steps when Jeb's angry bellow reached them.

"Ya cain't just walk off with my prop'ty!"

Pulling Linsey to a stop, the old man turned and stared at Jeb. Silence filled the camp. Four words were

31

spoken in a quiet voice that thundered through the air. With each one, Jeb seemed to shrink into himself, growing smaller before her eyes.

"She's for the Bear."

Chapter Two

Linsey watched the reactions of the trappers with bewilderment. As if the name Bear was an incentive, they suddenly seemed eager to return to their own affairs. They had drifted away from the stump during the argument between Jeb and the old man; but now some went inside the cabins, and a few shouldered their packs, making signs of leaving the settlement. They appeared totally unaware of Jeb's anger or Linsey's presence.

Zeke no longer stood quietly near the stump. He sidled close to his brother, his eyes darting from one spot to another as if he expected to see someone—or something—appear magically from the shadows. Jeb's look of fury melted to one of barely hidden fear.

"Ya cain't take her to the Bear," he whined.

The old man said nothing at first, his observant eyes noting the actions of the other trappers. "I'm beholdin' to the Bear." His voice was soft—deadly soft. "Kaleb Smith ain't a'owin' no man."

He turned his keen look to Linsey, seeing the apprehension and fear in her eyes. He remembered her fiery red hair and the soft, creamy flesh now hidden by the

33

cape. He turned back to Jeb. "Hit'll be a makin' us even."

"But . . . but I brung 'er all the way from 'delphie. I pertected 'er, kept 'er alive. Ya cain't just walk off with 'er!"

"I paid for 'er. Now she's belongin' to the Bear." Kaleb grinned sarcastically, startling white teeth sparkling between snearing lips. "If'n I 'members right, you tangled with the Bear a couple year back. Are you a'wantin' to try your luck with him agin by takin' his prop'ty?"

Jeb stepped back at the mention of the fight he'd had with the Bear. Not that it had been much of a fight. He remembered that with one mighty swing of a powerful right arm the Bear had sent him flying across the room to land in a heap against the far wall. His ears had rung for three days, and his head had hurt for over a week.

"We've got a debt to settle," Kaleb said quietly, his voice ringing with threatening promise. "After I see the girl to the Bear, I'll be back fer you. Ya can run far and fast but keep lookin' behind ya 'cause I'll be there."

Jeb's face whitened until it totally lacked color. Next to the Bear, Kaleb Smith was the last person he wanted to cross. All the rumors about the two men were firmly founded in fact. And somehow, somewhere, he had done something to cause Kaleb to hold a grudge. Jeb cared little about what he'd done, his prime concern was to get away before Kaleb could return and begin tracking him.

Kaleb turned and once again pushed Linsey down the trail toward the river. He settled her in the front of a well-made canoe, placed his pack and gear in the center and pushed away from the shore. He swiftly

34

jumped into the rear, picked up the paddle and guided the craft into the current.

Jeb watched his chance for riches disappear downstream. He made no attempt to stop them, even though Zeke could have easily shot the old man from that distance. There were too many witnesses that Kaleb had bought the girl for the Bear, and Jeb had no doubt that somehow the Bear would hear about it and come looking for her. Jeb decided to run from Kaleb's threat rather than have to face the Bear some future day. Only a stupid man knowingly tangled with the Bear. He had been stupid once.

"The Bear, Jebby," Zeke whined. "Where's the Bear?" His wildly moving eyes searched the area. "Zeke don't want to see the Bear. Don't let him hurt Zeke, Jebby."

"Shet up, Zeke," Jeb snarled, for once losing his patience with his brother. "The Bear ain't here. The old man done took our gal to him."

"Zeke scaired of the Bear, Jebby." He moved closer to Jeb, cowering at his side. "Ken we go somewhere's else?"

"The Bear ain't here!" Jeb looked at his brother with disgust and walked toward the cabin, mumbling with each step at the loss of the woman and at the building fear of reprisal from the old man. He felt that it had something to do with the women he regularly stole and sold to the longhunters. Everyone had to make a living, he justified to himself as he hastily made plans to leave the trading post.

Traveling in the well-maintained canoe was vastly different from the decaying flatboat. Linsey no longer had to worry about keeping her feet dry since water didn't trickle into the bottom of it. She felt her legs stiffen because of the folded position she was forced to use but Kaleb had not tied her, and Linsey relished the freedom.

Not content to drift with the current as Jeb had been, Kaleb paddled with a steady, powerful rhythm, putting mile after mile behind them.

Linsey tried not to think about her new fate. Obviously the old man had no intention of keeping her for himself, but no amount of questioning enlightened her to his plans. She knew only what she had heard him tell Jeb. He was taking her to the Bear. *Who, or what, is the Bear,* she wondered. The very mention of him had been enough to prevent Jeb from stopping them.

Tired beyond anything she had ever felt, exhausted by the weeks of travel and fear, Linsey let her mind drift as aimlessly as the gray clouds overhead. The river was alive with the sounds of nature: the raucous squawking of jays, the chattering of squirrels. Rounding a bend, they startled a buck at the river's edge. His proud head rose at their unexpected approach. He observed them for a moment before bounding away in a graceful flash of reddish brown.

Ever present was the hypnotically soothing rhythm of Kaleb's paddle rising and lowering to the water, moving them rapidly closer to their destination. The temperature dropped steadily as the afternoon grew later, and she began to shiver beneath the woolen cape.

"Take this, girl." Kaleb handed her a blanket from the bundle in the bottom of the canoe.

Linsey wrapped it around her head and shoulders. It was old, well used and smelled of wood smoke; but nothing crawled out of the folds, and she was grateful for its warmth.

When darkness made traveling dangerous, Kaleb

guided the canoe to the riverbank and jumped out. He made no effort to help her, and Linsey found her legs stiff and movement difficult after the long hours of sitting.

Kaleb ignored her as he went about setting up camp. She moved closer to the fire he lit and warmed her hands in its welcome heat. She watched him expertly prepare their meal from the food he had stored in the bottom of the canoe.

"Where are we headed?" she asked, hoping he would give her an answer this time. She had asked the same question numerous times already, but he had chosen not to answer.

"North."

Linsey sighed. It wasn't much of an answer. Accepting the plate he held out to her, she wondered if she was any better off with him than she had been with Jeb.

After they had eaten, Kaleb extinguished the fire and handed her a thick fur that was softer than velvet. "It'll be a long day tomorrow. Best be gettin' some sleep."

She took the fur, wrapping it and the blanket around her so that only her nose was exposed to the cold night air. From the sounds in the darkness, Linsey could tell that Kaleb was following his own advice.

"Aren't you going to tie me?"

"Nope."

Linsey's heart increased its tempo. "Aren't you afraid I'll try to escape?"

"Nope."

Freedom! She could almost taste its sweet flavor! Immediately, plans for escape began to formulate in her mind. She would wait until he was asleep, then quietly leave camp. Snuggling beneath the fur, she made a mental list of the things she would need to take along to assure survival. She had little fear of getting lost. Jeb had followed the river, so all she would need to do was keep it in sight. She didn't try to fool herself; it would not be easy to travel the distance by herself, but she had to try.

Food would be a major problem. She had no knowledge of hunting, cleaning or cooking wild game. In fact, she had no idea how to start a fire. Linsey decided she would have to depend on finding berries. It would be monotonous diet, but she'd manage if it meant she'd be going home! Almost at its inception she discarded the idea of using the canoe as a means of transportation. Since she had no idea of how to paddle or guide it, the canoe would be a hindrance rather than a help.

Kaleb shifted in the darkness, abruptly bringing Linsey back to the present. She would have to pretend she was asleep so that he would relax and sleep. Otherwise she might lose her only chance to escape.

"Don't forget a knife." Kaleb's soft voice shattered the stillness. "Hit's in the canoe."

"What?" Linsey asked, startled.

In the darkness, Kaleb smiled to himself. He would have been disappointed if the girl hadn't planned escape; he'd figured her for a spunky thing. If he'd had the time, he would have let her travel by herself for a day or so, staying just far enough behind her so that she wasn't aware of his presence. Even a day or two alone in the wilderness taught invaluable lessons.

"Won't give ya much pertection, but hit might be a help."

"Protection?" He couldn't know of her plans! She had said nothing to alert him of her plans for escape.

"Watch out for snakes."

"Snakes?" Linsey shivered, drawing her feet beneath her and trying to search the dark.

"Yep. They don't take too good to bein' stepped on when they's sleepin'."

Linsey listened to the sounds of the wind rustling through the leaves on the ground. Or was it the wind? Could it be a snake slithering ever closer to the warmth of her body?

"Knife might do on a snake if'n ya get close 'nough and aim real careful-like, but hit'd be like pissin' in the wind if'n ya meet up with a bear."

"Bear?"

"Yep. Bes' thin' to do is climb a tree—if'n there's one close 'nough."

"Oh, my God."

" 'Course a tree won't do ya no good a'tall if'n hits an Injun you're runnin' from."

"Indians. . . ." Linsey's voice lowered to an agonized whisper.

"Best mind ya don't get lost and wander to their huntin' grounds. Them Injun bucks surely would like that there hair of yours."

Stillness settled around her; even the wind quieted its whisper. She could not escape. She was as much of a captive as ever, even without the rope bindings.

Knowing sleep would be elusive, Linsey snuggled into her coverings, relishing their welcome warmth.

"Good night, Kaleb," she sighed dejectedly.

" 'Night."

In the early afternoon of the third day of traveling the river, Kaleb beached the canoe. He pulled it fully onto the sandy shore, unloaded a portion of its contents and covered it with branches and leaves. Without speaking to Linsey, he shouldered his pack, cradled his rifle and started walking. As the bitterly cold wind

39

played with her long skirt, she had no choice . . . she followed.

For two days Linsey tried to keep up with the taciturn old man who spoke only when giving directions. By the end of the first full day of walking, she no longer asked about their destination. Her only concerns became putting one foot in front of the other and not losing sight of Kaleb.

When they made camp at night, Kaleb no longer lit a fire, and Linsey soon wondered if she would ever again be warm. Even the heavy fur she kept snugly wrapped around her seemed to provide little protection from the constantly blowing cold wind.

Head down, doggedly putting one foot in front of the other, Linsey was not aware Kaleb had stopped until she collided with him. When he lowered the heavy pack from his back, she knew he had decided to stop for the night. Inelegantly dropping to the ground, Linsey rested her head on her bent knees.

She raised her head when Kaleb handed her a piece of jerky for their evening meal. Hungry as she was, Linsey found little strength to chew the dried meat.

"Please, can't you light a fire?" she pleaded through lips that would have trembled had it not been for her clenched teeth.

"Nope."

"Why?" Tentacles of long red hair reached out from beneath the hood of her cape, grasping at her face as if they possessed a will of their own. She made no effort to smooth them back, too tired and cold to care. "I'm freezing."

"Better cold than dead," he replied. "Injuns."

Linsey looked around the rapidly darkening area, suddenly forgetting her fatigue and the cold temperature. "Here?"

The old man did not try to hide a smile. "Little gal, we've been a'walkin' their huntin' ground since we hid the canoe."

Linsey began to shiver uncontrollably, more from fear than from the cold. For two days she had unknowingly followed Kaleb deeper and deeper into Indian territory. Savages! Dirty, filthy Indians! Everyone knew of the stories about their treatment of white captives.

As a child Linsey had spent hours with an older cousin who had filled her impressionable mind with vivid details of savage tortures and cruelties. When the eleven-year-old cousin refused to tell her what was done to the women captives, saying it was too horrible for her ears, the six-year-old Linsey did not realize that he knew little about what he spoke. In her eyes he was an adult, and she did not know that his exaggerations were mostly from his imagination. Now, at the age of nineteen, nothing had been done to erase the memories he had created, and she knew if she were captured her death would be slow in coming.

The fear she had known as a captive of Jeb and Zeke's could not begin to rival the sheer terror that coursed through her now. True, she had once stared across the river and had even wanted to flee to the Indians rather than face the fate Jeb had planned for her, but she would never have attempted it.

Linsey stared at the night-hidden figure across from her and wanted to beg and plead with him to take her safely back to her home. Experience had taught her it would be useless. Instead, she sat mutely, shivering with the cold and the terror that filled her.

"The Bear has a cabin pert near in the Injun village," Kaleb offered as he prepared for sleep. "Some be a-'sayin' he's part Injun hisself. I ain't knowin' fer certain; but I do know he's friendly-like with 'em, and

41

if'n they knows you're his woman, they won't be a botherin' us none."

Night sounds, familiar since the beginning of her nightmare journey, now became strange and magnified in her imagination. Knowing she would not sleep, she wrapped the blanket and fur more snugly around her. The night grew bitterly cold, and the wind seemed to find each hidden fold, creeping between them and chilling her further. Leaning against a tree, Linsey dozed, awakening when her exhausted body began to slump to the ground. As the night crawled past, Kaleb's snores and the lonely whistle of the wind through the trees kept companions with her terrified thoughts.

By late afternoon of the second full day of walking, a light snow began to fall. Linsey's lack of sleep the night before and five days of hard travel made it impossible for her to keep pace with the seasoned trapper. More than once she lost sight of him completely, and only her fear of the Indians kept her walking. When the cabin came into sight, she was beyond caring. She followed Kaleb inside and dropped onto a chair at the table while he started a fire.

"Bear must be a'checkin' his traps," Kaleb commented when the fire was burning merrily. "Should be back in a day or so now that hits fixin' to blow up a good storm."

Folding her arms on the table, Linsey lowered her head. The heat from the fire began to warm her, and the trembling that had threatened to overtake her body slowly stopped. She willed her eyes to remain open, and her stomach protested noisily when the smell of stew began to fill the room.

She slowly raised her head at Kaleb's next words.

"I'll be a'headin' back. Tell Bear we's even now. Kaleb Smith don't be a'owen him no more."

Her thoughts were sluggish as she watched him once more shoulder his pack. When he cradled his rifle in his arms and started toward the door, she finally realized just what he had said.

"Wait a minute!" Panic exploded through her. "You can't just leave me here!"

"I brung ya to the Bear. Past time for me to be a makin' winter camp." He reached for the rope that latched the door.

"But . . . but what about the Indians? You said their village was just a short distance away." Attempting to stand, Linsey tripped over her skirt and her uncooperative legs.

"Gal, they ain't gonna bother ya none," he replied with a hint of exasperation. "Stay inside and keep the fire goin' so's ya don't freeze. If'n the Injuns was to come out in the snow—which they ain't—you're in the cabin of the Bear, and they just ain't gonna bother ya." With a final nod, he pulled open the door and walked into the light snow.

"Shouldn't you wait here until the snow stops?" Linsey followed him a few steps outside. Being stranded in a cabin with the old man was preferable to staying by herself this close to an Indian village, not to mention waiting alone for the unknown Bear to return.

Kaleb looked at the light dusting of white on the ground and at the gray sky. He breathed deeply and knew there was the smell of snow in the air. He looked back at the frightened girl in the doorway. If he stayed with her until after the storm, it might be too late. After four years of searching, he was too close to stop now. Jeb would do his best to leave no trail to follow, but Kaleb knew, if he had to, he'd track Jeb to the

43

ends of the earth. He convinced himself that Linsey would be all right in the cabin by herself. Bear would return soon.

Soon, Mary, he whispered to the gentle image in his mind as he shifted his pack slightly. "Looks like hits a bad one comin'. I can be back at the river tomorrow. You'll do fine till Bear gets back."

Linsey watched her hopes disappear with him into the woods. It had taken them two full days of walking to reach the cabin, and yet he expected to be back to the river in only one. Had she slowed him down that much?

The snow blowing in her face made Linsey realize she was still standing outside. Reluctantly she walked back into the cabin, shutting the door behind her.

It was a small, one-room structure with a huge bed against one wall. On the opposite wall was a fireplace, and a table with two chairs sat in the center. An iron pot was suspended on a hook over the fire. As the stew began to warm, its delicious smells filled the room, reminding her needlessly that it had been days since she had eaten anything other than the dry jerky.

Using a piece of wood, Linsey swung the pot out of reach of the fire. She found a plate on a shelf beside the fireplace and heaped the stew onto it. A pan of water steamed beside the fire, but not knowing how to make coffee, she was forced to drink hot water.

Sitting at the table, her eyes drifted closed as the comfort of the fire, a full stomach and exhaustion took their toll. Her head snapped up abruptly; she had to stay awake. She had to keep the fire going. But more importantly, she had to watch for Indians!

Linsey stood and began to pace the room. Twelve steps from the fireplace to the edge of the bed; twelve steps to return. She pulled at the filthy dress clinging

44

to her and eyed the pan of warm water. It had been weeks since she had washed more than her face and hands. It would feel heavenly to be clean again . . . maybe it would help her stay awake.

Quickly undressing, she folded her torn chemise and dipped it into the water, washing as best she could. It would never substitute for a real bath, but it helped to remove some of the layers of grime.

As the cool air danced over her damp skin, Linsey realized she had no clothing other than the filthy dress lying in a heap on the dirt floor. Refusing to even consider putting it back on, she walked to the bed and wrapped herself in one of the wool blankets. It was rough and scratchy, but it would have to do for now.

Once more pacing the room, her eyes were drawn almost magnetically to the bed. A real bed! After weeks of sleeping on the hard ground, it looked too good to be true. She couldn't sleep, not with the ever present threat of Indians, but perhaps she could just sit on it, bundling up in the furs and blankets. She hesitated only briefly before climbing onto the bed.

The furs swallowed her in their softness. Sitting cross-legged, wrapped in a blanket, Linsey watched the burning fire. She could hear the storm intensify outside and was grateful for the security the cabin offered.

Warm, pleasantly full, cleaner than she had been in weeks, she could almost be content. . . .

Linsey's eyes slowly closed, and her head nodded. She felt herself falling and snapped her eyes open. But it felt so good, lying in the furs. She stretched her legs and wrapped more of the coverings over her.

She would not—could not—sleep. She *had* to stay awake. She had to be prepared in case of Indians.

Her eyes drifted closed. Sighing deeply, Linsey snuggled down in the softness and found a deep, dreamless sleep.

Wiggling beneath the furs, Linsey wondered why her maid, Betsy, had not lit the morning fire. Her room was usually toasty warm before she rose. She decided to stay in bed; Betsy must have overslept. She'd come soon.

Suddenly Linsey remembered. She was not in her room with its silk wall hangings and velvet draperies. Betsy would not come bounding cheerfully in at any moment, chattering while she efficiently made a fire. She was alone, in a cabin deep in the wilderness, surrounded by Indians. A cabin owned by an unknown man whose very name held the power to frighten fearless men.

Peeking from under the furs, Linsey saw that the door was standing wide open and snow had blown in during the night. The fire was cold ashes, the stew once more frozen solid.

The frigid air began to creep beneath the furs, forcing her to face the facts. The door was standing open, no one was around to close it but herself, and if she did not get a fire started, she would freeze to death. With a moan she climbed out of the warm nest, dragging one of the heavy furs with her.

The snow had thickened during the night and was now falling in fat, fluffy flakes. Linsey curled her toes away from the cold snow melting beneath her bare feet, bitterly regretting that she had removed her shoes and stockings. Shivering, disgusted because the snow blocked the door, she knelt and began clearing it away. By the time she finished, her hands were red and numb from the cold.

46

Linsey latched the door securely and blew on her hands. Wrapping the heavy fur around her, she turned toward the fireplace. Somehow she had to get a fire started, but how? It was not a requisite for graduation for the young ladies who attended Miss Mary Sarah Holland's School of Completion. Linsey could sew the most delicate of seams; she could sing and accompany herself on the pianoforte. She knew to the smallest detail how to plan a party and how to graciously instruct servants about their duties. She knew exactly how much material, lace and trim to order when designing a ball gown.

She could not start a fire.

Trying to remember what Kaleb had done the night before, Linsey piled heavy pieces of wood onto the cold ashes. After numerous tries, she managed to get a weak spark from the flint and steel, but to her frustration no roaring, warming flame followed.

The wind blew fiercely against the walls of the cabin, whistling through each hidden crack in the mud and clay chinking between the logs. Linsey could no longer stop her teeth from chattering, and her body shook uncontrollably. Each time she moved to strike flint against steel, the heavy fur slipped from her shoulders. She struggled to find the strength to pull it back into place.

Perspiration beaded her brow even as the frigid air teased around her. After what seemed like hours, she helplessly admitted defeat and climbed wearily to her feet. Dragging the fur with her, she climbed back into the bed, wrapping herself in the blankets and furs, praying for just a little warmth.

Linsey dozed off and on during the day, waking to find she had kicked off the covers while fleeing the terrors of her nightmares and was once again shaking from the bone chilling cold. Snuggling beneath the furs yet again, she waited for the warmth to comfort her, drifting into the nether world of unconsciousness.

When the cold again penetrated her sleep, she opened her eyes to total darkness. It took long minutes of concentration for her to remember where she was and to realize that night had come.

She ignored the grumblings of her stomach as it protested its lack of nourishment, and carelessly pulled the furs beneath her chin. Her eyes closed, fear of savage Indians swept from her mind.

It was mid-morning before Kaleb reached the river. He had walked until darkness and the falling snow had forced him to stop. He was too near his goal now to risk getting lost in the vast wilderness and die from the cold.

Wasting no time in uncovering the canoe, he pushed it into the river and jumped into the back. Turning it into the swiftly flowing current, he headed back the way he had come. The river fought his passing, making each mile seem like three as he used every ounce of his strength to paddle against the strong current.

By late afternoon, Kaleb knew he had no choice but to seek shelter. Sweating heavily from the exertion of fighting the current, he shivered each time the bitter wind crept into the folds of his coat. Squinting through the haze that lay thickly on the river, he searched for the long familiar landmarks that would lead him to cover.

Kaleb found the entrance to the nearly hidden stream that branched off the river and maneuvered the canoe past the overhanging branches. With a less strong current to fight, his paddling became easier, but with fewer trees overhead the snow fell thicker. It took the rest of the afternoon for him to find the lean-to he had constructed years earlier and used only occasionally. As an early evening turned the gray sky to black, Kaleb pulled up on shore, carefully secured the canoe and shouldered his heavy pack.

Inside, the lean-to was total darkness, but he moved with sure memory and soon had a small fire warming the tiny structure. Kaleb fed the fire from an ever-ready stack of dry wood at the back of the lean-to and cursed the fates that let him get so near before forcing him to stop.

For four years he had searched—a search that had taken him far and more than once should have cost him his life. He had known only their names, not their faces. It rankled that they had crossed his path once before but he had not known them for who they were. Now, through pure chance, he had found his enemy; he knew their faces. But for the early blizzard he would have begun his revenge.

The wind blew against the sides of the lean-to, and the fire danced in the darkness. He took some satisfaction from knowing they, too, would have to wait out the storm. As the blazing wood turned to glowing ashes, Kaleb Smith promised himself that Jeb and Zeke would never know spring.

Only by instinct and an overpowering will to survive was Luc LeClerc able to continue toward the promise of warmth. The unseasonably early blizzard had caught him unprepared several days from his cabin. He fluently cursed his own stupidity in three languages. His years of living with the Shawnee as well as being an experienced trapper had taught him to always be prepared for the unexpected.

Luc smiled grimly to himself as he walked head down. If he froze to death, the fault rested solely on his own shoulders. The signs of a storm had been clearly evident when he had been only a day away from the cabin, but he had chosen to ignore them. When the first gentle snow flakes had started to fall, he had cursed vividly but continued to set traps and check the ones already in place. By the time he started his journey back, the flakes were no longer gentle, and now he stumbled with exhaustion still more than two miles from the protection of his cabin.

His journey had been successful; several small animals had been in his traps. Their fur was not yet as thick as it would be later in the winter and therefore not as valuable, but the meat from the carcasses would be welcome.

If he lived long enough to eat it.

Doggedly, he trudged on, constantly looking for the familiar landmarks to guide him home. It was too late to stop and make shelter. He knew that he would be frozen before he could build a fire and make the protection of some kind of a lean-to.

His grim smile deepened. His Shawnee family would shake their heads sadly when they found his frozen body. They would wonder where they had failed and why he had not learned the simple lessons they had shared with him.

As darkness descended the storm intensified. The snow began to fall so thickly Luc could see only a few feet in front of him. Knowing that the cabin was just a short distance away, he determinedly continued, hoping that he had not strayed off the path in the blinding storm.

Watching as he put one foot in front of the other, he almost missed the cabin. It was only when he ran into the side of the structure that he realized he was home.

Using his hand as a guide along the outside wall, Luc walked to the door, pulling on the rope that released the guard bar inside. He stumbled into the room, discovering it was nearly as cold as the outside had been, but the promise of warmth beckoned.

Luc knelt wearily at the fireplace. In the gloom he saw the haphazardly stacked wood. Instantly alert, he reached for a small log with one hand and grabbed for the knife at his hip with the other. Moving in a blur of speed, Luc rose, turned and pulled the knife free. Fully prepared to face an unfriendly intruder, his alert gaze wandered around the room. There was no one in sight and no place large enough for a man to hide. When he was satisfied that there was no danger, he replaced the knife and turned again to the fire.

Sweeping aside the large logs, Luc replaced them with kindling. His only concern once more was the warmth now within his reach. A small spark turned to a golden blaze, and he added the larger logs slowly. He was careful to keep his frozen hands from the fire, knowing if he warmed them too quickly he risked losing them.

When the fire was burning brightly, he removed his heavy, ice-coated deerhide coat. The stew he had made before he left still hung on the hook beside the fireplace, and he moved the pot and its frozen contents toward the heat. His body cried out for sleep while his belly complained of hunger. He would wait until the food was warm, eat and then sleep until the storm abated.

As he stood near the fire, Luc realized he had carried the animal carcasses inside with him. He knew he

51

should take the time to clean them, but his tired body refused to make any unnecessary movements. Picking them up from the floor where he had dropped them, he carried them to the door and placed them outside the cabin. More than likely some animal would find them before he woke, but at the moment he did not begrudge losing them. The fight to get home had consumed his considerable strength to a point that he wanted only to rest.

The stew came to a bubbling boil, its aroma filling the cabin. When he found his cup and plate on the table instead of the shelf, he filled them, but his gaze continuously scanned the room. Someone had been in his cabin during his absence, someone who either did not know how to start a fire or had waited until the ashes were almost dead before adding more wood. It was not unusual for a traveler to seek shelter in someone else's cabin. It was unusual for that person to have moved on during a blizzard.

When his stomach was pleasantly full, he carefully added more logs to the blazing fire and turned toward the bed and its tumble of furs and blankets. The far side of the cabin lay in shadowed darkness, but already the heat was beginning to warm it. The ice coating his clothing began to melt, making the garments wet and heavy. Chilled by the dampness, he removed them as he crossed the room, falling nude into the bed. The furs warmed his body, the heat radiating from his shoulders to the tips of his toes.

With a contented sigh, grateful to have survived in spite of his own stupidity, Luc rolled from his side to his back. His hand lay on something in the bed beside him . . . something soft, warm.

Something alive.

Chapter Three

Run! Run! He's getting closer. Ground's uneven,
mustn't fall. Tripping. A tree root?
Snake!
No! No!
Zeke! . . . can't move . . . can't breathe. . . .
"Shet up, girlie, or Zeke'll have ta hug ya to deaf."
Behind him . . . an Indian! Garishly painted, mov-
ing without sound . . . reaching for Zeke's scraggly
hair. A feathered tomahawk slicing through the air.
A grisly tool of death aimed for his head.
Scream!
Scream of death.

Luc turned his head, his alert gaze searching for his
knife. It lay where he had left it, on the table in the
center of the room—another foolish error in judgement
that he had no time to berate himself for at the moment. He could depend only on his own strength and a
surprise attack.

Exhaustion forgotten, Luc whipped back the concealing furs, turned and threw himself on top of his

intruder. He stradled the body beneath his and pulled the arms above the head.

Linsey's nightmare turned to harsh reality as the breath exploded from her lungs. She struggled against his immense weight, trying to free her hands from his hold.

Luc judged that his captive's strength fell far short of his own, and in the flickering light he let his gaze roam. His eyes widened in amazement, and his hold slackened. A woman!

"*Mon dieu,*" he whispered in the French of his childhood. "What are you doing in my bed, little one?"

Too frightened to hear him, Linsey knew that she must fight for her life. A man, too large to be Zeke, was holding her down. That he spoke both English and French did not register in her mind. To her he had to be the thing she most feared . . . an Indian.

Taking advantage of the momentary easing of his hold, Linsey freed one hand and raked it down his chest. She twisted and turned, her hair streaming out around her, flipping over her face so that she could not see her captor.

Too startled to respond quickly, Luc looked down at his chest and the ragged trails of blood made by her fingernails. He grunted when her closed fist landed with surprising force in the center of his stomach. Grabbing her wildly flailing arm, he pulled it back with the other one above her head. The heaving of her slender body hardly moved his, and he leisurely studied her.

Even in the murky light it would have been impossible for him not to notice her hair. It was magnificent: a summer sunset of reds and golds; autumn leaves in the glory of full color; tarnished copper promising untold beauty. He searched for a description and could not find it. Her hair was a little of each and yet none.

An artist would despair never finding the shades and hues to paint it on canvas.

Her face was molded with delicate features, a tiny, slightly upturned nose and a light dusting of freckles across her cheeks. He longed to see the color of her eyes beneath the finely arched brows. His gaze drifted lower, to the creamy skin of her full breasts. Her chest rose and fell rapidly from her struggles, and he felt himself hardening as he dwelt on the tender buds peeking through the strands of long hair. He wanted to put his lips on them and sample their sweetness. Lower still was her narrow waist, gently rounded hips and flat stomach. His manhood throbbed with a life of its own when he realized it was nestled against the soft curls of her femininity.

"*Tukwàhkee Sh'kotai*, Autumn Fire," he whispered in Shawnee, his voice harsh with sudden longing. "Are you a gift from some god to warm my long, cold winter nights?"

Linsey heard his voice, and her fear intensified, nearing the breaking point. She no longer doubted that he was an Indian. The terrible tortures her cousin had hinted at were about to befall her. She stiffened, searching beyond her terror for hidden strength. If he planned to torture her, she might not be able to hide pain, but he would never see her fear.

Luc gasped when she opened her eyes . . . green eyes, sparkling with the vibrant color of emeralds or new leaves of spring. Again he was left wanting a description.

Linsey's defiant gaze saw hair as blue-black as a raven's wing, without the slightest hint of a curl. His face was hidden by the murky shadows, unveiled in the flickering light. Distorted by slopes and ridges where none should have been. A demonic specter created from the fires of hell.

Her scream splintered the silence. It echoed through the tiny cabin, reverberating off the walls. She screamed like one who had been touched by the burning hand of the devil.

"Easy, little one." His deeply husky voice was quietly soothing. "Do not struggle so hard. You will harm yourself."

There were many questions that needed an answer, but he knew that first he must reassure the girl, for he was well aware of the effect of his appearance on most people the first time they saw him.

"Shhh." He smoothed the silky mass of tangled hair from her face as Linsey struggled to free herself from his hold. Fearing she would injure herself while thrashing around, Luc held her firmly and talked quietly until she began to show signs of tiring.

"You grow weary of this struggle, eh, *petite ange*?" He cupped her cheek within his massive hand, rubbing her soft skin with his work-roughened thumb. He gritted his teeth when her breasts heaved against his chest, their pointed tips seeming to burn into his flesh. His stomach rested in the hollow of hers, and the throbbing hardness of his loins ground against her thigh, needlessly reminding him how long it had been since he'd shared his bed with a woman. He knew most men would take her in spite of her terror, perhaps deriving greater pleasure because of it. But it was not his way. He would find no satisfaction in rape.

Beneath him Linsey strained for each breath. Her eyes were tightly closed. She did not need to open them to remember the horror of the face above her. It was a nightmare visage, the thing mothers spoke of to threaten misbehaving children.

When her struggles stilled, Luc eased his hold, supporting himself on his elbow. "I am going to let you go, but I'm not moving far away, only to the other side of the bed."

Prepared for any sudden movement from her, he lifted up and rolled off her smooth body. He regretted the necessity of covering her obvious charms even as he pulled one of the furs over her.

Linsey grabbed the fur as if it would provide her the protection of a suit of armor. She wondered if her fear had heightened her imagination. Maybe he wasn't as horrible as she thought. She slowly opened her eyes and found herself staring into eyes as black as night.

"Hello," Luc said quietly, aware of the fear clouding her face.

"Hello," Linsey replied inanely, wanting to look at his face but too frightened to move her gaze from his.

"I'm going to get up and add more wood to the fire." Earlier he had prepared it for the night, but it was the only excuse he could find to leave the bed. And leave it he must before his lust overpowered his good intentions.

At Linsey's nod, he swiftly rolled over and stood. Dragging a fur with him, he wrapped it around his nude body as he walked across the room.

Linsey carefully kept him in view. She studied his profile as he knelt at the fire. The light from the golden flame danced over a classically sculptured, symmetrically beautiful face. She shook her head slightly, wondering at her imagination. There was no hint of the grotesque countenance she had thought she had seen earlier. In fact, his features were perfect, almost too perfect to be real. The fur draped over his shoulders seemed to accentuate their size, and she realized he was one of the largest men she had ever seen.

Deciding to use his distraction to her advantage, Linsey carefully wrapped a blanket around herself and stood. She knew he would return to the bed once he was satisfied with the fire, and she did not want their next confrontation to occur there. Keeping the table between herself and him, she slowly sat down in a chair. It was laughable to think that the sturdy table would provide any defense should he decide to attack, but it was the only obstacle she could set in his path.

A large knife lay on the edge of the table, and Linsey's eyes moved from it to the man and back again. She could use it as a weapon. Maybe, if she were lucky, she could provide herself with some protection. Her hand reached hesitantly toward it.

"I mean you no harm, Autumn Fire," he said quietly over his shoulder. "But if the knife makes you feel safer, hold on to it."

His back was toward her, and she wondered how he could have known she was reaching for the knife. As he turned, she raised startled eyes to his, and she saw the gentleness in his gaze, a slight smile tugging at the corners of his lips.

There was no mystery in his knowledge of her actions, only years of learning from his Shawnee friends. Luc could have told her that he had been aware of her every move since she had climbed out of bed. He had heard her wrap the blanket around herself and the quiet sound of her steps as she crossed the room. There had been total silence when she reached the table, and he had remembered the knife at the same instant a slight rustling told him she was reaching for it.

Linsey grabbed for the knife when he stood abruptly. Her blanket slipped, and she struggled to hold it in place with one hand while keeping the knife pointed at him with the other.

Luc's smile was one of gentle amusement. "Forget your nudity in battle," he advised softly. "There is no place for modesty when the life you are fighting to save is your own."

He turned away from the fire, and Linsey gasped, for the moment forgetting her struggles. It had not been her imagination. The flames seemed to flare, brightening the room. If one side of his face had been a thing of rare beauty, this side was flawed.

"It is only a face, little one. Skin and bone, scars earned in battle. It can not harm you."

His voice penetrated her mesmerized stare. As her eyes met his, she found that she wanted to erase his look of understanding. She wanted to apologize for staring so rudely, but not as much as she wanted to turn and run from the cabin so that she never had to see him again.

"I'm sorry," she said in a voice barely above a whisper.

"For what? For the scars? You were little more than a child when they happened, and I have come to accept them. For staring?" He shrugged lightly. "If I met me walking down a trail, I too would forget the lessons of my mother; I would stare."

"Does it hurt?" Linsey cringed mentally when she heard herself ask.

"Only when I frighten little children." Luc rubbed the side of his face in question. "It's been known to frighten some adults, too."

"You're the Bear." It was a statement.

"Some call me that. I was named Luc LeClerc. You may call me whichever you wish."

"I think always you are a little of both, but sometimes more one than the other." Linsey stated with perceptive cognition.

"Each of us is more than one person; we are the echo of many." He walked to the bed, pushed the furs away and sat down. Leaning back and stretching his big body, Luc sighed. It had been a long day; it would be a while yet before he could find sleep.

"The bed is big enough for both of us and much warmer than the table."

"No!" Linsey's hold on the knife tightened.

He shrugged and rolled to his side. The scarred half of his face was in full view, and she averted her eyes from it.

"How did you find my cabin? Why are you alone? Where is your family?"

He did not seem as threatening when he was lying down, and Linsey eased the hold on the knife. She snuggled beneath the blanket and became aware of the chill in the air. Pulling her bare feet up beneath her, she told him briefly of her kidnapping and of Kaleb buying her from Jeb and Zeke.

"He said to tell you he no longer owes you anything."

Luc nodded his understanding. "I saved him from the Iroquois. You are the paying of a debt."

"I don't want to be payment for a debt!" She stood and began pacing the room, one hand clutching the blanket at her neck, the other firmly holding the knife. "I want to return to Philadelphia. I must see about Elizabeth." Linsey stared into the flames of the fire, her thoughts hundreds of miles away from the cabin in the wilderness.

"I will take you home."

"When? Tomorrow?" Excitement rushed through her, and her eyes sparkled happily.

Luc grinned at her obvious excitement. "Come spring."

"Spring?" Linsey sputtered in agitation. "I can't wait until spring! That's months away!"

Rolling to his back and folding his hands beneath his head, Luc closed his eyes. "Spend tonight outside. In the morning we will again talk of this trip."

"Are you crazy? There's a blizzard going on out there!"

"True. And by tomorrow the snow will be hip deep." He turned his head and opened his eyes. "With adequate preparations I could survive. Could you?"

"I could try," she insisted stubbornly.

"We'd get halfway between the cabin and nowhere, and you would give up. I would then have to make the decision of whether to leave you to freeze to death or to try carrying you back here. You are a little thing, Autumn Fire, but I think in the snow you would quickly become very heavy."

"You arrogant, stubborn—you're so sure I couldn't make it. I'll have you know the trip getting here wasn't easy, but I made it." Linsey straightened her shoulders and raised her chin by several inches, trying to find dignity while wrapped in a blanket. "And my name is not Autumn Fire! It is Linsey Marie MacAdams!"

"You floated downriver in weather warmer than it will be again until spring. Now we have snow; soon the river will freeze solid. We would have to walk; . . . it would be foolish to even consider making the trip now."

A slight smile crossed his face as he looked at her hair shining with a life of its own and at her emerald eyes spitting more flames than the fire behind her. "You are Autumn Fire. The Indians change their names as the person changes. Autumn, the ending of a life cycle, shouted gloriously in colors unmatched by man, as if nature defies anyone to take her for granted.

61

The fire in you is just beneath the surface, flaming brightly for short moments before it hides again.

"Tonight you are Autumn Fire. Tomorrow? We will see."

"Comparing me to something that is dying, no matter how beautiful, is not a compliment!" she huffed. "I will pay you to take me home."

"Ah, but autumn does not just fade away. It fights desperately until the very end. Even now there are snow-covered leaves clinging to the trees. Nothing can match the beauty of those leaves in full color. So, Autumn Fire, spend the night outside. We will discuss your trip in the morning."

Linsey paced nervously around the room, the knife dangling uselessly from her fingers as it waved back and forth in agitation.

"Do not drop the knife; it is sharp and would easily remove your toes from your foot." Luc broke the silence, startling Linsey from her thoughts. "Come to bed. Tomorrow will come soon enough and find the solution for your dilemma. I am tired and would like to sleep this night."

"Bed?" Linsey clenched the knife tightly, careful to hold it away from her body. "You can't expect us to share the same bed!"

"It is the only one I have, but it is big enough for both of us."

"A gentleman would offer me sole use of the only bed."

"My father was a gentleman; I am not."

"Somehow that doesn't surprise me!"

Luc chuckled. "*Ain jel eè thàh*, I am too weary to fight you with words. Sleep where you will, but the bed is more comfortable."

62

"I shall be perfectly all right in a chair," Linsey stated haughtily, sitting down abruptly.

"As you wish." Luc yawned, stretched and grabbed a few of the furs, tossing them in her direction. "Good night."

She couldn't believe he was calmly going to go to sleep. Did he really expect her to spend the night sitting up in a chair? Linsey looked at the bundle lying on the floor halfway between the bed and the table. She walked over to it, picked it up and carried it back. The table! It would be hard, and even as small as she was, her feet would still hang over the end; but it was better than trying to sit up all night. She spread one of the thick furs on the table and used a chair to climb up on her make-shift bed.

"Take care that you don't fall off. The floor is only dirt, but you will find it is very hard dirt."

Linsey ignored him and settled herself for the night. The table was little wider than she, but it would do for tonight. It would have to. The only other choice was unthinkable! Tomorrow other arrangements would have to be made.

"What did you call me earlier?" she asked abruptly.

"*Ain jel eè thàh?*"

"What does that mean?"

"It is Shawnee and means 'my angel.' "

"I am not your angel!" she stated indignantly.

"Ah, but you are." His deep voice flowed gently around her, enveloping her in a sound as soft as silk. "You are an angel with the fire of the devil beneath the surface."

She refused—flatly refused—to give him the satisfaction of a reply. First he compared her to dead leaves, and now this. If he was looking for trouble, she'd be glad to give him all that he could handle . . . tomorrow. For now she would try to sleep.

Rolling to her side, knees bent so that her feet were under the coverings, Linsey clutched the knife and closed her eyes.

Sleep did not come instantly. She listened to the even breathing of the man across the room and slowly realized that her fear of him had vanished as quickly as it had come. His scars were dreadful, making him appear a demon, but he had seemed to make every effort to put her at her ease. She even felt an intangible sense of security knowing he was just across the room and would come instantly if she needed him.

The same situation would have been unthinkable in Philadelphia. Had she become a different person since she had left home? Could she now accept an intolerable situation as casually as she had once accepted new riding gloves? How could she find security with a terrifying stranger whose immense strength could easily break her in half?

The fire crackled as a log broke, sending sparks of light into the glowing embers. Outside the wind howled a reminder of its presence. Across the room Luc sneezed several times.

"God bless you," she murmured, too softly for him to hear. After all, any angel would do the same.

"Thank you."

Slowly opening her eyes, Linsey looked across the room, through the legs of the table, and watched the fire dance brightly. She could smell something cooking, and her stomach reminded her of its lack of nourishment. Snuggling deeper into the furs, she knew she would have to get up soon, but it felt so good to be warm and safe. And the bed was so soft.

Bed? Linsey sat up, her gaze roaming the small room. She was alone. Last night had not been a dream; the burning fire was proof enough of that. So where was her companion?

Her smooth brow wrinkled in concentration. She had fallen asleep on the table long after Bear's even breathing had told her he slept. Vaguely, she remembered being carried, snuggled against a massive chest, while a deep voice whispered soothing words into her ear. She had thought it was a dream. But now, waking in the bed, she realized he had carried her here before he left. Feeling safe for the first time in weeks, her sleep had been so deep it had almost been a stupor.

She was still wrapped in the blanket, and the fur that she had spread on the table was still beneath her. Linsey realized he had picked her up, furs and all, and carried her to the bed.

But where was he? Why had he left the cabin without waking her?

The noisily growling protest of her stomach put an end to her musing. She climbed out of the warm nest, once more wrapping the blanket around her. The dirty, tattered dress lay on the floor, and Linsey realized she would have to wear it. Maybe she could wash some of the dirt out of it before putting it back on. She certainly couldn't spend the rest of the winter wrapped in a blanket!

Linsey sat in a chair, her feet folded beneath her, finishing the last of her meal, when the door opened. Bear entered, looking very much like his name-sake and equally as large and powerful. He was wrapped in a coat made from a blackish-brown hide.

Flakes of snow clung to the long fur, and Linsey

knew without being told that it was a bear hide. She briefly wondered who had made it for him; it was beautiful, and she envied the hood that snugly covered his head.

Luc said nothing as he laid a wrapped package on the table and walked to the fire. Kneeling as he removed his coat and gloves, he stretched his hands toward the warmth.

The two windows on the front of the cabin were tightly shuttered to help keep out the cold; but even in the dim light, she saw a clearer picture of the disfiguring scars on his face, and once more Linsey felt a twinge of alarm. He was such a large man and so horribly scarred. Could he really be as gentle as she had credited him? His size alone was intimidating, but with the added scar he was truly terrifying.

His well-shaped hands were massive, and as Linsey watched him warm them, she realized for the first time that most of the little finger on his left hand was missing and the hand itself was as badly scarred as his face.

A sudden fit of coughing startled her from her observations as the big man doubled over, gasping for air. Linsey realized his face was flushed, but not from the cold outside or from the heat of the fire, and wondered if he were feverish.

Wanting to offer help but not knowing what to do, she waited.

"The package is for you." When his coughing had stopped, Luc stood, turning his back to the warmth of the fire.

"Are you all right?"

"Just a cough," he said, his voice considerably deeper and more ragged than normal.

"Where were you?"

His red, watery eyes seemed to twinkle at her.

"When I put you in the bed this morning, I remembered what you had been wearing the night before." Linsey's face turned a deep pink as she, too, remembered the fight, their nude bodies pressed intimately together. "Since you can't spend the winter wearing my blanket and even the most expertly skilled dressmaker can't make a dress in a few hours, I decided to get you some clothing."

His statement was interrupted several times with heavy racking coughs that sent a thrill of alarm down Linsey's spine. The man was sick!

"You shouldn't have gone out in the cold!"

He tried to answer; but chills sent a spasm of shudders racing down his body, and he clenched his teeth to prevent their chattering.

"Open the package."

Untying the wrappings, Linsey discovered a dress that revolted her even as she admired it. It was a pale yellow color, made of hides as soft as velvet. Long fringe hung from the bodice, down the sleeves and at the knee-length hem. Beaded moccasins and pieces of hide that Bear told her were leggings were also in the package and of the same yellow color. It was beautiful. She knew it would be soft against her skin. It would be warmer and more modest than the blanket.

She would not wear it; it belonged to an Indian.

Watching her reactions as he walked to the bed, Luc sat on the edge and rested his elbows on his knees. "It'll keep you warm until you can make something yourself." He shivered and wrapped a fur around his shoulders. "Add wood to the fire; it's cold in here."

Linsey forgot the dress in her concern for him. The cabin was already warm, almost too warm for the blanket she wore. And yet he was cold when covered by the heavy fur.

She reached for the wood nearest the fireplace and added several small pieces to the fire. "I'm not too sure what I'm doing."

"Is that why you had no fire when I arrived last night?" he asked, stopping again to cough.

"I'm afraid it was never necessary for me to learn the art of building a fire."

"Kindling first," he instructed as he lay down and pulled several blankets over him. "Then small sticks. When it's burning good, add the bigger logs."

Linsey carefully added several large logs to the fire and watched the greedy flame lick hungrily at them. Feeling a great sense of pride for her simple accomplishment, she turned to Luc, waiting for praise for her efforts.

His eyes were closed, and as she walked nearer, she heard his heavy, labored breathing. His face was deeply flushed, and beneath the furs his body shook uncontrollably.

"You can't get sick." Linsey felt panic race up her spine. "Promise me you won't get sick."

"Not sick," he muttered between coughs.

"Could have fooled me."

"Haven't been sick since I was a child."

She placed a hand near the unscarred side of his face, careful not to touch him, and was startled by the heat radiating from his skin. "Please," she pleaded softly. "I don't know how to take care of myself. How can I take care of both of us?"

He opened his eyes, his dark gaze locking with hers. A slight smile crossed the rugged face, and Linsey noticed a deep dimple in his cheek. "I just need sleep, Timid Deer. Keep the fire burning so we don't freeze."

"You just can't be sick."

"Not sick."

"If you get sick, you could die," Linsey's voice lowered to a whisper. "If you die, I'll never get home. I'll live here until the food runs out, and then I'll starve to death."

"Your concern for me is touching," Bear replied, his voice laced with sarcasm. "I am not sick!" His voice rose to a roar only to be broken by another fit of coughing.

"Sick and grumpy," Linsey moaned.

Bear gritted his teeth and tried to prevent another cough from escaping. "I will be well after a little sleep. I promise I won't die."

"Oh, please," she whispered, "I don't know what to do."

He lifted a hand toward her, but it fell back to the bed far short of its goal of her cheek. His feverish gaze locked with her worried one, and a gentle smile touched his mouth.

"It will pass, *mon ange*, after I sleep." His eyes drifted closed as the smile faded. "Keep the fire burning."

Chapter Four

The cold, crisp day gradually faded into the twilight of approaching night. Meticulously tending the fire while keeping a distant watch on the sleeping man, Linsey was unaware of the change and was startled when she realized it was growing dark. She had spent long hours fighting the panic that threatened to overwhelm her. Without the aid of the sick man across the room, she would be helpless in this wilderness; her very existence depended on him.

Each time Bear had wakened during the long day, he had seemed worse. His breathing was a harsh, labored wheeze, splintering the hush in the small cabin. Occasionally he muttered faintly, the words too indistinct for her to distinguish.

It had been several hours since he'd last been awake, and his sleep was becoming more restless, the muttering louder. She cautiously approached him and pulled the furs snugly beneath his chin.

"Bear? Are you awake?" She was unaware of her choice of names or that she never thought of him as Luc.

After trying several times to rouse him, Linsey reluctantly admitted to herself that the fever had sent him beyond normal sleep. She walked back to the fireplace and stared into the dancing flame, as if looking to it for guidance.

"You've got to do something," she mumbled to herself. "If you don't, he will probably die." She rubbed a hand wearily across her forehead. "Merciful God, what do I do?" It was a prayer, a plea for help.

Linsey sat down in the chair she had occupied most of the day, put her elbows on the table and supported her chin in her hands. She was sick so infrequently, and it had been years since Betsy had nursed her through an illness. Her brow wrinkled with concentration as she tried to remember what Betsy had done to help her.

"Water!" Linsey smacked the table with her hand, regretting it when her palm began to sting.

Looking around the cabin, she found several kettles and bowls . . . all empty. She added another log to the fire as she tried to think of the nearest water source. Surely Bear did not travel all the way to the river!

"Idiot!" she hissed loudly. "There's all the water anyone could ever need right outside!"

Carrying a large bucket, Linsey opened the door and took a couple of steps outside. The howling wind had stopped, leaving it eerily quiet. The snow sparkled brightly in the glow of a full moon while shadows from the trees danced darkly mysterious in a silent breeze. The air was bitterly cold but smelled invitingly fresh with a hint of wood smoke. A trail through the deep snow led toward the trees, showing the path Bear had taken that morning when he went for the dress.

Linsey knelt and began scooping snow into the bucket. Her long hair draped over her shoulders and dangled onto the ground. Several times she had to stop

71

to push it out of the way and decided the first thing she needed to do was to find some way to anchor it on top of her head.

Her hands were tingling from the cold by the time the bucket was filled. Carrying it back inside, Linsey was relieved to have the warmth and security of the cabin as she closed and latched the door.

She separated the snow into several smaller pots and kettles, placing them near the fire so that it could melt. She ran her fingers through her hair, trying to smooth the largest tangles. Twisting it into a long coil, she looped it around itself, forming a knot low on her neck.

Turning her back to the fire, her gaze came to rest on the buckskin dress still lying on the table. It was going to be a long night, tending both the man and the fire. The blanket wrapped around her would hamper her movements. It was bulky and constantly slipped down her shoulders.

Holding it gingerly with two fingers of each hand, she held up the dress. It was beautifully made, and closer inspection showed that the beadwork down the front was a series of tiny flowers, each vining into the next.

Biting the inside of her lower lip, Linsey looked across the room to assure herself that Bear still slept, then let the blanket drop and slid the dress over her head. A rawhide thong laced the front closed from the middle of her chest to just beneath her chin.

Linsey slipped on the moccasins while admiring the unfamiliar comfort of the dress. It hung lightly from her shoulders and flowed softly around her body. Its light touches were almost a caress against her skin where her curves swelled out to meet it. She felt nakedly exposed with so much of her legs uncovered; but the leggings were unfamiliar, and she had no idea how to put them on. Shrugging slightly, she decided she had more important things to worry about. Anyway, no one would see her highly unconventional mode of dress.

Wrapping the blanket over her head and shoulders for added warmth, Linsey carried the large bucket outside and refilled it. She placed it near the fire, tossed the blanket over a chair and waited impatiently for the snow in the smaller kettle to completely melt.

Across the room Bear moaned, tossing and turning, searching for a little coolness for his burning flesh. Linsey put the intimacy of touching him from her mind as she tested the water and found it no longer bitterly cold but still cool. She carried it to the bed and stood for long moments looking down at the feverish man.

It had to be done. . . .

Tearing the remainder of the ragged chemise into long strips. Linsey sat gingerly on the edge of the bed. She wet one of the rags, wrung it out and placed it on his broad forehead. Using another one, she dabbed it over the smooth side of his face, shrinking away from the thought of touching the other side even through the damp cloth.

As she talked softly, his restlessness ceased. She wondered if his reaction was to the cooling touch of the cloth against his heated skin, or if it was the sound of her voice that soothed him.

The rags warmed quickly, and Linsey soon set a rhythm of placing one on his forehead, sponging his face and then starting over. She carefully avoided acknowledging the existence of the left side of his face.

Her back began to ache from the bent position she was forced to maintain. Using the now warm water as an excuse, she stood, stretched and crossed the room.

The fire had burned down, and as she stooped to add several more logs, she felt a smug sense of pride in herself. She had managed to keep the fire going and had thought of a way to help relieve some of Bear's suffering. She was even willing to go without sleep if it became necessary. Tomorrow, if he was not better, she would have to see about fixing something for them to eat. For her evening meal she had eaten the last of the food he had prepared that morning. Even though she did not know how to cook, Linsey didn't let herself worry about it. For now, anyway, she felt that she could handle any situation.

Carrying a bowl of fresh water back to the bed, Linsey placed her hand against his smooth cheek, hoping for a noticeable drop in his temperature. She tried to swallow her disappointment when his skin felt as hot as ever.

With a sigh, Bear turned his face into the inviting coolness of her hand, trapping it between his cheek and the bed. Already his thick black hair had lost some of its glossy luster, as if the fever was draining the vitality from it. Linsey stared at his hair rather than the distorted skin now clearly in view. Hesitantly, her gaze dropped, and for the first time she really looked at his scars.

They began at his hairline above his ear, one scar joined at his cheek by a second and then a third near his jaw. They were evenly spaced, parallel scars barely missing the edge of his eye and the corner of his mouth. The surrounding skin was almost mockingly smooth.

It is only skin and bone; it can not harm you. As she studied his face, his words seemed to whisper through the room. *Only skin and bone . . . can not harm.*

"And an overactive imagination," Linsey muttered to herself with disgust. The scars were not nearly as terrifying as her overwrought mind had made them.

Linsey felt pity for his pain and suffering, but it

74

didn't begin to compare with the shame she felt at herself. She had been so noble, helping him when he was sick. Yet she had ignored a part of him that suffered all the more because of its damage. The scars were probably extremely sensitive to the heat of the fever. It was quite simply a face, and she had treated it as if it were something contagious.

"Forgive me, I'm so sorry," she whispered to the unconscious man. "I've been so selfish."

Sitting on the edge of the bed, she lifted her free hand and hesitantly traced the outline of his firm lips, delighted that the scars did not touch their perfection. The heat radiated against her skin, and her guilt soared. How could she have ignored this side of his face? He had shown nothing but kindness and thoughtfulness to her, even going out this morning to get the dress when he already showed signs of being sick.

"Konah?" Bear whispered through dry, cracked lips. "Konah *M'tuk o hee?*" He turned his cheek into the coolness of her hand.

"Bear?" Linsey called gently. "I don't understand you. Please, speak English."

"Snow?"

Her brow furled in puzzlement. "The blizzard has stopped, but there's several feet of snow on the ground."

"My Snow," he sighed, trying to wet his lips with his tongue. "Water, Snow—" A heaving cough racked painfully through his body.

Still confused by his reference to snow, Linsey stood, pulled her hand free and filled a cup with water. She lifted his head with one hand and held the cup to his mouth.

The water felt cool in his mouth, and his heated body cried for the moisture. Still held by the delirium, Bear

75

tried to swallow and choked, knocking the cup from her hand and spilling the water over his chest. He began to shake violently as the icy liquid touched his skin.

Linsey backed away, growing terrified as the choking grew worse. When she began to think he'd never breathe again, he stopped coughing, falling helplessly back onto the bed.

She saw the stain darkening the buckskin shirt and knew she would have to get it off of him. He was already so sick. He could not be allowed to stay in the wet shirt.

"Bear, you have to help me," she explained as her shaking hands unlaced the thong that closed the front of the shirt.

She tried pulling the shirt up, but his weight held it firmly in place. "Bear, sit up!" she ordered in a gruff voice that she hoped would penetrate his daze.

"Snow?"

"Sit up!" If he wouldn't, or couldn't, cooperate, there was no way she could do it by herself short of cutting it from him.

"Grouchy Snow," he whispered in a teasing voice. "Always in a hurry to get my clothes off!"

"So Snow is a woman," Linsey muttered as she pulled and tugged, hoping to get him upright. "I sure don't know why she'd be in a hurry to undress you."

After she got him sitting up, his fumblings to help her were more of a hindrance. Finally, in spite of his aid, Linsey managed to awkwardly pull the shirt over his head.

"Konah, my wife," he sighed, wrapping a massive arm around Linsey's waist and resting his head against her breasts.

"Wife?" Linsey's movements stopped abruptly. "Snow is your wife?"

76

He nuzzled against her breasts, his hand dropping down her back to caress rounded slopes. Linsey tried to push his head away from her breasts with one hand and stop his gentle touches with the other.

"How many hands do you have, anyway?" she questioned when she was unsuccessful in her attempt to catch his wandering hand.

"So long since we've loved," he mumbled, the delirium teasing his mind with long-ago memories. His hand slipped to the bare skin of her leg and began slowly creeping upward.

"Bear, stop!" Linsey gave up trying to move his head and reached for the hand nearing the apex of her thighs. "I'm not your Snow!"

"So long . . ." His voice trailed off into indistinct murmurs that Linsey realized must be Shawnee. He held her firmly but gently. A tender steel trap.

A startled squeal left her lips when his hand reached its goal. At the same time his lips found the bud of her breast. Even through the dress, Linsey felt her nipple harden to the unfamiliar, exciting tug of his lips.

"So warm."

"Stop!"

Linsey tried to squirm within his grasp, hoping to dislodge his hand . . . or mouth . . . or both. She was astonished by her body's response to his touch.

"No, Bear, you must stop."

"Come to bed, my wife."

"I'm not your wife!"

His caresses were awakening her body to exciting sensations she never knew existed. A warmth filled her, coursing like liquid fire through her veins, wanting to burst free.

Bear's mouth left her breast, nuzzling its way down

to her stomach. "The babe," he whispered reverently. "Our babe."

"Baby?" Linsey ceased struggling, her heart hammering an unnatural beat. "A baby?"

A gentle smile crossed his face as he laid his scarred cheek against her flat stomach. "We will raise enough little warriors to make their grandfathers proud. Our children will know the best of both worlds, my Snow: the dignity and pride of their mother's people, the elegance and knowledge of their father's. Deeply loved by their parents, could any child ask for more?"

Taking advantage of her sudden lack of resistance, Bear's hand slipped between her thighs to caress her rounded bottom. He lightly rubbed his scarred cheek against her abdomen, and Linsey knew it was a remembered response to a befogged mind. Sometime in his past he had rested his head against a swollen belly that held his growing child.

Linsey stroked his hair, offering comfort. Her eyes brimmed with unreleased tears. What secrets in his past tormented his present? He had deeper scars than the visible ones. Without being told, she knew that Snow and their child were dead. She had no doubt that if Snow still lived, Bear would be with her. The depth of love in his voice told Linsey that only death could have separated them.

Carefully, Linsey tried to dislodge his caressing hand. She knew that this was not an attempt at rape. His mind was in another place, another time. He was loving Snow. He was caressing the mother of his child, not the strange woman he had found in his cabin the night before.

"Don't leave!" His voice broke with anguish as he clutched her painfully to him. "So alone . . . not again."

Deep, rattling coughs rumbled through his massive frame, and he abruptly released her. Stumbling backward at the sudden freedom, Linsey watched him attempt to breathe. She was relieved to be free . . . and yet, her body tingled where he had touched. Her breasts throbbed for more of his exciting kisses.

When the coughing eased, Bear's chin dropped to his chest while deep shudders made his big body tremble like a leaf in the wind. He slowly raised his head, his dark eyes meeting hers . . . eyes filled with a haunting pain. Linsey realized that for the moment he was once again lucid.

"She's gone, she and the babe. I wasn't there when they needed me." His gaze left her, his eyes turning toward the fire. In its gentle glow, Linsey saw a tear streak down his cheek. "I failed them."

Whoever she had been, Snow was still very much loved by this gentle giant. Feeling his pain and grief, Linsey briefly envied Snow, wondering what it would be like to be so loved.

With a deep sigh, Bear fell back onto the bed. His eyes drifted close, the tear a silver memory on his cheek.

As she approached the bed, Linsey wondered at her lack of fear. If he had not started coughing, he could have easily raped her, never remembering the deed. She knew he would have been gentle with her. After all, he would have been loving his Snow again. For a momentary flash of time, Linsey regretted not knowing the experience of his love.

"What kind of a woman are you, Linsey Marie MacAdams?" she berated herself. She had been physically stimulated by a man that only moments earlier she had thought of as some kind of a monster. She had enjoyed the caresses he had thought he was giving to

79

his wife, a woman he deeply loved. And for a brief time, she had envied the woman—a woman who in death still retained his love.

Shaking herself out of her thoughts, Linsey called his name. When there was no response, she sighed and reached for the tangled furs. It was then that she looked at his massive chest. It was heavily muscled and thickly covered with crisp, curling hair.

And more badly scarred than his face.

The three scars that ended abruptly at his jaw started again just above the middle of his chest. Only here there were four lines that became five farther down his stomach. They continued on an angle from left to right, slashing down his body, turning into six scars where they disappeared beneath the pants low on his narrow hips.

"Ach mon, what have ye done?" she whispered, unconsciously using the long familiar brogue her father had brought with him from his native Scotland so many years earlier.

There were four newer marks slashing across the scars. Not nearly as deep as the older scars, they still showed signs of having bled. With a pang of regret, Linsey realized they were from her fingernails.

The incoherent ramblings of the man on the bed snapped her out of her shocked trance, and she quickly covered him with the furs. She turned and stumbled to the table, her trembling legs unable to support her slight weight. She sat down, looked at the fire and vaguely realized it needed another log, but her hands were shaking so much she knew she wouldn't be able to put a log in without risking burning herself.

Her reaction to Bear mystified her. She had never responded to any of her many escorts in Philadelphia with such abandon. How could she feel repulsion, pity and attraction all at the same time?

Across the room Bear rested quietly. The only sound in the cabin was the crackling of the fire, its light throwing a golden glow over the room and the anguished young woman who stared hypnotically into it.

Bear's feverish mind wove in and out of delirium, meshing reality and dreams as the long night slowly passed. The nightmares of past tragedies taunted him cruelly, memories of things never forgotten.

Linsey forgot time as she endlessly sponged him. She carefully tended the left side of his face and extended the baths down his chest. She felt reluctant, at first, to touch him—somehow it seemed too intimate even in its innocence—but as dawn approached, she was no longer hesitant. Taking special care in the areas around the scars, she worried that they were more sensitive than the surrounding skin and that she might inadvertently cause him pain.

Moving like someone older than time, she walked back to the fire to replace the warmed water. Linsey sat down, her head cradled on her folded arms. It had been a long night, and still Bear's fever raged. She fought sleep, knowing she must stay awake, but exhaustion was taking its toll, making her movements slow and clumsy.

"Autumn Fire?"

Linsey raised her head. The sound had been so soft she was not sure if she had heard it or imagined it. Her eyes met his, and for the first time in hours his dark, clouded gaze was rational.

"Bear?" Linsey stumbled in her haste to get up,

81

tripping over the chair and sending it crashing backward.

"Water?" A slight smile crossed his face as he watched her awkwardly hurry to do his bidding. The smile vanished when she reached the bed and he saw the dark circles beneath her eyes and the evidence of the long night.

Remembering the last time he had tried to drink, Linsey dipped a clean rag into a fresh pail of water. She held the cloth to his mouth, dampening his lips and letting him suck the liquid from it. She pushed the tangled hair from his face, unconsciously resting her hand on the scarred cheek to check the temperature. His skin was still hot, but she thought, or maybe just hoped, it was slightly cooler than it had been.

"You are tired, Autumn Fire," he whispered in a deep, gravelly voice, very aware of where her hand rested.

Linsey smiled softly at him. "I think you've been making up for all those healthy years."

Bear moved, wincing at the soreness throughout his body. "Have I been trampled by a herd of buffalo?"

"No buffalo, just a simple cold," she replied teasingly. "Simple colds always attack big, strong men the hardest."

His eyes fluttered closed, and he yawned widely. "I'm hungry."

She threaded her fingers through his hair, feeling very protective of him. "Sleep," she whispered quietly. "You can eat when you wake again."

Linsey sat beside him for a long while, watching him sleep. She let her hand rest in his hair, finding comfort in simply touching him. Deciding that his fever was no longer at a dangerous level, she sighed deeply and

82

stood. Stretching, easing the kinks out of her body, she had an overpowering feeling of exhilaration.

She had won! She had fought to save him and had done it. Carrying the pails to the door, she opened it and tossed the water outside, repacked them with snow and took them back to the fire.

Her exhaustion gone, she hummed lightly as she hung a large pot of snow on the hook and swung it toward the fire. Her prime concern now became food. Reasoning it out, Linsey knew that if he hadn't been able to swallow water, it would be impossible for him to eat much of anything. Not quite sure how, or with what, she decided to make a broth. Perhaps if she fed it to him slowly, he'd be able to have some nourishment.

Digging through various baskets and bowls, Linsey found nothing from which to make the broth. Finally, in Bear's backpack just inside the door, she found some strips of the dried meat she recognized as jerky.

Also in the pack were several small bags of herbs. She opened each bag and smelled its contents, wondering if she could add them to the broth for flavor. The first three were odorless, the next one was overly sweet, but the last was repugnant.

"Uck!" Linsey fanned the air in front of her nose as she quickly closed the bag. "If it smells that bad in the bag, what would it smell like cooking?" She shuddered at the thought and returned the bags to the pack, deciding that she'd remember the sweet one. If she couldn't find anything else, she would come back for it.

She dropped three small strips of the jerky into the large kettle and continued searching the cabin. In a large bag, she found a white, grainy substance, and hesitantly tasting it, Linsey discovered it was sugar. Delighted, she dragged the bag across to the fire and dumped a handful into the pot. When it quickly dissolved in the bubbling water, she wondered if she should use more. Not caring for overly sweet things herself, she nonetheless remembered that most people preferred extra sweetening. Maybe Bear would be more likely to eat the broth if it were slightly sweet. Shrugging, she scooped three more handfuls into the pot.

She found several carefully-labeled containers of herbs. Unfortunately he had written their names in French. Linsey could speak a few words of the language but could not read any of it. She smelled the herbs, and when she found one she liked, she added it to the pot. Sometimes, if the aroma was strong, she added only a little of the herb, others with a slighter scent she added in greater proportions. She stirred the concoction with a large wooden paddle, her stomach growling as the spicy, sweet odor filled the cabin.

Remembering that their Philadelphia cook had once complained that nothing tasted right if it was not salted, Linsey rummaged through the bags and baskets. Not finding the grainy powder she was familiar with, she was about to admit defeat when she discovered a large block of white crystals in a wooden box. She touched the tip of a finger to the block and then to her tongue.

It was most definitely salt, but in a block weighing several pounds. Linsey looked around the cabin searching for something to use to chip some pieces off the block. She spied Bear's hunting knife—his well-honed, carefully maintained hunting knife—on the table. She discovered that by scraping repeatedly over the top of the block she quickly had a handful of salt. Recovering the box, Linsey carried the precious seasoning to the pot, dropping it in.

As she stirred the broth, Linsey felt a quiet satisfaction steal over her. She had not panicked when Bear had needed her. She had thought the problems through and had been successful in finding solutions. In Philadelphia there were hired servants to see to her every need, but in the wilderness, with Bear so sick, she had only herself to depend on. When applied correctly a little common sense went a long way, she decided smugly.

The day dragged on, Bear waking only long enough to sip at water. Several times she poured him a cup of broth only to find that he had fallen asleep before it could cool enough for him to drink. Wanting to save the delicious smelling soup for Bear, Linsey chewed on pieces of jerky. She would sample her own cooking after being sure that Bear had eaten as much as possible.

Linsey walked to the bed for what she thought must have been the hundredth time that afternoon and lightly touched his cheek. He still felt warm, but not as dangerously hot as earlier. As if her touch had awakened him, Bear opened his eyes.

"Hungry," he muttered hoarsely.

"You must be getting better if your stomach is the first thing you think of when you wake," Linsey teased. She smoothed back the dark hair on his forehead. "Can you stay awake a little longer this time? Everytime I get the broth cool enough for you to drink, you're asleep again."

Bear started to roll to his side, but the aches and pains flowing through him convinced him it wasn't worth the effort. "Are you sure it wasn't a herd of buffalo?"

"Not even one tiny, baby buffalo." Linsey smiled before walking back to the fireplace. She spooned some of the broth into a cup and blew on it, wanting to cool it before he could go back to sleep.

She carried it and a spoon back to the bed and sat on the edge. She filled the spoon with the broth and raised it to his mouth. Bear opened his lips, and the flavor seemed to attack his senses. Intent on feeding him without spilling it, Linsey missed the startled expression that momentarily crossed his face.

"This is the first time I've ever cooked anything," she said proudly.

Bear swallowed the repugnant brew. At least its heat felt good on his raw throat. "What did you put in it?" he asked weakly as she held another spoonful to his mouth.

"Well, I found some jerky in your backpack—" Linsey began listing the various ingredients she had used.

Bear's hand came up, and with a surprisingly strong grasp, he clasped the hand holding the spoon at his mouth. "Backpack?"

"Yes."

"Did you use anything in it?"

"I already told you I used the jerky—"

"Did you use anything in the small bags?" His voice was threaded with exasperation and impatience.

"No, why?"

"Most of them, *mon ange*, are poison."

"Merciful God in heaven." Her hands began shaking so badly she was in danger of dropping the cup onto his bare chest.

"Easy, little one." Bear steadied her hands, guiding the spoon back into the cup. "It is of no importance. You did not use the poisons."

"I could have killed you!" Linsey jumped up from the bed and began to pace agitatedly through the room.

The repulsive bittersweet taste of the broth still lingered on his tongue, but Bear could see how hard she had worked to make it. He had no idea what she had put into it, but the only poisons were kept in his back-pack; as long as she hadn't used them there was no real danger. He shuddered at the taste even as he remembered the pride shining from her eyes when she had first sat down on the bed. With a mental shrug, he knew he would have to eat more . . . or at least try.

"Autumn Fire, will you not feed me your broth?"

Linsey turned and saw the pleading look on his face. "Are you sure I didn't use something in it that might kill you?"

"It will not kill me," *I hope*, he added under his breath.

Bear managed to drink half of the cup of broth. Fearing that any more would make him violently ill, he feigned sleep, forcing Linsey to stop feeding him.

When he felt her leave the bed, he opened his eyes and watched her walk away. He was not too sick to notice the shapely length of her bare legs or the way the dress clung lovingly to her curves. She moved gracefully, seeming to glide across the room. Bear tried to keep his eyes open, wanting to enjoy the pleasure he found in just watching her, but by the time she had made her way to the fireplace, his eyes had closed in earnest, returning him again to the healing arms of sleep.

Linsey placed the cup on the table and sat down, trembling with the knowledge of how close she had come to poisoning Bear. Only because she had not liked the smell of the herbs had she decided against using them. What if one had been pleasant smelling and she had added a generous portion to the broth? She shivered at the thought.

When she noticed that the fire had burned down, she stood and added more logs. Feeling anything but hungry, she knew she must eat so refilled the cup with broth for herself.

Trying to put the thought of what could have happened out of her mind, she set the cup on the table. Blowing on the broth to cool it, she decided that she would have to learn to make coffee. If Bear wasn't able to tell her how to do it, she would just have to experiment. After all, she had successfully made the broth, hadn't she? Coffee couldn't be harder since it was only water and coffee beans.

She glanced across the room and saw that Bear was sleeping peacefully. Exhaustion hit her, and she wondered where she would find the strength to make it through another night without sleep.

The steam from the broth rolled gently into the air, teasing her with its aroma. Using the same spoon she fed Bear with—in fact the only eating spoon she had found in the cabin—she began to eat.

The flavor of the broth rolled around her tongue. Gagging, she spit it out and quickly drank water from one of the bowls on the table, hoping to wash the taste from her mouth. It was horrible . . . both sweet and bitter, overlaid with the taste of salt.

How could Bear have eaten nearly half a cup? Linsey felt tears of self-pity prickle the back of her eyes. She was so tired. She had tried so hard, and it had smelled so good . . . and tasted so terrible!

Blinking away the tears, she rose with a sigh and moved the pot away from the fire. It would have to cool before she could carry it outside and pour it out. There was no reason to let it stay warm; it wasn't fit for human consumption!

Any sign of her former elation was gone as Linsey dragged herself to the bed. Bear's skin was still burning hot, but he seemed to be resting naturally. She again sat on the edge of the bed and placed a cool rag on his forehead. If she didn't do something, she risked falling asleep.

Linsey could not remember ever being so tired. Even during her time with Jeb and Zeke, she'd slept each night. Mostly it had been a light sleep that had been disturbed by the slightest sound, but it was sleep.

The night passed with incredible slowness. Linsey tried everything she could to stay awake. She added wood to the fire when it was not necessary, the noticeable reduction in the woodpile adding another worry. She stood in the open doorway, until her skin was icy to the touch. She tried to recite her favorite poems and even carried on conversations with herself, giggling at the absurdity of talking to herself.

Several hours before dawn, she lost the battle. Bear opened his eyes and found her sitting beside him. Her eyes were closed, her head hanging until her chin rested on her chest. He carefully slid over and pulled her down beside him.

Feeling herself falling, Linsey tried to open her eyes, but will-power alone was not enough to accomplish the herculean task.

"Fire," she mumbled as she snuggled into the warmth surrounding her.

Bear looked at the blazing fire that was making the cabin uncomfortably hot. "It will last awhile yet," he whispered in his husky voice. He cradled her head against his shoulder and pulled the furs over them both. "Sleep, little one."

"So tired."

"I know, *Ain jel ee.*"

"I tried so hard."

He smiled at the childlike voice. "You have done very well, Little Fawn."

"I want to go home."

"In the spring," he promised softly.

"Spring," Linsey murmured as she drifted into sleep.

Bear's hand felt like it was anchored with lead weights as he lifted it to smooth back her hair. He slowly worked the tresses free from their knot and spread the silky strands over the fur. The firelight danced around the auburn tresses, turning them into a burning flame of color. He twisted the clinging curls around his hand, sighing with pleasure at their softness.

He was not sure how long he'd been sick, but he knew she had been there beside him each time he woke, her voice soothing, her hands cool and gentle against his skin. The foul taste of the broth still teased his tongue, reminding him how hard she had tried to do the things that were unfamiliar to her.

She deserved some rest, he thought with a gentle smile, seriously doubting that he'd be able to wake her if he tried.

Bear closed his eyes, weary again. He felt Linsey's breath caressing the skin on his chest and found a contentment he had not known for years. And had only recently realized he had missed.

Linsey woke abruptly, an intense heat burning into her cheek. With a start, she realized she had fallen asleep and that Bear was once more burning with fever. His disjointed mumbling confirmed that he was again delirious.

She opened her eyes and found herself staring at a jaw, dark with several days' growth of beard. Her nose twitched at the coolness of the surrounding air, and she tried to turn her head, knowing before she looked that the fire was dead.

Finding it impossible to move her head without pulling her hair, Linsey reached up and encountered Bear's fingers firmly tangled in the snarled locks. Long minutes passed as she tediously unwrapped her hair from his hand. When she was free, she slid from the bed, careful to keep him covered.

Shivering, she forced her stiff legs to carry her across the frigid room. Cold ashes seemed to taunt her. At least this time she had a vague idea of how to start the fire, she thought dejectedly. After smoothing the ashes, she piled several pieces of kindling in the center and began striking flint against steel.

Several times a weak spark started a tiny flame that was destined to die before it took firm hold. Linsey shivered, grateful for the warmth of the buckskin dress. She knew she should stop long enough to wrap a blanket around her, but with each spark, she was sure this would be the one that would become a roaring flame.

Bear's mumbling became louder until she could distinguish several words. She clenched her teeth together; there was no one else to light the fire. If she didn't do it, they would freeze. Her stomach protested noisily, and she moaned at the thought of trying to cook again. She was so hungry—but not hungry enough to want to eat her own cooking!

Her hands shook, and her knees resting on the hard dirt floor began to ache. Each spark promised warmth only to leave a sense of despair. A feeling of impending doom spread through her. She decided she was destined to die in this forbidding wilderness, either from starvation or from the cold. She wondered why she even bothered to try to delay the inevitable. Only the instinct for survival kept her trying repeatedly to start the fire when her teeth chattered, her hands shook uncontrollably and the knowledge of warmth, even if it was false warmth, beckoned from across the room.

"Dear God," she prayed softly, desperation ringing with each word, "help me to—"

Without warning the door crashed open and slammed violently against the wall. The frozen leather hinges creaked protestingly, one tearing free to leave the door hanging crookedly.

Linsey swung around to face the new threat, her long hair settling around her in a shimmering veil of red. Her morbid thoughts of death fled as she stared at reality.

Framed in the sparkling daylight was the sinister jackal of her nightmares, in search of her soul, the final test of her diminished strength and failing courage.

Her scream splintered the quiet, unheard by the one person who might have been able to save her.

Chapter Five

"*Nèe lah neè kah nàh!*"

The Indian's hand raised threateningly, and a feathered tomahawk sliced through the air in front of him, effectively silencing Linsey. Tightly clenched in his other hand was a wicked-looking knife, the blade shining razor sharp. He stood as if poised to spring into action, his piercing black eyes surveying the room, intently scrutinizing the shadowed interior. His wide, heavily muscled shoulders stiffened at the sound of a moan from the bed, and his alert gaze moved to that corner of the room.

"*N'tha thàh!*"

His harsh, guttural words grated on Linsey's ears, making her tremble.

With a threatening stare in her direction, he moved gracefully to the bed. Still poised like a mountain cat expecting danger, he swiftly threw back the furs.

As Linsey watched, she desperately searched for a plan to protect the defenseless man. Bear's hunting knife lay on the table, and without conscious thought, she crept slowly toward it. The Indian continued his survey of Bear, his back toward her.

Her hand closed around the knife, and without sound, Linsey rose to her feet, her body seeming to act on its own accord. She had fought too hard to save Bear's life from the fever to sit back and watch him be killed by a savage.

Linsey took two hesitant steps toward the vulnerable copper back, the knife raised above her head. She knew she had made no sound; she had never moved quieter in her life. But instinct must have alerted the Indian to danger.

He turned abruptly, a wicked sneer crossing over his face.

"I'll not let you kill him," Linsey whispered.

As if he understood her, his sneer deepened to a grin, his eyes seeming to dance with enjoyment. Slowly he hooked the tomahawk through his breechcloth and sheathed his knife. As graceful as a panther, he began to stalk her.

With each step the Indian took forward, Linsey took one backward until she felt the mantel from the fireplace pushing into her head. She could go no farther, and still the Indian silently approached.

"Damn you! Only a savage would torture a sick man."

Linsey held the knife at waist level, both trembling hands wrapped around it. "I've never killed anything before, but as God is my witness, if you touch him, I'll put this knife so deep in you it will come out the other side!"

The Indian stood relaxed, the smile never leaving his face. His black eyes sparkled as they stared into hers. He spoke in his fiendish language, his hand outstretched, palm up.

"You want my knife, do you?" Linsey snarled. "Well

have it you shall," she raised the knife slightly, "but it will be in your belly, not your hand."

From the bed Bear moaned loudly, and for a fraction of time the Indian turned his head. Linsey sprung, realizing this was the opportunity for which she had waited. The Indian returned his attention to her just as she moved. Grabbing her hands effortlessly, he removed the knife. With a flick of his wrist, he threw it into the wall across the room, where it hit and quivered before becoming still.

Face to face they stood, the proud fierce warrior holding her easily. Her chin raised even as shear terror dilated her eyes.

"*Pel áh wee o skeès a kwèe.*" His voice was soft, the smile gone.

"You will never know of my fear." Linsey tried to make her voice firm, but a quiver sounded in spite of her effort. "I'll never give you the satisfaction of seeing me afraid."

Again he spoke quietly while almost reverently wrapping a strand of her long hair around his finger. As if breaking out of a trance, his big body shook, and he freed her hair and gently set her aside.

He walked toward the fireplace, and for the first time Linsey noticed that he limped. How could he appear to move so gracefully that she only now saw his limp?

Having expected to be instantly tortured, Linsey's terror-fogged mind jumped from one scattered thought to another. Why was he taking time to make a fire? Dressed only in pants and a breechcloth, his bronzed chest bare, she wondered if he was cold. Perhaps he liked to be comfortable when he tortured captives, she thought, fighting to swallow a nearly hysterical impulse to giggle.

Without realizing she was doing so, Linsey watched

the Indian light the fire. When a spark caught, he blew gently, adding larger pieces of kindling as the flame grew.

"He didn't tell me to blow on it," she moaned in a whisper, seeing her error in trying to start the fire.

A hungry golden blaze quickly began to devour the logs. The Indian broke the ice covering the top of one of the buckets and poured the water into an empty kettle. He removed the kettle of broth from the hook and set it near the fire, placed the kettle of water on the hook and swung it directly over the blaze.

When everything was to his satisfaction, he stood and limped to the open door. He walked into the snow, disappearing around the side of the cabin, returning quickly with a heavy fur slung over his shoulders. In one hand he carried some frozen raw meat; the other held a wrapped bundle.

Without looking at Linsey, he set the package on the table and began cutting chunks of meat off the bones, adding them to the pot of water. He opened a pouch at his waist and removed several small bags.

The Indian set another pot of water in the now glowing coals and added what looked like dried leaves from some of the bags to it.

Linsey took advantage of his turned back and moved quietly over to the wall. She reached for the knife above her head and tried pulling, twisting and turning it, but it was sunk so deeply into the log that she could not budge it. She leaned her head against the rough wood, her hand clutching the knife hilt, despair running rampant through her slender body. Turning, she slowly slid down the wall, sitting with her arms wrapped around her legs. She knew that the true test of her strength would begin soon.

At least she would be warm when she died, she

thought apathetically. Maybe he'd even feed her first. Her stomach did not seem aware of the danger facing the rest of her as it growled in protest of the delicious smells beginning to float through the cabin.

The Indian glanced in her direction, and seeing that she presented no danger, he walked once more to the bed where Bear lay delirious, innocent of the danger surrounding him. The Indian removed his knife, and Linsey stifled a scream as she watched it descend.

A tearing sound filled the hushed silence, and Linsey's eyes widened when she saw the Indian's hand come back up—holding what remained of Bear's pants. He quickly dropped them onto the floor and kicked them out of his way.

Growing more mystified by the minute, Linsey watched as he walked to the fire and returned to the bed, carrying the small pot of steaming water with him. He set it near the bed, shifting Bear until the steam drifted into his face. Pouring some of the liquid into a cup, he lifted Bear's head, forcing him to drink. She realized that they were speaking when she heard the rumble of Bear's deep voice.

When he decided Bear had drunk enough, the Indian slowly lowered him back to the bed. She watched as he ran his hands searchingly over Bear's body. Satisfied that there was no hidden damage, he covered the shivering man with all of the blankets and furs on the bed. When Bear attempted to throw off the coverings, the Indian raised his voice and spoke harshly.

From her corner, Linsey realized that the cabin was growing increasingly warmer. Dressed in pants and breechcloth, the Indian's copper skin glistened with a light covering of perspiration. Linsey wiped her hand across her forehead and found that it, too, was wet.

Bear no longer seemed in life-threatening danger; in

fact, the Indian seemed to be trying to help him. Lowering her head to her knees, Linsey waited with resignation for whatever was to come. When moccasin-covered feet entered her line of vision, she lifted her head, startled to find a bowl being held out to her. With a grunt, the Indian pushed it toward her.

Feeling light-headed from fear and hunger, Linsey accepted the bowl. Not waiting for the steaming food to cool, she burnt her fingers in her haste to eat. It was simply meat and broth, but she swore she had never tasted anything so good. Only as she was drinking the last of the broth did she stop to wonder if one of the ingredients he had added was poison.

With a shrug, Linsey decided it was too late to be concerned. She had all but licked the bowl clean.

Across the room Bear moaned, tossing and turning while sweat ran down his face. The Indian frequently forced him to drink from the prepared water, maintaining a constant watch that the furs stayed in place over the thrashing man.

As the day grew on, Linsey's thoughts of imminent torture faded. She began to wonder if he were not known to Bear. No man, Indian or white, would give a stranger the kind of care the Indian was giving Bear.

"Do you speak English?" Maybe, if he was a friend, Bear had taught him a few basic words.

When there was no reply, she tried again. "Who are you? You must have a name."

Except to occasionally check on her whereabouts—which was simple for him to do since she hadn't moved in hours—the Indian ignored her and concentrated on nursing Bear.

"Divil take ye, mon, be ye not going to torture me?" Her agitation showed in the brogue she unknowingly used.

The Indian turned slowly, his eyes glittering brightly. "Do you wish for me to do so?" he asked in perfect English. "You will have to forgive me that in my concern for my brother I neglected to begin your torture. What did you have in mind, Summer Eyes?" He crossed his arms over his chest, an amused smile showing straight white teeth.

"Why, you . . . you. . . ." Linsey's rage made it impossible for her to speak or to form a clear thought.

"If I may make a few suggestions as to the type and method of your torture?" he offered. "My forefathers spent years refining their techniques."

Linsey slowly stood, her building anger noting and magnifying his enjoyment. "Ye bloody whoreson savage," she yelled, her brogue so thick that he could understand only a few words. "Ya dinna intend torture! I hae spent the day long waiting for something that wasna to happen!"

It was fortunate that the Indian could not understand her as she paced toward him, speaking in a brogue so thick it would have pleased any Highlander while she cursed his ancestors, his future generations and even the ground he stood on.

They stood face to face, the tall majestic warrior and the small, furiously angry woman. One smiled, one raged. He was fascinated by her fiery hair but in awe of her summer leaf eyes. Her size was little more than a half-grown child, and yet he could detect the womanly curves beneath the dress of his tribe. Never had he encountered such a violent temper in a woman, a temper capable of wiping any other emotion from her mind. If she were not the woman of his brother, he would take her for his own. Except for the man on the bed, he had no love for the white race, but he would enjoy the challenge of channelling her temper in another direction—a direction that would make him the envy of many warriors when they heard her screams and moans of passion through the darkness of night. That he already had a wife mattered little. His people accepted multiple marriages as a fact of life. Many hands made the work lighter. That he loved his wife and had chosen her from many others because of that love did not enter his mind.

Linsey would never know the thoughts that raced through his mind as she cursed at him. Nor would she be aware that the thoughts were discarded as quickly as they came. In the mind of the Indian, she was the woman of his brother. He would accept her as a sister-in-law. As she ranted and raved at him, she did not know that his trust, respect and protection were extended to her as a sister. Nor did she realize the extent of affection she would one day feel toward him.

At a feeble sound from the bed, the Indian turned his attention from Linsey. "You are healing," he said quietly when he saw that Bear's eyes were open and the delirium was gone.

"It's easy with all the noise in here," Bear mumbled. "I see you've met my woman."

"Summer Eyes is a woman to walk the trails with."

Bear nodded in quiet agreement. He already knew that Linsey was a woman who would enrich the life of any man fortunate enough to spend it with her. That she had survived her captivity showed her strength. He knew she would protect those she loved as fiercely as she now ranted at the Indian warrior. With the passing of time, she would grow into the woman she was meant to be, and lucky would be the man who could claim her as his own.

When her angry tirade continued unabated, Bear couldn't prevent a grin. "Could never take her hunting; . . . her screeching would scare all the game away. You seem to have upset her, *N'tha thàh,* my brother."

"Summer Eyes is angry."

"Obviously. Would you know why?"

"I did not torture her," he explained with a shrug.

"Not the usual reason for such anger; most people would be relieved to discover they weren't to suffer such a fate."

"Not a usual woman." He turned and looked down at Bear. "I think my brother, Bear Who Walks Alone, has found a mate worthy of him."

Bear could understand most of Linsey's thick brogue, and his eyebrow rose in amusement. He was glad his brother did not realize exactly what she was saying. His relationship with Limping Wolf might not be able to survive the abuse Linsey was heaping on it.

"She is beginning to repeat herself, Limping Wolf," Bear said as both men listened to the ranting woman.

"You will find much pleasure in taming her, I think."

"My days—and nights—will not be boring!"

Bear began to cough, the sound penetrating through Linsey's red haze of rage. She suddenly felt drained of all emotion. Even the fact that she was standing face to face with the fierce warrior did not rouse her fear. She turned toward the bed and the man who seemed unable to draw a breath.

Perspiration ran down his face, a sign that the fever had broken once again. Linsey wondered if he would become feverish as night drew nearer or if, this time, the fever would stay down.

Without a word to either man, she turned and picked up one of the rags she had used for sponging him down. Wetting it, she began to run it soothingly over his face. She kept her eyes turned from his. There was a noticeable difference between sponging a man who was delirious with fever and one who was aware of every move she made.

"We need to get the wet bedding from beneath him." She motioned to the Indian, who stood quietly observing her. "If you'll help him to stand, I'll change it."

"I don't need help to stand!" Bear stated as firmly as his weakened voice would allow.

Linsey moved away and waited. After several attempts, Bear admitted he needed help, finding he was so weak he could barely sit up by himself. As he slid his legs off the side, he realized he was nude. He sat on the edge, regaining his breath and trying to decide how to stand without offending Linsey. He knew Wolf would think nothing of his nudity and wouldn't understand Linsey's reaction to it.

"My brother, I seem to have lost my pants," Bear said in the Shawnee language, "and unless you want to start Summer Eyes up again, I think we had better find a way to keep me covered."

Wolf looked puzzled and questioned Bear. His look turned to one of utter amazement, and he shook his head in disbelief. He would never understand the way of the white man—or woman!

As Linsey watched them wrap a blanket around Bear's waist, she remembered Wolf cutting off his pants, and her face flamed scarlet. When Wolf put Bear's arm around his shoulders and started to pull him off the bed, Linsey turned her back.

"It is safe to look now, little one," Bear said, trying to hide his grin. Wolf helped him cross the room, stopping frequently when Bear began to cough helplessly. As she replaced the wet bedding, she tried to ignore the sounds from across the cabin, sounds that told her

102

all too clearly that she should be grateful for the help of the Indian.

When Linsey heard the shuffling sounds of them returning, she quickly finished smoothing the bedding. Turning, she carefully kept her eyes lowered until a pair of bare feet and ones covered by moccasins came into view.

Slowly raising her eyes, she studied the two men. Their coloring was similar with blue-black hair and eyes so dark brown they appeared black. Wolf's skin was a deep copper shade while a dark tan attested to Bear's preference of doing without clothing. They were nearly the same height, with Bear perhaps an inch or two taller, but that was where the similarities ended. Bear's massive size would have dwarfed a smaller man and made even the muscular Indian appear insignificant. The muscles of his arms and shoulders rippled with each movement, and Linsey knew his upper arm was as big as her waist. She realized she had been staring only when her gaze met Bear's amused eyes.

Hastily backing away, she stumbled over the discarded pants. A strong arm came out to grab her when she started to fall, and she found herself staring into the eyes of the Shawnee brave. Years of terror could not be eradicated in a few short hours, and without her emotions submerged beneath a cloak of rage, Linsey's deep-rooted fear returned full force. She pulled away from Wolf, once more seeing only the savage Indian.

Bear lowered himself to the bed and lay back with a sigh, unaware of the tension until he turned his head in her direction. Her fear was easy to read but difficult to accept. This was the woman who had stood face to face with Wolf and used her sharp tongue as her only weapon. Now she stood immobile at the foot of the bed, her eyes dilated with fear.

"Little one, there is nothing here to cause you such fear." Bear offered her his hand, motioning for her to come to him. "You are safe. Wolf will not harm you. He would protect you with his life."

The men exchanged glances, Wolf's questioning, Bear's without answers. Finally Wolf turned and walked back to the fireplace. Linsey kept her eyes on him as she edged around the bed and grabbed at Bear's hand.

Aware of the trembling hand in his, Bear pulled her to the bed, closing his eyes as she sat down. He wanted to reassure her, but his excursion across the room and back had left him exhausted. Holding her cold hand tightly in his, he drifted back to sleep.

Linsey felt ridiculously secure holding Bear's hand. Common sense told her he was too weak to provide any kind of protection. It also told her that Wolf offered no threat, but common sense held little value in the face of deeply ingrained fear.

Sitting beside Bear, her hand tightly clenching his, she watched Wolf as he knelt to add wood to the fire. He stirred the kettle of soup he had made and turned his attention to the pot of broth whose sweet fragrance now drifted through the cabin.

Wolf stirred it with a wooden spoon, bent and inhaled deeply. His wide brow furled as he tried to identify the contents. Dipping the spoon back into the liquid, he raised it to his lips, blew gently to cool it and tasted.

Revenge! It was unintended and unplanned. Her mouth tingled with remembered revulsion. It was unsubtle torture!

"Pfftt!" Wolf spat the offensive broth back into the pot. He slowly turned his head, his fierce gaze meeting

104

the twinkle of amusement she could not hide in her own.

"You fed my brother this?"

Linsey nodded.

Wolf stood, crossing his arms over his chest, and a proud expression lit his sculptured countenance. "My son's sons will sing of his strength. Until now even I did not know how truly strong he was."

Bear twined his fingers together beneath his head and stretched his big body. He could feel his strength slowly returning with each passing day, but he had begun to chafe at the inactivity. For now he felt content as he watched Linsey across the room. Using the ornately decorated silver brush and comb that had belonged to his mother, she carefully worked the tangles from her hair. Each stroke of the brush through the glorious mane was as soothing to him as it was to her. The silver brush and comb were the only things he had that had been his mother's. It seemed to him that his earliest memories were of them flowing rhythmically through her long, dark hair.

He closed his eyes as a remembered pain flashed through his mind. For a moment he let his thoughts dwell on the spring he had turned fourteen. He could almost feel the warmth of the sun on his face as he rode beside his father on their return from town. The snow had melted sufficiently for them to take the trip, the dwindling of their supplies making it necessary. In a few weeks game would again be plentiful, but until then they had purchased enough to restock their depleted larder.

The smell of smoke drifted on the wind long before their cabin came into sight. For as long as he lived,

Bear would never forget the horror of seeing the smoldering structure and finding the violated bodies of his beloved mother and sisters. There were many signs around the ruins telling that it had been the handiwork of Iroquois braves raiding at the first spring thaw.

Three lonely graves were dug in the frozen earth beneath the spreading branches of a giant elm. Only a few yellow crocuses had ventured above the ground, their blossoms vibrant against the backdrop of the glittering snow, promising that spring was near. They were the only flowers he could find to decorate their graves. Almost a man, his body showing signs of his future size, he bowed his head and let his tears drop onto the flowers in his hand.

Broken-hearted at the loss of his beloved wife and daughters, Bear's father salvaged what he could from the ruin of his home. When he found the silver brush and comb beneath a smoldering down mattress, he had at first cradled them in his work-roughened hands. Then, in anger at his loss, he threw them violently into the woods surrounding them. Bear carefully searched out the treasured items, hiding them in his pack when they left the clearing. It was years later before his father became aware that he had them.

Now as he watched Linsey smooth her hair with his mother's brush he wondered why it seemed so right. He had never given them to his wife. Snow had known of their existence and had admired their ornate silvering. She never asked about them, respecting his privacy and seeming to know of their value to him.

But now, without hesitation, he had offered them to Linsey. When she had washed her hair earlier and sat combing her fingers through the tangled strands, Bear had dug them out of their place of safe keeping and given them to her. It had been years since he'd packed

106

them away, and rarely did he think of them; yet it seemed as if they had been waiting for this moment in time.

It was not dark hair they caressed, but hair with the warmth of flames, golden strands mingling with sunset red. The motions were the same as those from his memories, totally feminine, but now instead of maternally soothing, they were sensuously arousing.

Each time she lifted her arms, her unbound breasts bounced gently, the beaded bodice clearly showing the rounded fullness it should have concealed. Bear found himself staring at the enticing movements until he finally forced his eyes away. His gaze then traveled down her slender body to where the hem of her skirt rested at the tops of her knees. Having quickly grown accustomed to bare legs, Linsey had neglected to ask him how to wear the leggings. Now he lay in the bed, appreciating the sight of her shapely legs demurely crossed at the ankle.

Bear felt his blood begin to heat when he thought of those slender legs wrapped around his body, his hand shaping her tender breasts while his tongue teased a soft peak into pebble hardness.

He closed his eyes, trying to capture a picture from the past, but it merged with the reality of the present. With a low moan, Bear rolled to his stomach, fighting the urge to leave the bed, only to return with her in his arms.

"Are you all right?" Linsey stopped brushing her hair when she heard the sound from the bed. Bear's fever had not returned since Wolf had left two days earlier. He seemed to be improving rapidly, but perhaps it had only been wishful thinking. Perhaps the fever had come back.

Carefully setting the brush and comb on the table,

Linsey walked to the bed and laid a hand against his cheek. His skin was cool.

When she touched him, Bear had to bite back another moan, his hand clenching and unclenching the fur beneath it. His body felt out of control, his thoughts only on satisfying the need his body demanded.

"Are you in pain?" Linsey watched his hand open and close on the fur. She lightly ran her hand down his buckskin-covered back. "Can I help?"

Bear's knuckles turned white from the force of his grip. He wanted to laugh—or cry—with frustration. She was the only one who could help, but he knew she'd be horrified and frightened if he were to tell her exactly what kind of help he needed.

Since Snow's death almost five years before, Bear had been celibate. It was by choice that he took no other woman to his bed. He had loved his gentle wife and had met no other woman who made his blood burn with desire . . . until now.

"I'm tired of being in this bed." He forced his hand to ease its hold and rolled over, sitting up. He rested his elbows on his knees and supported his head in his hands.

Linsey understood his restlessness. Her father had been a terrible patient the few times she could remember him being sick. After a couple of days in bed, he became extremely irritable, complaining about the simplest thing.

"I need to start dinner." Linsey stood and nonchalantly smoothed her dress, repressing a smile at the nearly muffled moan from him. "Why don't you come sit at the table? Maybe you can make some suggestions that will improve my cooking."

Bear watched her walk away and shuddered. He'd do more than make suggestions. He'd watch like a hawk surveying its dinner and make sure of each ingredient she put into the pot. His tongue nearly curled at the remembered taste of her last attempt.

An hour later a large kettle boiled, filled with carrots and potatoes. Bear sat at the table, carefully sharpening his knife.

"Do you have any idea how long it takes to sharpen a knife?" he asked, sending accusing looks in her direction.

"Not nearly as long as it took to dull it," she replied sassily. "How was I supposed to know that scraping it across the salt would dull it?"

"You could have asked."

"Who? You?" Her eyes began to glow with building temper. "You certainly didn't complain when it spent three days stuck in the wall!"

"I'm surprised it didn't just bounce off!"

Linsey picked up a log to add to the fire and momentarily considered hitting him with it. Wouldn't be fair to the log, she decided, placing it in the blazing coals.

"We need more firewood," she stated, looking at the depleted pile.

" 'Round the side of the cabin." Bear carefully tested the blade, then returned to sharpening it. He had several other knives, one of which he decided to give to her. It would be for her sole use. She could scrape all the salt or sand or anything else she wanted to scrape with it, just as long as she left this knife alone.

A muffled scream interrupted his thoughts. Moving with cautious speed, Bear reached for his rifle beside the open door, loaded it and stepped out into the snow. The setting sun turned the snow to a glittering pink. Looking carefully to the right and then left, he quickly realized there was no danger. The snow was unbroken

109

except for the trail left by the arrival and departure of Wolf . . . and the path leading around the side of the cabin.

Another muffled scream came from that direction, and Bear followed the trail. In places the snow had blown into drifts nearly waist high, and he wondered how Linsey had managed to wade through it. His greater weight sunk him ankle deep with each step.

When he rounded the cabin, he was greeted by a sight that brought a smile to his lips. Two bare legs protruded from the snowbank. A bare foot waved frantically. Another muffled scream broke him from his amused trance, and he grabbed a handful of her dress and easily pulled her free.

Linsey spit and sputtered, wiping the cold wetness from her face with one hand while holding firmly onto him with the other. When she could see again, her temper flared from the humor dancing in his eyes.

"It . . . is . . . not . . . funny!" She stamped her foot, and snow fell from her hair, some of it going down the back of her dress.

"I was just thinking I had never seen a more attractive snow . . . ah . . . woman."

"I want to go home . . . now!" Linsey turned from his grinning face to return to the cabin. Her battered dignity was further tested when her foot slipped and she would have fallen again had he not reached out and grabbed her.

"In the spring," Bear replied with a chuckle. "Surely you can see the grave dangers we would face should we begin the journey now." His gaze traveled from the top of her wet head to her foot . . . her bare foot. "I would spend too much of my time pulling you out of snowbanks. We'd never get to our destination."

Raising her nose haughtily, Linsey stamped away,

110

careful where she stepped so that she did not fall. Each time her bare foot stepped into the snow, she quickly lifted it, so that her usual graceful glide became reminiscent of a hop-step movement.

"You did not gather the firewood," Bear reminded her needlessly, retrieving her moccasin from several feet away.

Stepping into the doorway, she turned disdainfully. "You're outside. You get it."

His grin widened as he walked past her to the other side of the cabin. Linsey realized that the snow was not nearly as deep there. He walked only half the distance she had covered on the far side of the cabin and stopped before a place where the snow was mound nearly to the roof. Working quickly, he brushed it away, revealing a neatly stacked woodpile covered by a heavy canvas tarp.

"The snow always piles up higher on the other side because there are no trees to cause a wind break." He loaded his arms with logs and turned back to her. "I put the woodpile here so that it would stay drier." He passed her in the doorway, a grin teasing the dimple in his cheek. "And so that I wouldn't have to worry about falling down the slope on that side of the cabin."

"I'm going home!" Linsey slammed the door, testing the newly repaired hinge. "The divil take ye and yon snowbank. If I canna walk or float, then it's wings I'll sprout and fly myself home!"

Chapter Six

An hour after going to bed, Linsey was still awake, wiggling on her make-shift bed. Finding a comfortable position on the hard table was impossible, she decided with a huff as she rolled from her back to her side. The remembered softness of the bed taunted her as she pulled a heavy fur up to her chin. Each time she moved, one of the furs or blankets started sliding to the floor, and she had to make a quick grab for it, which usually dislodged others.

The discomfort did nothing toward improving her already frayed temper. The dip in the snowbank still rankled, and all evening she had searched for a way to release some of her frustration. Bear had given her no opposition when she tried picking an argument with him, thwarting her simply by being patient. Now, as she searched for sleep, unable to relax, she blamed it on the table . . . and the man who refused to be a gentleman and offer her the bed.

Across the room, snug and warm in his massive bed, Bear listened to Linsey tossing and turning. Occasionally a muffled word reached him, and he judged her building temper as the unintelligible murmurs became distinct curses. He wondered how long her anger would burn before it either exploded or faded away. At the rate she was going, it would still be white hot in the morning!

Bear rolled to his side so that he could watch her in the glow of the banked fire. In a short span of time, he watched as she turned from one side to the other and back again, grumbling each time she moved. His quiet sigh was one of resignation. If either of them was to get any sleep, she would have to find a release from her agitation.

Had Linsey been able to see his eyes, she would have found a gleam of anticipation in them.

The tranquil quiet in the small cabin held the promise of the calm before a storm, disturbed only as Linsey again changed positions. The fury of the storm broke over Bear's head with his quiet words.

"Take care, Wiggle Worm, or you will fall off your bed."

Worm? Linsey threw off the heavy fur, swung her legs over the side of the table and sat up. She stared into the corner and through the darkness could see a vague outline of his massive body. All evening she had waited for him to say something, anything, that would give her an excuse to unleash her anger. Worm wasn't much, but it would do!

She jumped down and began pacing the room, Gaelic curses flowing freely from her tongue. She had learned them from her father during one of his frequent bursts of temper. When she began repeating herself, she switched to English, easily remembering the flowery curses she had overheard at various times in her life.

Bear waited patiently for a lull. He recognized the Gaelic for what it was but was unfamiliar with the language. However, her English was bruisingly clear, and

113

he raised an eyebrow, a smile crossing his face at her colorful rantings.

Linsey began to feel rather sheepish as the towering rage washed away.

"Do you get angry very often?" Bear asked quietly.

Linsey found herself at the foot of the bed and leaned against one of its tall posts. "I didn't even know I had a temper until I was kidnapped."

"That is hard to believe, little one," Bear replied with a chuckle.

"One of the few things I can remember about my mother was her temper." Linsey smiled, the memories happy ones. "My father seemed to enjoy her outbursts, and they always ended with both of them smiling at each other." She pushed her tangled hair away from her face. "My father's temper is almost legend in Philadelphia. But I really thought I hadn't inherited it from either of them. I've never been angry until the afternoon Jeb and Zeke stopped our carriage."

The horror of that afternoon quickly erased the smile from her face. Sensing her change of mood, Bear sat up and held his hand out to her. "Come here, *petit chat.*"

"*Petit chat?*" Linsey moved slowly toward him, her hand reaching for his.

His big hand engulfed hers, and he pulled her to the edge of the bed. "You were hissing and spitting like a little kitten."

Once more, simply touching him brought a feeling of security to her. "I was angry," she finally replied.

"That is an understatement." Bear chuckled. "What were you saying in . . . Gaelic, I believe?"

She nodded affirmation as a roguish smile dimpled her cheeks. "I'm not sure exactly what I said. My father would never translate those particular words for

114

me, though he did turn an attractive shade of red when I repeated them to him and asked their meaning.''

Bear threw back his head and roared with laughter. Linsey joined in, her sense of humor quickly restored. He released her hand and wrapped an arm around her shoulders, hugging her tightly as they shared their amusement. Finding her face turned up to his, Bear bent and lightly kissed her lips. It was a natural reaction, without conscious thought. He meant it to go no further. But when his lips met hers, laughter was wiped from their faces. He raised his head, and their eyes met; and as he watched, the sparkle in hers was replaced by a startled, wary expression. His gaze lowered to her slightly parted lips, and he was drawn to them by a force as powerful as life itself.

Linsey raised her hands defensively to his bare chest, but any thought of resistance was drained away as her lips met his. It began as gently as a spring shower, his lips softly teasing hers, barely touching as they rubbed lightly back and forth. He deepened the kiss gradually as her lips parted. He nibbled lightly at her lips, the tip of his tongue soothing the sensuous bites.

The softness of his lips against hers and the warmth of his breath against her cheek made Linsey feel as if she were floating. It came as a shock when she realized he had picked her up and set her on his lap. It seemed natural for her hands to slide up his chest until her arms wrapped around his neck. Her fingers found their way into the long hair on his nape and teased at the thick strands.

Taking care not to alarm her, wanting the magic to go on and on, Bear deepened the kiss further, carefully introducing her to the sensation of his tongue sampling the sweetness of her mouth.

Linsey hesitantly met it with the tip of hers, feeling

his startled reaction in the tightening of the muscles in his shoulders. She began to withdraw when his hand moved to the back of her head and lightly, but firmly, held her in place.

Her long hair spread around her like a cape, and Bear tangled his hands in the silken curls. His moan was lost in her mouth when she innocently moved and her breasts flattened against his chest. Only the thickness of her deerhide dress separated their bodies—a fact that offered its own torment to Bear's whirling thoughts.

Linsey's mind reeled at the new sensations running wild fire hot through her body. Touching him had always brought a feeling of security to her. Now it brought a different kind of feeling altogether as she lightly traced the tight muscles of his shoulders.

She had grown accustomed to touching his scarred face and felt no hesitation in moving her hand from his neck to gently cup his cheek. He moaned softly at the touch and covered her hand with his, holding her palm against his cheek.

Bear fought for control as he felt the heat raging through his body. Knowing he had to stop before it was too late, he slowly ended the kiss, withdrawing first his tongue and then easing the pressure of his lips against hers. He slowly, reluctantly, raised his head, his passion-filled eyes burning into hers.

Linsey traced the three scars on his face, her fingers feather soft against the damaged skin. Bending slightly she placed light kisses along the length of each one. "Only flesh and bone. So badly hurt," she murmured. Her hand returned to its place against his cheek.

Bear shivered at the intensity of the feelings flowing through him. He knew how monstrous his face was. He could not take her caress lightly; to him it was almost a declaration.

He pulled her hand from the back of his head and at the same time turned his face so that her palm covered his mouth. He worshipped her hand with his lips, lightly tracing the center with his tongue, before pulling both of them down to her lap.

He had to clear his throat several times before he could speak, and then his voice was deeply raspy. "I think we should stop this and try to get some sleep."

Linsey felt bewildered. Why had he suddenly stopped kissing her? Had she been wrong to touch his cheek? She had not planned to do it, but it had felt so good, so natural, and she wanted him to know that she no longer feared his scars.

Bear read the questions in her gaze and lightly traced the slope of her cheek. "That is only the beginning, sweet angel."

"The beginning of what?"

His gaze roamed the molding of her face, and he softly kissed the end of her up-turned nose before picking her up off his lap and setting her on her feet. "The beginning of something you are not yet ready for." He turned her toward the table and gave her a little push.

"I hate it when people talk in riddles," Linsey mumbled childishly as she climbed back up on the table.

Bear's hands clenched until the knuckles showed white as he fought the urge to take her back into his arms and show her exactly what he meant. But if he once loved her, made her his, he'd never take her back to the city. And he had no doubt that Linsey did not belong in his wilderness. Fourteen years of his mother's gentle teachings forced him to relax and wait for sleep.

It would be a long winter, with many days of them

snowed in together. The cabin was tiny even for one person. How long could he resist her . . . and himself?

Linsey sat at the table, her chin in her hand, her elbow against the rough wood surface. She watched intently as Bear shaved the week's growth of hair from his face. Using the now razor sharp knife, he quickly dispensed with the smooth side of his face and worked slowly on the time-consuming scarred side. The hair had grown quite long in only a week and had begun to cover the scars.

"Why do you bother to shave?" Linsey was finally forced to ask, after he had cut himself for the third time. "It takes forever, and you appear to be adding more scars."

"It doesn't take nearly as long if I do it every day." He contorted his face, looked into the small mirror and resumed shaving.

"A beard would cover the worst of the scars," she commented innocently.

Bear stopped, lowered the knife and turned to her. "Even covered with hair, they would still be there, little one. I will not hide something that is a part of me. *Nèe lah e nèe nee làh*, I am that I am."

"It's really not that bad."

He raised a dark eyebrow in her direction. "It was enough to scare you witless the first time you saw it."

"At that point anything would have scared me witless! In fact, at that point I was witless." She stood and walked over to him. Raising a hand, Linsey lightly touched the scar. "I think your imagination has made it more than it is. If you scare children, it's probably more because of your size than your face." She looked up impishly, her hand resting on his cheek.

Bear gritted his teeth as her innocent touch sent far from innocent thoughts racing through his mind. His voice was far harsher than he intended as he fought to control the urge to crush her in his arms.

"If you will move your hand, I can finish this task sometime today."

Linsey lowered her hand. "I'm sorry, I didn't—"

"I know, sweet." He turned back to the mirror and grimaced at the traces of blood from the nicks he had inflicted on himself. "Why don't you open the package Wolf brought while I finish this?"

Linsey picked up the package from the floor and set it on the table. Using the knife Bear had given her, she worked open the knotted thong tying it closed. Inside was a heavy coat similar to Bear's only much smaller. The fur side was out, the longish hair hanging thick and sleek. Linsey slipped it on, delighted by its warmth. She swirled around in circles until she was dizzy, laughing when she had to grab the table to steady herself.

"Put on the leggings, and we will see what the outside world has to offer."

Linsey reluctantly removed the coat and reached for the bulky pieces of fur. She tried unsuccessfully to wrap them around her legs, and as she began to lace them they slid down her slender leg.

Wiping the traces of lather from his face, Bear grinned when he heard the muttered Gaelic. Taking pity on her, and himself, he knelt on the dirt floor at her feet and lifted the shoe-encased foot onto his bent leg. He tried to ignore the warm flesh beneath his hands as he quickly tightened the thong.

"Sit still or I'll never get these things laced." Bear grinned as Linsey wiggled like a small child, impatient with the stubborn pieces of fur, wanting only to be outside.

With a happy sigh, Linsey stood when he had finished, grabbed the hooded, fur coat and headed for the door. Bear's grin widened at the absurdity of her clothing and her innocent acceptance of it; the leather shoes combined with the dress, coat and leggings of the Shawnee. Her long hair, coiled like a rope and knotted through itself, peeked from beneath the hood.

Linsey opened the door, breathing deeply of the crisp, clean air. Only when she had taken a few steps outside did she remember the dangers that waited for someone who was not familiar with the terrain. She turned pleading eyes toward Bear, silently asking him to come out with her.

Grabbing his coat, Bear accepted the silent invitation. He, too, was unaccustomed to the enforced inactivity and needed to feel the sun against his face.

"You lead; I'll follow," Linsey stated as he walked toward her.

"What if I lead you off a cliff?"

"Since you'll fall first, I'll just have to be sure to land on top of you!"

Bear chuckled and headed down the path. He had no destination in mind, just enjoying the freedom from the cabin.

Linsey walked behind Bear, snuggled deeply into the coat. The only sound was the crisp crunch of the snow beneath their feet and the occasional plop of snow dropping from the limbs above them.

The giant trees seemed to reach for the deep blue sky. The sun sparkled on the snow like untold numbers of fabulous jewels, so bright it hurt their eyes. Linsey stopped to look at an ice-encased bush, its remaining leaves covered in a layer of sparkling crystals.

When Bear no longer heard her accompanying footsteps, he turned and watched as she stared in fascination. One hand appeared from the sleeve of the enveloping coat to trace the ice formation that hung from the bush. Her childish enthusiasm touched a deeply buried longing in him, and he smiled gently as he watched.

Linsey turned and answered his smile with an impish one of her own. Just as she started to move toward him, a ball of snow from the trees above fell and landed in her face. Linsey spit and sputtered with surprise and yelped as some of the icy wetness found its way down her neck and under the fur.

Bear chuckled as he watched her trying to wipe the snow away. "When there is snow on the trees above, it is better not to look up too often."

"Now you tell me!" Linsey started walking toward him as she wiped the snow away.

"I would have told you sooner if you had asked."

A grin split his face as he turned and continued down the trail. With the fur once again in position tightly around her neck, Linsey watched the broad back in front of her. Enjoying the fresh air on his head, Bear had not pulled the hood of his coat in place, and she contemplated her actions only briefly before bending and grabbing a handful of snow. She formed it into a good-size ball and lobbed it toward his unprotected head, bending for another glob of snow as the first one left her hand.

The snowball hit the back of his head with a satisfying plop, and as he turned to face his attacker, another one, also intended for the back of his head, hit him squarely in the face.

"I . . . I didn't think you'd turn so quickly," Linsey said in way of an apology as she took a few steps backward. "I meant it to hit your head, not your face."

Bear wiped the snow away, fighting not to let his amusement show. The look on her face was so horrified he wanted to throw his head back and roar with laughter. But not yet. . . .

"So you want to play, eh, my snow bunny?" He bent and grabbed a handful of snow. Before she could turn, a well-aimed snowball hit her face.

"No fair!" Linsey yelled as she wiped her face a second time. "It was an accident!"

"An accident that you threw a snowball?" he asked as he made another one. "Or an accident that your aim was better than you thought it would be?"

Linsey turned in time to prevent his next missile from landing in her face. Instead it hit the side of her head, falling harmlessly against the heavy fur.

"You realize you just declared war, don't you?" She bent, and grabbed a handful of snow. She threw carefully, but it landed several feet short of its destination.

The fight quickly escalated into a full-blown war. Few of Linsey's poorly constructed missiles found their way to her opponent, while few of Bear's missed. He was careful that he didn't pack the snow too tightly, wanting them to land and splinter instead of hurting. It had been years since he'd had a snowball fight. Not since that long-ago time when he had been a child for such a few short years.

"I yield!" Linsey yelled as another glob of snow dripped down her neck. The only exposed part of her body was her face, and each of his snowballs had landed on or near it, most of the snow finding its way inside her coat.

"Surrender?" Bear threw again and chuckled at her squeal.

"Never!" A quickly thrown ball fell short. "I surrender to no man!"

"Then to the death!" Bear pelted her with several more snowballs.

"I yield! I yield!" Laughing, Linsey turned and started running back down the trail toward the cabin.

A few steps and Bear caught up with her. Linsey's leather shoes slipped on the slick ground, and when he tried to prevent her fall, they both tumbled into the snow.

Using a small portion of his weight, Bear carefully held her down, but the contest was done. His dark eyes were lost in the picture of her. Her cheeks were rosy, the tip of her nose red. Her eyes sparkled with the brilliance no emerald could ever claim, and her hair had come unbound, lying flame bright against the white backdrop.

She giggled helplessly, her breath coming in short spurts and gasps. When her eyes met his, the giggles abruptly ceased, but the breath came no easier to her lungs.

The harsh light of day showed her more clearly than ever the scars that marred the perfection of his face. Freeing a hand from beneath his chest, she traced the hardened ridges from their beginning in his hair to the edge of his jaw. She lightly touched each scar and ran her fingers across them, finding the height of the ridges and the depth of the valleys between.

How lucky he had been not to have lost an eye, she thought, lightly touching the edge of his brow. She traced a line down to the edge of his mouth, her finger following the outline of his lips.

Bear lay perfectly still above her, supporting his

weight so that he did not crush her. His agitation showed only in the depth of his breathing. He closed his eyes so that he did not have to see the expression in hers. Be it pity, revulsion, disgust, they were not the emotions he wanted from her.

. Linsey almost moaned at the thought of the pain he had endured. How had he survived such damage? She knew that the scars were on his body as well as his face. Were there also hidden scars? Scars of hatred because of the destruction of something once so perfect?

Her gaze moved to the other side of his face. Only a few hours earlier, when she had watched with avid curiosity as he shaved, she had wanted to turn her eyes away from the contortions he had made as he worked on the damaged side of his face. She had not wanted him to see the fear in her eyes—fear that he would seriously cut himself and cause more pain. The wholly masculine activity had fascinated her even as she feared for him.

She compared the two sides of his face. The finely arched brows were the same as were the long lashes that lay against his cheeks. As if dividing good from evil, his high-bridged, slightly off-center nose separated the two sides. She remembered the softness of his lips against hers as she stared at his firm, well-shaped mouth.

When she remained still and did not speak, Bear knew he had to open his eyes, force himself to look at her. His eyes, so dark and troubled, met hers and found an emotion as unexpected as it was surprising. Tenderness shined from her as a gentle smile rested on her lips.

"Do you plan to keep me here until I surrender?" she asked impishly. "I must warn you that if that is your intention, we will slowly die of starvation, for I will never surrender."

"You will not surrender, but you will yield?" He felt off balance at her abrupt return to their game. He had expected pity or repugnance; she was giving him teasing smiles and gentle touches.

"Your aim is far better than mine, I yield."

A smile crossed his face, one that had started at his toes and spread its warming strength through his body before finding its way to his mouth. "Perhaps my aim is better because I don't let a giggle interfere."

"But you laughed! I heard you!"

"Yes, little one." His voice deepened, the smile lingering only in his eyes. "With you I think I will always find much to laugh about."

Linsey lifted a hand and once more traced the scars. "Did it hurt very badly?" she asked softly.

"I have had other things hurt much worse and for far longer."

"I wish I could take all your hurts away," she whispered.

Bear closed his eyes. He already knew she would bring her own form of pain to him . . . in the spring.

The quiet mood was interrupted as the coldness of the ground finally penetrated Linsey's thick fur coat. Bear felt the shivering of the form beneath his and stood, pulling her up with him.

"You are cold," he stated, wrapping the coat securely around her. "We will go back and get warm."

It felt natural to both of them to walk toward the cabin hand in hand. Bear shortened his stride so that she had no trouble keeping up with him. Overhead, the sun shone brightly; the snow crunched loudly beneath their feet.

"Waging war sure makes a man hungry."

"I'm so glad to hear you say that. I'm starving!"

"Good, we'll eat our noon meal a little early today."

"You cook."

A shudder rippled through his massive body. "Of course!"

Kaleb left the three cabins behind him as he headed down the trail toward the river. Three families had carved their spot in the wilderness. Clearing the land and building their one-room log cabins, they had started their own future.

Guardedly welcoming strangers, anxious for any news that might be filtered to them, they were careful to protect what they had sacrificed so much to build.

Kaleb felt a deep envy for what they had, for the goals they had set and worked endlessly to achieve. He had once built the same kind of dreams; but they had crumbled to dust at his feet, and his life now had only one purpose.

Revenge.

He was getting closer. Each settlement or trading post he stopped at had seen Jeb and Zeke. He used as much patience in tracking them as he used in tracking game. It was a contest of wits . . . with no doubt as to the winner.

Reaching the river, Kaleb pulled the canoe firmly onto shore. He had discovered that Jeb and Zeke were now on foot, so he could no longer use the river. He shouldered his pack and walked away from the canoe without looking back. The people at the settlement had said he could leave it on shore, but he had little hope of ever seeing it again. It was well made, carefully crafted. Someone would see it and take it for their own.

He had little regret at losing the canoe. If he lived, he could build another one.

His long muscular legs easily ate up the miles, the limp hardly noticeable. The heavy pack was a familiar weight on his back. It was a big wilderness, and he had only a vague idea of the direction they had taken; but he would find them. Then his revenge would begin. He had not spent four years searching to give up now that he was so close.

"They'll pay with their lives fer what they did to you, Mary," Kaleb whispered to the face in his mind. "They'll suffer fer what they did to us. . . . I will make certain they welcome their death long before it comes."

Chapter Seven

Linsey discovered that playing in the snow with the abandonment of a mischievous child made it difficult to remember simple table manners. When Bear placed the plate of food in front of her, she ate as if she were starved. And, she was relieved to see, so did he.

When it came time to clean up, Linsey volunteered to wash the dishes, using some liquid soap that had a light wild flower fragrance. Bear told her how the Indians made it out of roots and used it for anything that needed to be washed.

Linsey made careful note of where he stored it so that she would not have to ask. In the back of her mind played the idea that at the first opportunity she would use it—on herself.

"Get your coat and we'll take another walk. If someone behaves herself, we may get a little farther than we did this morning."

"Are you implying that I prevented us from taking a walk this morning?"

"You threw the first snowball."

"But you started the war!"

"How so?"

"You threw the second one, therefore I had no choice but to defend myself."

"Your logic escapes me." He shook his head. "Blame me if you must, but get your coat."

Not waiting for another invitation, Linsey grabbed her coat, swung it around her shoulders and stood waiting at the door for him.

"Don't you even want to know where we're going?" he asked as he pulled on his heavy fur coat, picked up his rifle and opened the door.

"Hunting?" Linsey nodded toward the gun.

"Nope."

"Then, why take your rifle?"

"Because, little one, you never know who, or what, you might meet on the trail. In this land it is best to be prepared for anything."

He easily carried the heavy, long rifle in his right hand, careful to keep Linsey on his left and slightly behind him. Should it become necessary, Bear would not hesitate to put himself between her and unexpected trouble.

The world was covered in a glittering blanket of white, drifted deep in some places while nearly bare ground showed in others. As the trail sloped downward, Linsey found it more and more difficult to maintain her balance. Her slick leather shoes were not made for walking on the slippery snow. When she started to fall, Bear reached for her hand, supporting her until she regained her balance. Instead of releasing her hand, he twined his long fingers through hers, and as always, she felt comforted by his firm grasp.

They walked quietly, the only sounds the gentle rustle of the breeze through the trees and the crunch of snow beneath their feet. Linsey was not concerned with their destination. She was content to follow Bear wherever he led, placing her trust in him without question.

The trees parted suddenly, and they were standing on a slight incline. Nestled in a deep hollow was a settlement with hundreds of houses, placed in orderly rows, one beside the other. From most of the structures, smoke drifted in a ghostly dance until it merged with the blue of the sky.

"Why didn't you tell me you lived so near a settlement?" Linsey stared with wide-eyed wonder at the quiet setting, noticing how neatly laid-out it was. The houses were built differently than those she was accustomed to in Philadelphia. They were long, low, windowless structures with thatched roofs. Skins were stretched on a frame to make the doors of the mud-colored dwellings. There were fenced fields and garden spots behind most of the houses, with well-defined roads weaving throughout.

From their vantage point, they could see the entire settlement that seemed to stretch endlessly. In one of the fields, several small children were playing in the snow. Slipping and sliding, their game appeared to have no rules except that it be enjoyed by participants as well as spectators. The high-pitched screams and squeals drifted to them, and Linsey smiled at their obvious pleasure.

"Maybe I can talk the children into forming an army, and we'll challenge you to a battle," Linsey teased, eager to meet Bear's neighbors.

"You and all of them against only me?" Bear raised an eyebrow, his eyes twinkling as he looked down at her. "Doesn't sound like fair odds to me."

"Depends on whose side you're on. From my point of view, twenty or so to one sounds fair."

"But you're the twenty or so, I'm the one!"

Linsey scanned his massive form and pretended to shudder. "Maybe it would be better if I enlist more than those few children down there before I engage you in battle!"

"There is no need for anyone but you, Timid Deer. I have seen you battle Wolf. I surrender!"

Linsey blushed, remembering the anger she had felt and shown. She turned her eyes again to the settlement. Several adults had joined the children, and even from this distance she could see that the adults were willing to let the children defeat them. She wasn't sure when she finally realized what she was seeing. No one thing stood out to give her a clue; rather it was a series of small things. The few words that drifted up to them were not English or any of the foreign languages she had heard throughout her life. The sun shone brightly on tiny, uncovered heads, clearly showing no golds or reds. There was no shine from leather shoes, no sparkle of frilly white drawers.

"They're Indians." It was a statement of fact from a voice almost paralyzed by fear. For nearly as far as she could see were the neat fields and strange houses. "Thousands and thousands of Indians."

"Not nearly that many," Bear replied, unaware of the terror building in the woman beside him. "Several hundred, maybe, but not thousands."

Linsey dropped his hand and started backing away. Bear turned when he realized she had moved, and saw the stark horror on her face. Her eyes remained glued on the scene below as every evil she had ever heard replayed through her mind. He had brought her to an Indian village! To the very home of the savage!

"Linsey, come to me." Bear held out his hand, hoping his voice would penetrate her terror. "Come to me, little one." He prepared to spring should she turn and

131

run. Too many things could happen to her in her present frame of mind should she panic.

Linsey tore her eyes away from the village and saw his hand reaching out to her. Like a light in the dark, it offered security, protection.

She threw herself into his arms, buried her face in the thick fur coat and held on to him as if her life depended on him.

"Easy, *mon ange*, there is nothing here to hurt you." Through the thickness of her cape, he could feel the shuddering of her body.

"Take me home. Please, Bear, take me home!"

Bear glanced around them. To the side of the trail was a large boulder, clear of snow. He bent and picked her up, carrying her to the clearing. When he tried to put her down, Linsey tightened her hold until he was forced to sit with her on his lap.

"Is your fear because of the Indians?"

Linsey nodded, her face still deeply buried in his coat.

The hood of her coat had fallen back, and Bear rubbed a cheek against the softness of her hair. "They are people just like you or me."

Linsey shook her head violently. "Savages!"

"Only because their lifestyle is different from ours do they seem savage to strangers."

"They torture innocent people!"

Bear was glad she couldn't see the smile crossing his face as he remembered her anger when Wolf had not tortured her. "There is an old lady down there. Her name has been forgotten, and everyone calls her Grandmother. She is so old that all of her family has died. She is a highly respected member of the tribe, not only because of her age, but because of her wisdom. The only torture I have ever known her to com-

132

mit was when she doctored me." His big body shook with revulsion. "I was feverish and everything else had failed. She forced me to drink a concoction that would have made your broth taste good!"

Linsey almost smiled. Nothing could have made her broth edible.

"There's a man who has six daughters and no sons. He married three times hoping that one of his wives would give him a son. He is the one who is tortured every day because his wives don't like each other and occasionally forget to hide it from him."

"Three wives!" She raised her head, her eyes wide with disbelief.

"It is one of their customs. There is a lot of work involved in just living from day to day, so if a man can provide for them, he is allowed more than one wife. Usually the wives get along fine; but sometimes the man is not careful in his choices, and it can become very uncomfortable around his house. I have heard his voice raised in pleading prayer with Manitou to give him the strength to deal with so many females."

"Manitou?" In spite of her fear, Linsey found herself becoming interested in the Indians.

"Manitou." Bear hesitated, trying to find the right words. "It is similar to our God. Manitou is the mysterious, unexplainable force in their lives."

Linsey rested her head against him, enjoying the comfort of his embrace. "They believe in God?"

"Not our God perhaps, but one that to them is as strong, as right, as powerful as ours."

"Then, why do they torture?"

Bear lightly kissed the auburn head beneath his chin, then rested his cheek on it. "They torture only those they think have committed a crime against them. To them it is no more cruel than it is to us when our courts hang a criminal. Perhaps it is even kinder than our punishment of putting men in prisons. The Shawnee could not live without the freedom of the sky overhead, to come and go as they please."

They sat quietly for long minutes, both enjoying the closeness. Bear wondered if she would trust him enough to overcome her terror and follow him to the village. He wanted her to meet the people he considered friends.

"As with every group of people, they are neither all good nor all bad. They are different from us, so some of their customs seem strange, even cruel. But they are people, little one, not some evil sent to earth to punish innocent bystanders."

With a gentle hand beneath her chin he raised her head. "Will you come with me to visit my friends?" When he saw the renewed terror in her eyes, his voice softened. "You've met Wolf. Wouldn't you like to meet his wife and children? He has a tiny son . . . little more than a babe, who will steal your heart."

Linsey wanted to jump to her feet, run back to the cabin and hide until spring. But she could see how badly he wanted her to accept his friends. How could she willingly walk into the middle of an Indian village?

"Will you hold my hand?" she whispered.

Her fear was so clearly etched on her face that Bear was tempted to take her home. He slowly lowered his head until his lips met hers. It was a gentle kiss of tender understanding. Setting her on her feet, Bear stood, raised his hand and offered it to her.

"I will hold your hand until you let go."

Linsey grabbed the comforting security, entwining her fingers through his. "I don't think I'll let go until we're home again."

Without another word, holding tightly to her cold

hand, Bear turned and started down the trail. Behind him Linsey searched for courage, but failing to find any, she clung more tightly to him with each step they took nearer to the village.

The children were the first to spot them. When their games ceased abruptly, the adults turned, instantly alert to danger. The children recognized the massive man and normally would have run to him. To them he was as much a member of the tribe as they. He was greatly respected as a fierce warrior. Stories of his strength were always begged for when long winter nights came early and the children gathered around the fires of their grandfathers to hear of days long past or just beyond yesterday. They knew him to be fearless in battle and unforgiving toward enemies. They knew him as a legend who walked among them.

And the children knew him as a friend. They had seen him kneel in the dirt to play a game of stones with the smallest boy. Several of them had been given guidance by him as they tried to master a new skill. They had seen him hold a new baby gently in his huge hands, hands that could have crushed its tiny body as easily as the children crushed ants beneath their moccasined feet.

The older boys had once tried to bring him down. Six or seven of them had clung to his massive body, but he continued walking as if unaware of the extra weight added to his stride.

Linsey did not know that she was the reason the children had not come running with greeting, inviting Bear to play with them. She knew they stared at her but not the reason for their awed hush. They stared opened mouthed at her hair, amazed by its color of the setting sun. Never before had they known anything but shades of black. Manitou had given her a crown the sacred color. Surely she was the perfect mate for the man they knew as Bear Who Walks Alone.

Linsey lifted her head proudly, defiantly, pretending a courage she did not feel. Her eyes remained lowered as she listened to the children's whispers, not knowing that they marvelled at her hair or compared her skin to the whiteness of the snow. She did not understand how different she appeared. Most of the people had never seen a white man except for Bear. Never had they seen someone whose coloring was so different from their own.

Curiosity overcoming their fear, the children slowly gathered closer. Bear stopped walking and cordially greeted the adults. He smiled at the children even as he felt Linsey's hand tighten its grip on his own.

"They are only children," Bear said quietly. "And as all children, they are very curious about a stranger in their village."

The children began to giggle amongst themselves, and one, slightly braver than the others, reached a timid hand out to touch Linsey's hair. He pulled back his hand and checked to see if the color had rubbed off on his fingers. He missed Linsey raising her head at the gentle tug on her hair. When the child turned back to touch her again, he found his eyes impaled by hers.

The little boy's mouth gaped open, and he muttered something to the others. As a group the children stepped away from her. Taking one final terrified look at her, they turned and ran away as fast as the snow and their frightened legs would let them.

"They fear you," Bear explained when she raised questioning eyes to him.

"Me? Why would they fear me?" She looked down the row of houses and saw people coming out of them, standing near the protection they provided and staring toward her.

"Few of these people have seen a white man other than me. The warriors on raids have crossed paths with the whites, but few of the women and probably none of the children have every seen any." He turned and started walking down the road, nodding to those he knew only slightly, verbally greeting those he called friend.

"Look at them, Linsey. Their skin is dark, their hair is black and their eyes brown. Your skin is as white as the snow, your hair is their sacred color, but most strange to them are your eyes. They have never seen green eyes!"

Linsey looked at the people watching her. When her eyes chanced to meet someone's, she could see the shock they experienced. As they approached the middle of the village, she saw the only person she knew.

Wolf stood at the door of his house, legs spread, arms crossed over his chest. When they reached him, he greeted Bear with a nod and turned his dark eyes to Linsey.

"Have you come to hurt my children, Summer Eyes?"

"Hurt your children?" Linsey looked to see if he was teasing her but could read no humor in his face. "Why would I hurt your children?"

"The children of the village whisper that surely you must be a witch woman sent to punish them."

"Witch?" Linsey's voice rose in amazement, and she noticed the children ducking behind their parents.

Linsey saw his eyes meet with Bear's, and for a moment she thought she detected a sparkle; but when they returned to hers, she could read nothing in the dark depths.

137

"Wolf, I could never hurt any child." Linsey was truly bewildered. She had come to the village full of fear only to discover that she was causing the children to be frightened. She turned to those nearest her and saw that some of the adults were also showing signs of fear. She turned back to Wolf and pleaded with the proud Indian. "Please, tell the children I would never, ever hurt them."

No hint of softening crossed his features as his eyes scanned hers. After long minutes of intently studying her, Wolf raised his head to his people and spoke words she could not understand. Slowly they began to return to their own homes.

"Enter my home, woman of Bear Who Walks Alone, and know that you are among friends and family." Wolf turned, pulled back the hide covering the door and entered.

Linsey looked at Bear, wanting to question him, but he gave her no opportunity as he reached for the hide and held it open.

The house was toasty warm after the coolness of the outside. Linsey was greeted by two pairs of dark, leary eyes and a pair of honey-brown ones that sparkled with mischief.

Wolf motioned for them to be seated, and Bear led her to woven mats near the fire. When she was settled, he introduced Wolf's wife. Morning Moon smiled shyly at Linsey while their young daughter, Spring Flower, hid behind her mother's skirt. Linsey said hello to the two and was surprised when both greeted her in English.

Linsey's attention was then diverted to Wolf's small son. Too young to know fear because of her hair or eyes, the baby threw himself onto her lap. Linsey was forced to relinquish her hold on Bear's hand in order

138

to prevent the child from banging his head on the hard ground.

The baby turned to her, grinned a wide, toothy smile and chattered as if she were an old friend.

"This gabby little fellow is Chattering Squirrel." Bear lifted the toddler from her lap and held him high in the air until the baby squealed with delight.

When Bear carefully set him back on his feet, he again launched himself at Linsey. There had been few opportunities for her to hold an infant and even fewer for entertaining one. Not quite sure what to do, Linsey settled the baby on her crossed legs.

Chattering Squirrel studied this new person intently. One chubby finger reached toward her eyes. Linsey grabbed his hand and held it firmly in her own, watching as his soft forehead furled in concentration. Finally his brow smoothed, and the sparkle returned to his eyes. He looked at her and chattered happily, his vocabulary a confusing mixture of English, French, Shawnee and infant gibberish.

"Good heavens." Linsey giggled in amazement. "What is he saying?"

Bear translated with a smile, "From what I can understand, he has decided you are a tree."

"A tree!" Linsey sighed. "I guess that's somewhat better than being a witch."

Morning Moon tried to coax her son off Linsey's lap, with little success. "My son mix words," she said softly. "My husband and his brother teach me English and French because I not know what my baby say, but sometime we still mix words."

"You speak very well," Linsey ruffled the straight black hair of the toddler who sat enthroned on her lap. "But why did he call me a tree?"

Morning Moon smiled and shrugged. "Your eyes must remind him of one."

As the afternoon wore on, Chattering Squirrel left Linsey's lap only for short excursions, quickly returning and climbing freely back in his place. While Bear and Wolf spoke quietly, Morning Moon served refreshments with the shy help of Spring Flower. The little girl handed Linsey a white ball, sticky with thick maple syrup.

"What is this?" She tore a piece of it free and hesitantly put it in her mouth. The crunchy sweetness was a delight, and she eagerly ate more.

"We call it a snowball," Spring Flower answered shyly. "I made it. You like?"

"Yes, very much!" Linsey replied, licking the sticky sweet syrup from her fingers.

"It is one of the first things a little girl learns to make," Morning Moon said softly. "It is made by cooking corn until it pops white, then coating it with the syrup and making it into a ball."

Chattering Squirrel was obviously familiar with the sweet. He reached eagerly for Linsey's and smacked his lips loudly when she put a small piece in his mouth.

Sharing her treat with the baby, Linsey had time to study the interior of the dwelling. Shelves of different heights and widths were suspended from the walls. Some held neatly folded furs, and Linsey correctly guessed they were for sleeping. Others held articles of clothing, colorful bowls and baskets. In the center of the room, a small pit had been dug, and a fire burned brightly, the smoke disappearing out a hole in the thatched roof.

Suddenly realizing that Chattering Squirrel had become heavier, Linsey looked down at the toddler. One chubby hand firmly clutched a fistful of red hair while he sucked contentedly on the other fist. His head rested against her breasts, long thick lashes forming soft shadows against his cheeks.

Linsey gently kissed the head resting so trustingly against her. She raised her eyes and met Bear's. They shared a long silent look, neither questioning nor denying the feeling of oneness that flowed between them. She pulled her gaze away from his and found her eyes meeting Wolf's.

"My son trust in you. He knows you are different than others he has met, but he does not judge because of that difference."

Linsey lowered her eyes to the baby, feeling that Wolf was telling her that she should not judge without first knowing a person. Difference alone was not reason enough to condemn a whole race of people.

"Chattering Squirrel is aptly named." She rubbed her cheek against the top of his head. "I don't think I've ever heard anyone speak in three languages the way he does."

"My husband and his brother, Bear Who Walks Alone, have decided Chattering Squirrel will become a great chief. Since the night of his birth, they have talked to him in the languages they know. They think any truly great chief must know the words of others." Morning Moon grinned impishly at her glowering husband. "They forget that all great chiefs begin as small babies."

"He will grow up knowing the languages of many," Wolf defended, straightening his shoulders and sitting taller.

"He will grow up never knowing how to speak his own language," Morning Moon teased. "He will think he is speaking a language and not understand why only his father and uncle understand what he says."

141

Linsey hid her smile in the baby's thick hair even as she marvelled that Wolf could stare at his wife so fiercely but Morning Moon did not hide in terror. She had never before considered that Indians could love, but it was quite obvious that Wolf and Morning Moon not only loved each other and their children but extended that love to Bear. The gentle teasing, the fierce expressions, the pride in their children . . . Linsey had seen it all before, on the faces of her friends in Philadelphia.

When it was time for them to leave, Linsey regretfully handed her valuable bundle to his mother. Chattering Squirrel opened his eyes, rubbed sleepily and began to chatter. He reached for Linsey, and his bottom lip protruded stubbornly when he was told no.

Wolf and Bear walked outside while Linsey lingered for a moment with Morning Moon. "Thank you for the dress and coat," she said quietly. "I will return them as soon as I can make something else to wear."

"Among my people, when a gift is freely given, it is an insult if it is returned," Morning Moon replied.

"Oh, I didn't mean to insult you!" Linsey was horrified at the thought.

"I know you did not, woman of Bear. Perhaps you will come to learn our ways and not think them so strange."

"My name is Linsey; I would be happy if you would call me that."

"Lin Zee," Morning Moon tried the unfamiliar word on her tongue, giggling at its strangeness. "It has a meaning for your people?"

Linsey had never given her name much thought and was startled when she realized exactly what her name had meant to her father. "Linsey woolsey is a type of cloth commonly used by my people. It is sturdy and

142

long lasting. My father came from a land far across the ocean where many men were ruled by one man. I think he named me Linsey so that I would remember always that I lived in a land where every man is the same and no man is ruled by a king."

"You have many names," her dark eyes sparkled, looking remarkably like the mischievous ones of her son. "Lin Zee must be better than witch!"

"Will the children ever trust me?" Linsey was truly horrified at the thought of frightening all the children. She was to be the thing of their nightmares as Indians had been of hers.

Morning Moon's eyes showed the gentleness of her nature. She understood Linsey's horror. "When they forget you are different and see you only as a person, they will come to love you as my son already does."

"I hope you're right."

They left the house and found the two men standing just outside, patiently waiting. They said good-bye and headed back to the cabin. Linsey had little to say on the trip home. As she walked behind Bear, her thoughts were centered on the Indian village. The people she had met had been like people everywhere. They were not the frightening savages she had feared all her life. But there had to be a basis of foundation for the horror stories she had been told.

Her confused thoughts tumbled over themselves. Which was true? The savage bent on torture or the loving parents proudly showing off their children? How could the same people leave two such totally opposing impressions?

She quickened her steps until she walked beside Bear. "I tried to thank Morning Moon for the dress and found I had insulted her when I offered to return it."

143

Bear caught her hand and held it tightly. "It would be appropriate if you gave her something instead," he offered.

"Like what? I have nothing to give!"

"You could make a dress for her or Spring Flower. I have some hides at the cabin you could use. Or you could make something for the new baby."

"New baby? Morning Moon is going to have another baby?"

"In the spring," he replied with a smile.

"But I won't be here in the spring." A stab of disappointment ran through her at the thought. She would never know if Morning Moon's baby was a boy or a girl.

Linsey walked quietly, hand in hand with Bear, still deep in thought when the cabin came into view. She sighed deeply, deciding to wait until another day before she examined her confused feelings.

Darkness fell quickly once they were inside the warm haven of safety.

"How did you become Wolf's brother?" Linsey's abrupt question broke the comfortable silence of the room. Bear looked up from the trap he was repairing, his thoughts drifting back nearly twelve years. He told her briefly about the deaths of his mother and sisters and how he and his father had started trapping.

"The first snow of the winter had fallen, and we were working our lines back toward our winter camp," Bear said, his voice deep with memory. "I almost stumbled on Wolf in the darkness. He had carelessly stepped in one of our steel traps."

Bear grinned. "To this day, he swears he wasn't careless, just intent on following a deer.

144

"It's amazing that the trap didn't cut off his foot. As it was, if we hadn't found him when we did, he would have bled to death. We built a fire and kept him warm, doing our best to stop the bleeding. In the morning I carried him to the village.

"He was delirious by the time we arrived, and there were a few rather uncomfortable days while we waited to see if he'd live or die.

"When he recovered, we were invited to spend the winter in the village. My father decided it would be a good experience for both of us and accepted."

He became quiet, and Linsey waited for him to continue. "Is that it?" she asked when it became obvious he was finished with his story.

Bear smiled at her curiosity. "Not really," he said. "I was the first white man Wolf had ever seen while he was the first Indian I had ever had the chance to know. We had to prove our strengths to each other; after all, I couldn't let him think he was stronger than I was. We spent that first winter doing more fighting than anything else.

"I won most of the fights simply because I was almost twice his size, but when it came to tracking—" Bear shook his head, chuckling—"he'd lose me in the woods every time we went out. Even with the snow thick on the ground, he'd get away from me. More than once I spent the night out in the cold because he had managed to get me lost and then drifted away like a shadow. I'd spend the night sitting with my arms wrapped around me, shivering and cursing while he'd be in the village, warm and toasty."

Linsey had to wait for Bear to finish chuckling before he continued. "That first winter we were more enemies than friends. While he felt great respect for my father, considering it was his aid that had saved

145

him, Wolf thought I was rather like a stupid bear. He was the first one to call me Bear, and believe me it was not a compliment!

"We wintered with the tribe every year for the next five. Each new winter Wolf and I felt we had to prove ourselves to each other. Finally, one winter I could not out fight him; he couldn't lose me in the woods. We tracked game equally as well; I was only slightly more accurate with a gun, he with a bow and arrow. We became friends."

Bear set the finished trap on the floor and leaned back in the chair. "That spring before we left, we became blood brothers." He held up his left arm, and almost lost among the other scars was a thin straight one just above his wrist.

His face clouded, and Linsey knew the new memory was bringing pain to him. "The next winter my father was dying by the time we reached the village. I had carried him for miles while he fought to breathe. Even the old Grandmother couldn't save him.

"I wintered alone with the tribe that year. When spring came, Wolf invited me to stay." He looked up at her and shrugged lightly. "I did."

The fire crackled, filling the silence with its familiar sound. Linsey watched Bear as he stared into the fire, and the question that had haunted her since his illness sprang unwittingly to her lips.

"Who was Snow?" she asked softly.

Bear was startled by her quiet question and wondered where Linsey had heard about Snow. "Snow On The Trees was Wolf's younger sister," he answered quietly. "She became my wife two winters after my father's death. I had to prove to her father that I was worthy of his only daughter."

Bear stood and walked to the fire. He knelt in front

of it and added several logs. When he said nothing more, Linsey knew he was not ready yet to tell her about his beloved wife.

"In the morning, if you'll show me how to work with hides, I'd like to try making something for either Morning Moon or her baby," Linsey said, abruptly changing the subject. "I can embroider fairly well on cloth, but I've never had the opportunity to work with hides."

Bear sighed quietly and shook the melancholy thoughts from his mind. He was relieved that she had changed the subject but knew he would someday tell her of Snow. He would have to.

"It will give you something to do while I'm gone." At her startled expression he grinned. "I am a trapper. It has been too many days since I've checked my traps. If I expect to have any to sell come spring, I have to get busy."

Linsey closed her eyes, hiding their expression. She had spent several days alone in the cabin before he arrived, so why did she suddenly worry about being alone again. "Fine," she said firmly. "I'll be just fine."

"Of course you will, *mon ange*. I will be gone only during the day. I will not leave you here alone at night."

"I'll be fine." She tried to hide the shudder from his too observant eyes . . . and failed.

Kaleb stared at the ceiling above his head and wished he had not decided to spend the night in the abandoned cabin. He hated sleeping inside, even on cold winter nights. He preferred to look up and see the stars, watch them twinkle so far away until he drifted to sleep.

He was getting closer. Jeb and Zeke were making no attempt to hide their trail. Kaleb's job had become easier with their arrogance. He knew Jeb had decided Kaleb had given up the search. He had begun to find dead campfires, and they had used this cabin. Kaleb had felt the dead ashes in the fireplace and detected a slight warmth. He doubted if he was farther than a day behind them now.

Kaleb closed his eyes, but the memories wouldn't let him sleep. Somehow Mary's battered face combined with Linsey's terrified one. He was glad he had taken the time to save the girl from the clutches of Jeb and Zeke. He had lost only a few days by taking her to Bear's cabin.

In the silence Kaleb chuckled, wondering at Bear's reaction when he returned to his cabin and found the girl. Maybe after he finished with Jeb and Zeke he'd go back, just to check on her.

She'd be quite a woman someday, Kaleb decided. She had grit and backbone. Couldn't have made it as far as she had if she'd been a prissy city girl. She'd be the kind of woman a man could plan a future with, just like Mary.

A pain lanced through Kaleb, so deep he had no choice but to wait it out. The pain didn't come as often any more. Almost as if time was healing a wound little by little, he could remember Mary more often without feeling like he was going to die from the loneliness that engulfed him.

"Soon, my sweet Mary," Kaleb whispered through the darkness. "I promise ya, hit will be soon."

He closed his eyes and tried to find sleep.

Chapter Eight

It had seemed strange being in the cabin without Bear. Constant reminders of his presence were reassuring; his shirt, a spare hat, the pipe that she'd seen him smoke only once. Knowing that he had promised to return each night had helped, but it wasn't the same as having him there all day. The first day had been the hardest. Every noise had made Linsey jump, and with little to occupy her time, the hours had dragged by.

The next morning, before he left, Bear showed her where he kept needles and thread, and she spent the long afternoon repairing the damage to her dress. One evening he carved several buttons for her to replace the ones that were missing, and after a good washing the dress was serviceable if not attractive.

Now, after almost a week of him leaving each morning and returning just before dark, Linsey was becoming accustomed to his absences. She found that she enjoyed the solitude and realized she had never truly been alone before. There had always been someone just within calling distance, and even when she sought the quiet of her room, someone else was in the house.

The last few days, she had worked on a gown for

Morning Moon's new baby. After carefully cutting the white deerhide into the desired shapes using a razor sharp knife, Linsey punched small holes along the edges. Bear had shown her how to use an awl to make the holes and then sew the pieces together using narrow strips of sinew.

Linsey had been pleased with the finished product until she realized Bear had nothing she could use to embroider the tiny gown. She could not give it to Morning Moon without some sort of decoration. During her visit in the village, she had noticed that each piece of clothing was heavily decorated. Some of the clothing had intricate geometrical patterns while others had flowers, animals or birds. Colorful beads made of various materials were skillfully worked into the pattern.

Linsey put the gown on the table and looked around the room, searching for something to use. She did not want to sew beads on the gown, fearing that the baby would pick at them until they came loose, put one in his mouth and choke.

Sighing with exasperation, she ran her fingers through her hair, testing it to see if it had dried yet from being washed earlier that morning. Shortly after Bear left, Linsey heated several pots of water. Her hair had not been given a good wash since leaving Philadelphia, so she indulged herself, using the flowery scented soap. It was a time-consuming project, nearly impossible for one person. Her almost hip-length hair was thick and full of hidden tangles, and by the time she finished, she felt slightly dizzy from hanging nearly upside down. She had gotten as much water on herself and the floor as she had on her hair, but for the first time in weeks, it was truly clean and, after hours of patient combing, tangle free. As her fingers wove through the slightly damp strands, an idea came to mind.

Sitting down, Linsey pulled several pieces of hair free. Working slowly she twisted them together making a long thread of red. She tested the thread on a spare piece of hide, using the needle Bear had given her. After several attempts, Linsey found that five pieces of hair twisted together made the right thickness for the embroidery. Delighted with her discovery, she spent the remainder of the afternoon happily occupied.

Darkness was descending when Bear reached the cabin. He had managed to return each evening before dark, but he knew that soon he would have to stay out overnight. His traplines stretched for miles, and it was impossible for him to work the farthest traps and still return at night. He worried about leaving Linsey alone in the cabin and thought about taking her with him; but he knew she would slow him down considerably, and he wasn't sure how her tender heart would react to the animals caught in his traps.

Linsey put the gown down when she heard noises outside the cabin. She picked up the knife she had been using and held it defensively in front of her. When Bear's familiar voice demanded that she let him in, she dropped the knife and ran to open the door. Wanting her to have a feeling of security while he was away, Bear had made a heavy wood bar that could be dropped across the door, making it impossible for someone to open it from the outside.

Bear entered the cabin, looking as big as a mountain and comfortingly familiar. Linsey did not like to admit even to herself that she waited eagerly for his return each evening. After several days of being left by herself, she had become accustomed to being alone, but as darkness descended, she was relieved by his return. The cabin was warm and cozy while he was in it but very lonely when he was gone.

Another thought worried Bear as he took off his coat and hung it on the hook beside the door. He liked coming home to her. Her smile always welcomed him, and the smells of something cooking awaited his arrival.

Evidence of her presence was everywhere. Her sewing lay on the table; her coat hung from a hook beside his. The shelf he had put up for her was slowly filling with her possessions.

He looked forward to coming home . . . to her. He liked it . . . he was afraid he was beginning to like it too much. He wanted to ask her to stay. To make a home with him in the wilderness. To be his wife, his friend, the mother of his children.

Spring would come, and he would take her back to the city. Bear closed his eyes at the knowledge of the loneliness waiting for him once she was gone. He had known such loneliness before when Snow had died, and vowed never again to depend on someone else. Somehow, without his consent or knowledge, Linsey had wedged herself into his life. And the suffering would not wait for spring.

"Are you hungry? What did you get today? Look at the baby's dress; I'm almost finished with it. Can we—"

"Slow down, little one," Bear said with a grin. "You begin to sound like Chattering Squirrel."

Linsey blushed lightly, but grinned back at him. After a day by herself, she could barely wait for him to get inside the cabin before she started talking.

"To answer your first question, yes, I am starving." He walked to the fire and bent, breathing deeply. The aroma of the thick rich stew filled his nostrils. "Now that you can make stew perfectly, I think it is time I taught you how to make something else."

"Better not chance it. At least my stew is edible!"

152

Bear chuckled. "I'll check everything you put in—just to make sure you don't add the wrong herb."

Linsey shivered at the thought of how close she had come to poisoning him. "Stick to the stew," she advised.

Linsey cleared her sewing from the table and dished up their dinner while Bear washed from the pot of water she kept warm by the fire. They talked quietly while they ate, Bear telling of his day, she of hers.

During the evening, Bear worked on his furs. The new ones had to be cleaned of any lingering flesh before they were placed on stretchers. Linsey sat near him, finishing the baby gown.

"It's almost done," she said, holding up the gown for his inspection. "Do you think you could come home a little early tomorrow so that I can take it to Morning Moon?"

"Why do you not go yourself? The trail is clearly marked; you can't get lost." It was a test. Had she come to accept the Indians as friends, or did she still think of them as enemies?

"By myself?" Linsey stared at the gown as she felt a flicker of fear run through her. She wanted to lean against Bear, beg him to take her. They had gone twice to the village since their first visit, and each time she had been warmly welcomed. Could she go by herself, without the security of Bear?

"I guess I could," she stammered.

"Nothing will happen to you, *mon ange*," Bear said quietly. "You know the people now. They will welcome you." He felt an almost overpowering urge to enfold her in his arms and chase away her fear. Clutching his knife tightly, he remained where he was. He wanted to hold her close to him. Much too often during the day, he found himself thinking of holding her, loving her

153

through the long night. If he ever made her his, nothing on earth could force him to take her back in the spring. And staying had to be her decision.

Linsey ran her hand lightly over the velvet-soft gown and raised shadowed emerald eyes to him. "I'll think about it," she whispered. "It isn't easy to change your thoughts about a group of people, and I've been terrified by Indians for so long."

A muscle jumped in Bear's jaw as he fought the urge to go to her. Trying to appear casual he nodded and returned to the fur in front of him. "I'll try to get home earlier tomorrow." He scraped on the hide for several minutes. "There are signs of another storm brewing. So I had planned not to work too far away." He raised his head and grinned at her. "I don't want to take the chance of catching another cold."

Linsey carried the wrapped package by the thong that tied it closed. Wearing her own dress and cape, she carefully watched the trail in front of her so that she didn't accidentally venture off and get lost. Since the night before, when Bear suggested she make the short trip alone, she had struggled to find the courage to go. The last thing she wanted to do was lose her way and wander alone into the vast wilderness.

Most of the snow from the blizzard had melted, leaving only small patches of white under trees where the sun did not reach. The last of the leaves had fallen, and skeletal branches stretched toward the sky as if searching for warmth. A light breeze rustled through the leaves and tugged at Linsey's knotted hair, its cool caress a needless reminder of cold winter winds.

The path between Bear's cabin and the Indian village had been used for years and could not have been clearer had it been a cobbled Philadelphia road.

Linsey tried to keep her mind clear of thought as she followed the path. If she tried hard enough, she could pretend she was taking the shortcut through the woods that separated her Philadelphia home from that of her nearest neighbors. It was a path she had taken hundreds of times to visit with childhood friends.

"Ée kwài wah!"

The silence was shattered by the harsh guttural words of the ugliest Indian Linsey had ever seen. His dirty, matted hair hung around narrow shoulders, and even from the distance still separating them, her nose easily detected his stench. His eyes narrowed appraisingly, and his evil smile showed missing teeth.

Linsey hugged the package to her breasts as he slowly approached her. Her first instinct was to turn and run, but she fought it, her chin raised proudly. She kept her eyes on him and tried to prevent herself from gagging when he stopped directly in front of her.

"I am the woman of Bear." Her voice was strong and clear, showing no sign of the quiver lurking in her throat.

"Bear! Pfftt!" He spit in the dirt at her feet, showing all too clearly that he recognized the name and exactly what he thought.

He said unintelligible Shawnee words as he reached for her hair. His smile returned at her scream of pain as he wrapped his fingers hurtfully in the silken strands. His free hand pulled open the cape and tore at the neckline of her dress, grabbing harshly at the soft mounds he uncovered.

Linsey screamed again, twisting and turning, but his hold on her hair tightened, easily keeping her in place. When he plucked at a distended nipple, she kicked,

155

her hard leather shoe catching him on the shin and making him grunt at the pain. He pulled back his hand from her breasts and hit her face with his closed fist.

Linsey reeled, nearly unconscious, but his hold on her hair prevented her from falling. He began pushing her down the trail, kicking at her when she stumbled, holding her up by the hair on her head.

The Indian village was a welcome sight to her blurred and swollen eyes. As he led her stumbling and tripping to the center of the village, word spread, and the villagers appeared at their doors. Linsey saw several people who knew her as Bear's woman, but no one interfered with their progress. When they approached the house she recognized, Linsey screamed one word.

"Wolf!"

What seemed an eternity to her was actually only seconds as she waited for the door to open. Wolf stepped out and directly into their path, arms folded across his bare chest, feet spread in a wide stance.

The exchange that followed was in Shawnee, but Linsey had no trouble understanding the argument. The ugly Indian holding her refused to relinquish his prize. The hand in her hair tightened, and he raised a tomahawk in his other hand. Wolf grabbed the weapon, throwing it into a tree several feet away. Finally, the Indian released her, pushing her violently into Wolf's arms. He swaggered away, talking and laughing loudly to a few of his friends who had gathered around.

Wolf helped Linsey into his house, where she fell into Morning Moon's comforting embrace. Large crystalline tears ran silently down her cheeks as she fought to control her sobs.

After a quiet exchange between Wolf and his wife, he left the house. Chattering Squirrel toddled to Linsey on chubby legs, his dark eyes wide with concern. He

156

patted her legs through her thick dress and cape, mumbling baby words of comfort. Spring Flower sat silently by the fire, her black eyes sparkling with curiosity.

Morning Moon led Linsey to a sleeping shelf and removed her cape. When she saw the torn and tattered dress, she offered one of her own. Linsey refused, pulling the ripped bodice up to her chin and holding it in place. It was then that she realized she still clutched tightly to the package.

"I was bringing this to you," she whispered through her sobs. She held it out to Morning Moon, her hand trembling from reaction. "Who was he? Why did he attack me?"

Morning Moon took the package and set it to the side until later. "He is called Small Dog." Using one of the precious steel needles Bear had given her and a fine strand of sinew, she worked quickly to repair Linsey's dress. "He is not liked in the village. He beats his wife and children without cause, and he enjoys torturing his slaves and prisoners." Her movements were sure as she sewed the dress together, careful to keep the needle away from Linsey's skin.

Linsey shivered. "He seemed to understand that I belong to Bear, and yet he didn't appear to care."

"He knew," Morning Moon replied. "Small Dog has no honor or respect. He claims you as his, refusing to accept Bear's claim. He argued with Wolf, but there is little he can do against the son of the chief. For now you are safe, and soon Wolf will return with Bear."

Linsey wrapped her arms around her shaking body and was grateful when Morning Moon draped a fur over her. In the center of the room, Morning Moon poured some warm water into a cup. She added several crushed leaves and stirred gently. Returning to Linsey, she handed her the cup, insisting that Linsey drink.

157

"It will help warm you," Morning Moon said gently.

The liquid was slightly bitter, but not unpleasant. Linsey drank slowly, feeling the warmth flow through her body. "Wolf went to find Bear?"

Morning Moon nodded. "Small Dog has challenged Bear to a fight. The winner will claim you."

"A fight?"

"Do you fear for yourself or for Bear?"

Linsey blinked, startled by the question. Her thoughts had all been centered on Bear. "He's been hurt so badly in the past. I don't think I could live knowing he was hurt again because of me."

Morning Moon's smile was gentle. "He is a fierce warrior, Lin Zee. There are few men who could stand against him in battle. Small Dog has lost the fight before it is begun."

She saw that the cup was empty and took it from Linsey's hands. She placed it on a shelf and reached for the package. "May I open this now?"

At Linsey's nod, Morning Moon knelt on the floor by her feet and carefully untied the package. She was so quiet that Linsey was afraid she did not like the gown. Beginning to feel uneasy, she searched for something to say to break the silence, when Morning Moon raised her head.

"It's for your new baby," Linsey offered inanely.

Morning Moon examined the gown carefully. She saw that some of the stitches were uneven and the edges slightly ragged, evidence of a person working with unfamiliar tools. But her eyes were glued to the embroidering. She realized it was worked with Linsey's hair; the colors were as vibrant on the soft hide as they were on Linsey's head.

"Red is our sacred color," she said softly. "It protects our warriors in battle, honors both our living and dead." She lightly traced the design with a finger. "You have brought my child great honor by presenting him a gift of yourself. As he grows I will rework the gown so that it becomes a shirt. It will grow with him, and he will always carry your protection."

She carefully folded the gown and held it close to her slightly protruding stomach. "I thank you, Lin Zee. It is a gift to be treasured by my son's sons."

Linsey was delighted to have so pleased her new friend. Smiling, she was startled by a huge yawn.

"You must rest." Morning Moon rose and placed the gown on a shelf. She motioned for Linsey to lie down and spread another fur over her. Chattering Squirrel, amazingly quiet, climbed up beside her and wiggled beneath the fur. He reached for her hair, wrapped his fingers in it and contentedly sucked his free fist. With a sigh of pure pleasure, his eyes closed.

Morning Moon smiled. "It seems my son plans to take his nap with you. I will move him if he bothers you."

Linsey lightly caressed his dark head. "Please don't," she whispered, bending to kiss his soft cheek, snuggling the tiny, warm body against hers. Yawning again, she lay her head down. "We will comfort each other."

Sleep slipped in on silent feet; Linsey closed her eyes, unaware that Morning Moon's warm drink was the cause.

Bear stood in the doorway, captivated by the sight that greeted his eyes. Bright red hair and snowy white skin peeked from beneath a dark fur. Nestled under her chin was a head of black hair and a rosy, plump cheek. He silently crossed the room and knelt beside

159

the sleeping shelf. A killing fury darkened his eyes when he saw the swelling on the side of her jaw, the delicate skin turning an angry purple. His hands knotted into tight fists as he struggled to control his raging temper. Small Dog would die . . . slowly!

He leaned across the baby and placed soft kisses on her jaw, wanting to take the pain away. Linsey sleepily opened her eyes and smiled gently into the tender eyes seeming to caress her with their gaze.

"You are all right?" he questioned softly.

"Now that you're here."

She lightly licked her dry lips, and his gaze was drawn to her mouth. Linsey held her breath as his head slowly lowered to hers. She seemed to wait an eternity before she felt the soft touch of his lips against hers. With a sigh of contentment, Linsey opened her mouth to him, meeting his caressing tongue with her own, venturing into the warm recess of his mouth. Fighting to breathe, Bear raised his head, his eyes blazing with passion into hers.

"Please don't fight him," she pleaded softly.

"I must, sweet."

"You'll be hurt because of me."

"No, Autumn Fire. He will not touch me." He smiled, confident in his own abilities. "You must try to understand; I must prove that no one can touch what is mine. If I were to back down, nothing would stop some of these braves from attacking you or me. They would see it as a weakness. They respect strength. Small Dog knew you were mine, and yet he tried to claim you for his own. He will learn the hard way that no one touches what is mine!"

Bear felt the wiggling and kicking of the small body beneath his belly. Chattering Squirrel opened his eyes and his mouth. Seeing who held him down, he thought it a new kind of game from his giant friend and squealed with glee.

Bear tickled the chubby baby, lifting him free from the fur. Chattering Squirrel chattered happily, showing no signs of the sleep he had just left.

"Come, my gabby friend. Let us see if we can find your maman." He held the squirming child away from him. "You seem to have sprung a leak!"

"Leak! Leak!" Chattering Squirrel clapped his hands, delighted with the new word.

Bear carried the dripping child across the room and set him down. "I'll be back." He smiled at Linsey and left.

Chattering Squirrel watched the door swing closed and turned, running to Linsey as fast as his baby legs would carry him. She hugged the bundle of joy, grimacing at his dripping bottom.

"Leak! Leak!"

"Ah oh." Linsey nodded in agreement.

Chattering Squirrel's eyes widened, and he grinned a toothy smile. "Ah oh, me leak!" he squealed. "Ah oh, me leak!"

"My son has learned new words," Morning Moon said with a smile. She had entered so quietly Linsey had not been aware of her presence.

"Blame it on Bear when you grow tired of hearing it!"

"Me leak! Ah oh, me leak!"

Linsey watched Morning Moon care for her son while her thoughts turned to the coming fight. Would she have to witness it? How could she watch Bear fight, knowing she was the cause? But how could she stay away when he would be fighting for his life? How could she live if something happened to him, knowing she was responsible?

161

Bear and Wolf entered together, both wearing identical expressions of fierce pride. They would make formidable enemies, and Linsey had trouble believing she had once stood face to face with Wolf with no weapon but her tongue.

"We are ready." Wolf looked at his wife, turned and left.

Morning Moon smiled reassuringly at Linsey, picked up Chattering Squirrel and followed her husband.

"I would spare you this," Bear said quietly, his face softening as he looked at her, "but they must know that my woman stands beside me."

"Am I your woman, Luc LeClerc?" she asked softly.

He stared down at her, his gaze warm and caressing. "You will be when the time is right."

"When will that be?" She walked to him, wrapped her arms around his waist and rested her head against his massive chest. "I'm more scared now than I've ever been in my life."

"You have been through so much in such a short time." He put his arms around her and pulled her tightly against him. "This will be over quickly, and we will go home."

"Promise?" She raised her head, her eyes pleading childlike for reassurance.

"Promise." Bear lowered his mouth to hers, tasting the sweetness she offered. He slowly released her, entwining her fingers through his. "Hold your head up and show no fear."

Linsey nodded once, raised her chin proudly and followed him from the house. They walked to the center of the village, the people parting to let them pass. It looked as if everyone from the village had turned out for the fight. It was a break from the long, boring winter inactivity. The Indians loved to gamble, but very few bets had been placed on the match. Except for a few of Small Dog's friends, no one would bet against Bear. They had seen him fight before.

Linsey looked at no one as she walked beside Bear. At the edge of the crowd, he squeezed her hand tightly before dropping it and going on without her. Wolf and Small Dog waited in the center of the ring formed by the people. Bear stripped to the waist, throwing his shirt to the edge of the crowd. Small Dog wore only a breechcloth and knee-high moccasins.

Bear was over a head taller and almost twice as broad as the smaller man, which was something Small Dog considered to his advantage. He could move quicker, springing in and out, gone before Bear could move. If it had been a wrestling match, Small Dog would have no chance, but with a knife, the odds were in his favor.

A stake had been pounded into the ground, and short ropes of equal length were tied to it and to the combatants' ankles. Armed with knives, they faced each other as Wolf backed away.

Small Dog attacked quickly, thrusting with the wicked knife. Bear turned so that it slid past him, sweeping up with his knife at the same time, but the blade deflected off a rib. Small Dog grunted at the pain, but ignored the blood flowing down his side. He sprang again, and Bear felt the bite of the blade as it left a long, thin red line down his chest.

Linsey bit the inside of her lip until she tasted blood. She wanted to look away, but her eyes were glued to the two men tied to the stake. All around her were cheers and yells, urging the men on.

Bear balanced lightly on the balls of his feet, prepared for the next attack. Linsey closed her eyes, praying for it to be finished, but the yells of the crowd forced her to look. In the short space her eyes had been

163

closed, Bear had brought Small Dog down. Straddling the smaller man, he flicked his knife and cut off Small Dog's ear. He held the knife at his throat, the point pressing into the flesh and causing a small pool of blood to form.

"You are not worth killing," Bear said loudly enough for all to hear.

He rose to his feet, cut the thong tied to his ankle and walked toward Linsey. Wolf entered the center of the ring, spoke loudly and spit at the man in the dirt.

"You're all right—oh, God—you're all right," Linsey whispered, her eyes searching for signs of wounds other than the thin one on his chest.

Someone handed Bear his shirt, and he slid it on. "Let's go home."

"Oh, yes, please," Linsey pleaded, trying to prevent the tears filling her eyes from flowing down her cheeks. "I want to go home."

Bear grabbed her hand, entwining his fingers with hers. "Hang on just a little longer, Autumn Fire. Don't let them see your tears."

Linsey nodded, clearing her throat several times before she could speak. "What will happen to Small Dog?"

"I should have killed him," Bear snarled, walking away from the crowd. "I'll probably be sorry later. He's a troublemaker, and I'm sure this won't be the last we see of him.

"He has been banished from the tribe. He and whatever friends want to follow will no longer be allowed to live here. They'll probably roam around, causing trouble wherever they choose to go."

"Why didn't you kill him?"

Bear sighed and shrugged. How could he tell her she was the reason he had let Small Dog live? He had no doubt that Small Dog would be back. He had caused the Indian greater shame and humiliation by letting him live; death in honest combat was a reward Bear would not give to him. Small Dog would want revenge.

Killing was not the issue. Bear had killed before, and he knew he would probably be forced to do so again. It was a fact of which he felt neither pride nor shame. The unsettled wilderness bred an untamed violence, and few men lived there without meeting that trouble from time to time. They handled the situations as they arose, the only judgement between God and the man.

Bear had not killed Small Dog because he did not want it to stay forever in Linsey's mind. He hoped time would lessen the incident to just an unpleasant memory. More importantly, he wanted nothing to damage her trust in him.

In front of Wolf's house, Bear shouldered his pack and cradled his rifle in his free arm. His other remained firmly clutched by Linsey. He spoke in Shawnee with Wolf for several minutes before turning down the path toward his cabin.

Linsey followed Bear out of the village. Several warriors stopped and beat him on the back, offering congratulations. She sighed with relief as they entered the woods, leaving all signs of the village behind.

When they reached the cabin, Linsey instantly headed for the warm water. She made Bear sit down so that she could clean up his wound. The blade had barely reached him, leaving only a red line in places, not even cutting the skin in others. She wiped the blood away and applied a soothing salve. When she was finished, tossing the water out and putting the cream away, her hands began to shake. Kneeling in front of the fire while Bear finished cleaning himself up, she let her tears flow.

"If I could have reached Small Dog when Wolf first found me, I would have wrung his flat head from his scrawny neck," Bear said between clenched teeth. His back to her, he ranted and raved as he pulled on his shirt. Turning as he laced the thong, he saw her at the fire and knew from her shaking shoulders that she had finally given in to her terror.

"Easy, little one, it is over," he murmured as he knelt beside her.

"He tore my dress," she cried, rubbing her fingers over the hastily mended dress. "I just got it fixed, and he tore it again!"

Bear smiled at her little girl voice until Linsey turned tear-filled eyes to him and his heart turned over. Taking her into his arms, he held her tightly, her face against his chest. He whispered soothingly to her and gently rubbed her back. When there was no sign that her tears would end any time soon, Bear stood and easily picked her up, carrying her to the bed. He sat on the edge, cradling her in his lap.

The bruise on her jaw had darkened, the swelling distorting her face. Bear cursed himself for not killing the bastard that had done this to her. He placed light kisses on her temple, pushing her long hair back from her face.

He felt her tears dampen his chest as the sobs shook her slender body. He had been so proud of her, standing straight and tall in front of the tribe. He pulled her tighter against him, alarmed when he heard her moan.

"What? Did I hurt you?"

Linsey shook her head and kept her face buried in his chest. "Small Dog," she mumbled through her tears.

"Small Dog hurt you?" The muscle in his jaw began to jump. "Where? Show me!"

Linsey blushed as she opened several buttons of her

dress. Pulling it back so that he could see the bruises marring the creamy flesh of her shoulders and the tops of her breasts, she kept her eyes lowered.

"*Mon Dieu*, the bastard!"

Bear rose, laid Linsey on the bed and walked outside. He returned quickly with a large handful of snow which he placed in a rag. He carried it to the bed and sat down. He opened Linsey's dress farther so that he could put the cold rag on her bruised flesh.

Linsey moaned when the coldness reached her. He held it firmly in place when she wiggled, trying to dislodge it.

"It's cold!"

"I know, *mon ange*, but it will help." His long fingers rested on the soft skin of her breast. He lowered his eyes and found a hint of dark pink nipple peeking enticingly from her dress.

Her eyes raised to his, and with a moan of defeat, Bear lowered his head. He tasted the tears on her cheeks and kissed them away. His fingers slid farther to touch the tender bud. Linsey moaned at the touch, arching her back so that it fit more tightly in his hand.

Bear moved his mouth to hers, wanting to devour her but only tasting lightly. If he didn't stop soon, he wouldn't be able to stop at all.

"Is this the time?" Linsey asked softly.

He lowered his head to her shoulder and kissed the bruises. He had won the fight with Small Dog but couldn't begin to win the one against himself.

"Yes," he whispered, admitting defeat.

Chapter Nine

Leaning over Linsey and staring down into the swirling depths of emerald green eyes, Bear regretted his answer. She looked at him in such a trusting manner he wondered if she would accept his change of mind.

"Luc, kiss me?" Linsey whispered. "Please?"

With a moan he complied, and regret was swept into oblivion. Lowering his head to hers, he softly stroked her lips with his, just barely touching. The tip of his tongue traced the shape of her lips, tasting, sampling.

Linsey opened her mouth, urging him to deepen the kiss. His teasing continued until she was nearly mindless, wanting more than the light touches he was offering.

His lips left her mouth, gently kissing her bruised jaw and making a trail up her cheek, over her nose then back to her lips. He raised his head, his burning eyes meeting hers.

"If I make you mine, my angel, I may not be able to let you go in the spring." His voice was husky with his rapidly rising passion.

"Spring is far away," she replied in a whisper. "I may not want to go."

His eyes remained on hers as his hand slipped to the buttons of her dress. Slowly, giving her time to protest—hoping she would, praying she wouldn't—he opened them. As he pushed the tattered garment aside, his lips closed on hers.

It was the kiss she had asked for. His tongue invaded her mouth, searching each hidden recess. His hand moved to cup her chin, his arm resting heavily between her breasts. Linsey had not realized she had quit breathing until his lips moved to the tender skin of her neck and she gasped with pleasure.

Sitting up, Bear pulled his shirt over his head. He threw it on the floor as he lifted her onto his lap. He slowly lowered the bodice of her dress, his eyes caressing her. The firelight played across her skin, dancing gold on the creamy flesh. He gritted his teeth at the sight of the finger-shaped bruises on her shoulders. One full breast was badly bruised from Small Dog's rough handling.

He soothed the marks on her shoulders, his tongue delighting in her taste. Linsey turned her head, offering him easier access to her neck as flames of fire danced through her. He kissed his way across to her other shoulder, giving it the same tender treatment. Slowly, lingeringly he made a path to the slope of her breasts, cradling the feminine flesh in his big hand. He ran his work-roughened thumb over one peak until it hardened, eager for his touch.

He raised his head slightly until he could see the precious mounds. Her breasts looked small cupped in his massive hand; the hardened buds of her nipples were inviting, enticing. He delayed no longer, taking one of the nipples in his mouth and teasing it with his tongue.

Linsey moaned as he tugged and pulled, his lips gentle, his tongue rough. She found it harder and harder to breathe as he licked and suckled her breasts, first one and then the other. Never had she imagined the sensations that flowed wave after wave through her body. She was hot, burning with fever—the fever of passion.

Bear lifted her from his lap and laid her on the bed. He slid the dress down over her hips and removed her tattered drawers. When she was nude, he studied her as an artist studies the great masters.

"You are beautiful, *mon ange*, more beautiful than anything I have ever seen."

Working quickly, he unlaced and removed his knee-high moccasins and then his pants. He lay down beside her and was pleasurably startled when Linsey pushed him back and leaned over him. With a feather-light touch, she followed the path of the scars. Beginning at his temple and across his cheek, they dropped abruptly from his jaw. She heard his moan as her fingers traveled down his chest. Her hand moved slowly lower, and Bear grabbed it when it reached his belly.

His eyes were tender as he lifted her hand and placed a kiss in her palm. He then put it on the middle of his chest and held it firmly with his own.

"I am going to love you, little one." His voice was filled with desire, and his eyes lowered to her pointed breasts bobbing invitingly near his face. "I am going to make you mine."

He gently pushed her back on the bed and leaned over her. Throwing a leg across her flat stomach, he rubbed his throbbing hardness against her hip. He kissed the puckered nipples, a growl rumbling from deep in his chest as she arched her back in eager response. Moving his leg to between her thighs, he caressed her soft stomach and rested his hand at the moist entrance he longed to know.

Linsey was startled by the unfamiliar warmth throbbing against her hip, but Bear's caressing hands and lips caused too many other sensations for her to give it much thought. Her breath came in short gasps when his knowing fingers found her femininity, quickly driving her to a frenzy of need.

"Open your eyes, sweet," Bear whispered. "You are very tiny here—" he rubbed his fingers gently through the moist warmth—"and I am very big."

He bent and suckled a nipple, unable to resist its tempting invitation. "When I make you mine the first time, it will be more painful than pleasant. I will try to make it easy for you, but there can be no help for it; it will hurt."

Her emerald eyes were so glazed with passion Bear doubted she understood what he said. He raised himself up and slid between her parted thighs. Slowly he entered her until he felt the thin barrier impeding his progress. Holding his weight on his elbows, he kissed her open mouth and gave a final, swift, sure thrust.

Linsey gasped at the agony burning through her middle. Brought abruptly back to reality, her passion fled from the force of the pain.

Bear lay still, deeply embedded in her raging heat. He waited for the pain to ease and for her to become familiar with the new sensation. Whispering words of love in both French and Shawnee, he nuzzled her neck, making trails to her breasts. As he said the words, their truth wove around him like a shimmering veil. Against his will, knowing the pain that would come in the spring, he had fallen in love with her.

It had been a long time since he had been with a woman, and before he wanted it to, his control splintered. Unable to resist the invitation of her warmth, he began a gentle rhythm.

As the pain eased for Linsey, the passion returned. She caught his rhythm and followed it, meeting and returning each thrust. She willingly followed where he led to a world of their own, spinning through time past the stars, toward the horizon of eternity. Together they climbed the summit of desire and found the release their bodies demanded.

Fearing that he couldn't support his weight and would crush her, Bear rolled onto his back and pulled her into his arms. Their breathing was slow to return to normal, and the chilled air played over their nude bodies. Feeling like it took superhuman strength, Bear reached for a blanket and pulled it over them.

"That was nice." Linsey put her head on his shoulder; her small hand rested on his chest. Cuddling against him, she felt like a rag doll in his embrace.

"Nice?" Bear chuckled, the sound rumbling through his chest beneath her ear. "You call it nice?"

"There's a better word?" she asked impishly.

"My sweet, I don't think there is a word in any language to adequately describe what we just shared."

"Then, it was nice!"

"Nice is too tame."

"Well—" Linsey yawned—"you think of the word and let me know. I'm going to sleep." She wiggled slightly, grimacing at the burning discomfort between her thighs.

Noting the fleeting expression and hearing her muffled moan, Bear twisted his head, looking for the snow-filled rag he had used earlier. It lay discarded on the furs beside them, the snow having melted from the heat of the room.

"Be right back," he whispered, kissing her nose and climbing out of bed. Linsey was too near sleep to ask questions, but she missed him immediately.

Bear knelt at the fire and added several logs. As the flame blazed, he looked down at himself and saw the evidence of her virginity smeared on his thighs. It was a badge he would like to wear for the rest of his life, but he dipped the rag in the pot of warm water she always kept near the fire and reluctantly washed the stains away.

He carried the water and rag to the bed, setting them on the floor. Linsey slept quietly, her lips slightly parted, seeming to invite him to taste again of their sweetness.

Sitting on the edge of the bed, Bear pulled the blanket up above her waist and carefully tended to her. Linsey woke at his first touch, and embarrassment colored her cheeks as she felt him part her thighs; but the warmth was so comforting that she sighed deeply.

"Next time there will be little pain," Bear said softly, acknowledging that he knew she was awake.

"When will that be?" she asked in a husky whisper.

Bear chuckled. "You are in a hurry?" He dropped the rag into the bucket and lay down beside her, pulling the blanket around him. Linsey snuggled against him, her head pillowed on his shoulder.

Bear kissed the top of her head. "Sleep, little one."

Wrapped in the arms of blissful contentment, the two were unaware as the night drifted past. One by one the stars were slowly covered as gray storm clouds filled the sky. When morning came, the sun was lost behind a curtain of white, for winter had returned to stay until spring.

Linsey leaned back against the wall, a fur pulled to beneath her chin, and watched as Bear knelt to add wood to the fire. He seemed oblivious to the chill of the room, his naked body gleaming in the glow of the dancing flames. Rising, he stood and watched as the logs were consumed by the hungry blaze.

Linsey wondered what words could be used to describe him. He could not be called beautiful; it was too feminine a word for the masculine perfection of broad shoulders rippling with muscles, narrow waist and tight hips. Thighs bigger around than her waist firmly supported him, the muscles so well defined they appeared rock hard even as he stood relaxed.

Bear turned and walked to the door, uncaring of his nudity as he opened it and breathed deeply.

"It's snowing," he called to her. The gray clouds were heavy with snow, and he knew it would be several inches deep on the ground before it stopped.

He closed the door and walked back to her, raised the furs and climbed into the bed. Linsey shivered as his cold skin touched hers.

"You're freezing!"

Bear pulled her against him, his long body touching hers in as many places as possible. "Not anymore!"

"No, now I'm freezing!"

Bear chuckled until she bit his shoulder. "Why did you do that?" he asked, rubbing the offended area.

"Guess I'm just hungry. . . ."

"Hmmm, sounds like a good idea." He bent slightly and tenderly bit the soft underside of her breast. He nuzzled and suckled her puckered nipples, making her moan and arch her back. "Someday these will be filled with milk and will give nourishment to a babe. For now, let them feed me. . . ."

It was hours later before they again thought of food.

Evening had come, and outside the cozy cabin the snow continued to fall quietly. Linsey marvelled that they had spent most of the day in bed. They had made love then drifted to sleep only to wake and reach hungrily for each other again.

Her lips made a moist path down the trail of scars on his chest, and she raised tender eyes to him. "Will you tell me how you got these?"

Bear pulled her head down to his shoulder and captured her wandering hand in one of his. He delighted in how freely she touched him, but he could not answer her question with her hand lying so warmly against his groin.

"Behave if you want me to answer your question," he admonished when she threw her thigh over him, rubbing it firmly against his all-too-willing flesh. "Five winters ago a rogue bear attacked the village," he began quietly, the memories flooding his mind.

"I thought bears hibernated all winter."

He shrugged. "It is not unusual for one to leave his sleep. This bear was old, and maybe his pains of age would not allow him to sleep peacefully. It wasn't the first time he had entered the village in search of food. He had destroyed lodges and possessions but had never hurt any of the people. They even had a name for him, called him Six Toes. One paw was deformed and had an extra claw. He was a wily old bear, always seemed to sense when the warriors were gone. He never came to the village when they were there. . ."

It was one of those beautiful crisp winter days with a clear blue sky overhead and a solid layer of snow on the ground. Wolf and Bear had walked for miles, searching for deer. They and several other warriors had decided to take advantage of the day to do a little hunting. Already beginning to be bored with the inactivity of winter, they welcomed the opportunity to do something . . . anything.

The trip was more for pleasure than necessity. The winter had been mild and food plentiful. But they were young and used it as their reason to leave the village.

Time would never soften the agony Bear suffered when they returned to the village. Toting a buck they had killed, laughing and teasing the warriors who had not been as lucky, they quickened their steps as they heard the moaning death cries.

The path of destruction was painfully obvious, heading in an almost straight line toward the center of the village. His blood burning through his veins, Bear dropped the buck and walked toward his home. Somehow he knew what he would find before he reached it. With each step that drew him nearer, he wanted to turn and run, deny the truth.

His stride was sure, moving quickly but refusing to break into a run. The faces of the people he passed would have told him what he was to find . . . if he had bothered to turn and look at them. His gaze remained glued on the lodge in the distance.

From the outside there was little destruction. Only the door had been torn free, lying on the snow several feet away, shredded by a massive claw. The inside also showed little of what had happened. Almost ironically, everything was neatly in its place. As if he had been searching for only one thing, the bear had found it and destroyed it, leaving everything else untouched.

Bear slowly knelt by the fur-covered figure lying so still on their sleeping shelf. He knew, without looking, that Snow had not survived the attack of the marauding animal. Their time together had been all too short. Never again would he hear her laugh, see her smile or feel her gentle loving touches. His breath coming in shallow gasps, he slowly pulled back the fur. Little beauty remained of his gentle, vibrant Snow. Had the bear tried, he could not have destroyed her any more than he had.

Bear's eyes moved to the ominously still mound of her belly. His child. Snow's soft voice whispered in his mind as he remembered their joy when they knew his seed had found fertile ground and in the spring they would be parents. They had shared the excitement of the baby's first movement, and only that morning he had teased her about her waddling walk. Their child, trapped in the body of its mother, had died before it had taken its first breath.

The entire village heard the death wail of Bear. None remembered that he was white as they shared his loss of both wife and child.

Bear gently covered the woman who had been his wife with the white fur and left the lodge he would never again enter. He passed the villagers, friend or enemy, without acknowledging their presence. Only when he came to the lodge of Wolf did he stop. His eyes turned toward the woods and the obvious track of the grizzly. It was the only time since he and Wolf had become brothers that they fought.

"See that she is buried," Bear ordered in a voice

little resembling his own. "I will not return until I have revenged her death."

Wolf nodded. "It will be done, but I go with you to track the bear."

"No!" Bear turned his head, his eyes glazed with the pain of his loss. "I go alone."

Wolf grabbed Bear's arm. "She was my sister. I demand the right to seek revenge!"

"She was my wife," Bear whispered in an agonized voice. "She carried my child. I go alone, my brother."

It had been easy to follow the animal, its lumbering tracks clear in the snow. When darkness forced him to cease his search, Bear rested against the trunk of a tree. His eyes remained open through the long hours of darkness, his mind blank of everything but the picture of Snow as he had last seen her as she lay dead on their bed.

Memories taunted him, teased him. The hours until dawn were spent remembering Snow, both as a captivating child and as the breathtaking woman she became. The light wind rustling through the trees became her voice, promising the pleasures of love as it whispered around him.

When the morning sun lightened the sky, Bear had armored himself with single-minded determination. He would destroy that which had destroyed his wife and child. His search continued. He found the old animal at the edge of the river. With a fierce war cry, Bear attacked, fighting with only his knife and his towering rage. Lost in his thirst for revenge, Bear did not feel the massive claw as it slashed cruelly down his face and body. In a fight that should have left the grizzly the winner, Bear killed an animal feared by all men, both red and white.

Leaving the animal where it lay, his knife embedded

to the hilt in its throat, Bear turned back toward the village. He took only a few steps before the loss of blood caused him to collapse in a heap near the dead animal. Wolf had followed, knowing that the contest was unequal and that Bear had left the village without sufficient weapons. He found Bear, more dead than alive, his flesh torn open to the bone in places.

It had taken all the knowledge the Grandmother had known to save him. She bathed his body to bring down the fever and applied salves to his wounds. It was she who fought to save him, refusing to let him die, making him eat and drink . . . forcing him to live. It was the old Grandmother who heard his feverish whisperings and who knew how greatly he suffered through guilt. When he was well, it was she who convinced him that it was meant to happen and eased his guilt because he had been away from camp.

It was the old Grandmother who gave him a new name. "You are now Bear Who Walks Alone. Your life has changed directions beyond those you desired. You must follow its path wherever it leads, mighty Bear."

"It was mid-summer before I had the strength to walk more than ten steps," Bear said quietly, not elaborating on the extent of his injuries or the nearness of his own death.

"I came here and spent nearly two months building a lean-to. I was so weak it took days for me just to cut down a tree. By the time the first snow came, I had a rough shelter made, and I wintered here alone."

"I'm so sorry," Linsey whispered, knowing the words inadequate.

He nuzzled against her breasts. "It is over, little one. I have buried Snow, and time has a way of making the

179

pain less." A gentle smile crossed his lips. "She was so young and our time together so short, nothing can erase the memories I have of her. But I can't live in the past, and she would not want me to; so I have let her go."

Linsey leaned over him and looked deeply into his dark eyes. She saw that he spoke the truth. The agony of Snow's death would always be with him, but he had accepted his loss.

Moving slowly, allowing instinct to guide her, Linsey brought her head down to his. She caressed the scars with her lips, her touch soft against the sensitive skin. All thought of pity was also forgotten. It was skin and bone, as he had said, battle scars honorably won against a mighty opponent.

With her mouth and hands, she paid homage to a fierce warrior. Her inexperience was no barrier as she applied recently learned skills to take them both beyond the gates of reality, into the land of lovers.

The fierceness of the winter storm outside the snug cabin could not begin to compare with the fiery battle of love within.

Chapter Ten

The thick gray clouds filled the sky to overflowing, telling a tale for anyone willing to listen. The wilderness was unforgiving to those who did not or would not heed the warnings of nature.

Kaleb Smith was not ignoring the signs; he simply refused to obey their command to seek shelter. Hunching his coat more snugly around his neck, he was thankful for the thick leather gloves lined with soft rabbit fur that protected his hands. His lungs ached in protest of the bitterly cold air as his labored breathing made a thick white mist that gathered in tiny ice droplets from his beard.

For weeks he'd followed the trail, and now he knew it was only a matter of time before he found Jeb and Zeke. At mid-morning he'd come across the campfire they had used the night before. Cursing their carelessness in leaving live coals, he threw dirt over the smoldering embers. Wild fire spreading uncontrolled through the wilderness was something all hunters feared. Kaleb had lived through one once and had no desire to repeat the experience.

Kaleb knew that his quarry had lost their way. They

had come full circle and were actually a few miles above Big Jim's trading post. Jeb no longer took the time and effort to hide their trail, making Kaleb's job that much easier. A child could follow the path of broken limbs, trampled grass and human waste.

Alert ears detected a noise unnatural to the quiet woods. Kaleb stopped, his eyes narrowing as he listened carefully. The few animals and birds that stayed in the area during the winter were aware of the approaching storm and had sought shelter. The only sound was the wind whistling mournfully through the leafless trees. Kaleb cocked his head slightly. The noise had come from his left, and as he listened it came again: a human voice, too far away to distinguish the words, but still identifiable. Quietly, Kaleb moved forward. It was possible that the voices were from men other than the ones he sought. If so, he would cautiously seek information and move on.

But the instinct that had sharpened and grown with each passing year in the wilderness told Kaleb that he had found his prey. He lowered his pack to the ground, hiding it out of sight in the hollow of a dead tree. Cradling his loaded rifle, he cautiously walked to the edge of a clearing.

A smile of grim satisfaction spread through the puddled creases of his face. His search was finished; . . . now he would have vengeance. Across the clearing, arguing loudly, Jeb and Zeke were unaware that their lives had dwindled to a few short, extremely painful days.

"But Jebby . . ." Zeke whined, shuffling his foot in the dirt.

"Ya ain't gonna go back," Jeb said firmly. "There's a storm a'comin', and we's gotta be ready for hit."

"But hit was a purty red fox just a'waitin' for me to let hit outta the wood, Jebby."

Jeb snorted with disgust. "That purty red fox tweren't nothin' but a piece a brokin' tree branch. If Ma'a knowed what trouble hit was gonna cause, she'd never gived ya that knife and showed ya how to carve. Now ya won't let me burn a piece a wood to keep us warm if'n it looks like some animal to ya."

He raised his head and looked at the gathering clouds. "Ya do like I tolt ya. Go get us a lotta wood so we don't have to worry none about freezin' afore the snow stops."

"But Jebby, hits just back down the trail a ways. I can get hit and still get some wood."

"I said forget hit! Hit ain't down the trail a ways; we passed hit two days back, and ya ain't quit complainin' 'bout hit since." Jeb turned and began setting up camp. The temperature had dropped steadily all afternoon, and he had started to worry about finding a good place to build a shelter. The small clearing had not seemed a likely location until he discovered a natural cave dug into the rock.

"Go get all the wood ya can find," he ordered Zeke. "I'll make sure there's no animal a'nestin' in the cave."

From his hiding place, Kaleb freed his knife from its sheath and rested his rifle against a tree. He watched as Zeke passed within sight of him and breathed a silent sigh when Zeke kept his eyes on the ground, never looking right or left.

"Poor little foxy," Zeke mumbled as he kicked at a pine cone. "Got caught in that piece of wood and Jebby won't let me go get ya."

Kaleb silently followed Zeke and realized from listening to his mumblings that the other man intended to ignore his brother's orders and go back down the

183

trail for a particular piece of wood that had caught his fancy. Kaleb knew Zeke's mind was slow and without Jeb to care for him he would soon die in the wilderness. Weighing the idea, he decided to let Zeke go. His death from freezing would come much quicker than the fate Kaleb had planned, but now he could put all his attention on the man he held responsible for Mary.

For almost an hour Kaleb followed Zeke. When he was sure Zeke would not return to camp, Kaleb left him and made his way back. The first few gentle flakes of snow began to fall by the time he took up his hiding place again.

Jeb had cleared the cave of debris and made a covering for the front entrance by tying four sturdy branches together and covering them with one of their blankets. It would stop the wind and snow from blowing into the cave and keep some of the heat inside. As he worked, he was unaware of time passing, and only as the falling snow thickened did he realize Zeke had not returned.

He carried their packs inside then returned to begin gathering wood. His eyes constantly scanned the area, hoping to catch sight of Zeke. Even as he considered going in search of him, the snow became a veil of white. Jeb knew if he left the cave now he might never find it again. He carried the last armload of wood inside and pulled the blanket-covered barrier into place.

"Gawdamn ya, Zeke!" Jeb swore as he lit a fire near the front of the shallow cave. "I been a'takin' care a ya since ya tweren't no more'n a tadpole. I protected ya when Ma's men wanted to wop ya 'en she'd had too much rotgut to know what were goin' on. Ma never had no truck with me 'cause I knew she tweren't nothin' but a whore; but ya were special-like to her,

184

and I promised I'd watch out for ya. But how em I gonna do that when ya don't mind what I say?"

He slowly added logs to the flame. "I done tolt ya hit was gonna come a storm! I done tolt ya ya coun't go back for that piece of wood! Now you're out in the snow, 'en you're too stupid to find a place to hole up! You're gonna freeze your gizzard for a gawdamn piece a wood!"

Jeb stared into the golden flame as he cursed the only person who had ever looked up to him or ever needed him . . . the only person he had ever loved. Noises were hidden beneath the building fury of the storm as the wind howled fiercely. Jeb didn't know he was no longer alone until the covering at the front of the cave was violently thrown open.

"Zeke?" Blinded from staring into the fire, he looked up and grinned with relief. "You had me worried that you woun't be a findin' your way back here."

When his vision cleared, the grin left his face and he found himself staring into the business end of a long rifle. As his hand moved to the knife at his hip the gun pressed firmly against his chest.

"Throw the knife, careful like, past the fire," Kaleb said in a deadly soft voice.

Using only two fingers, Jeb tossed the knife, handle first, beyond the fire. His gaze rested briefly on his own rifle only an arm's length away.

"What'd I ever do to you?" Jeb whined. "Why you been a trackin' us?"

"It's a long story." Kaleb rested the rifle on his arm, his finger firmly on the trigger. "One you just might live long 'nough to hear."

"I ain't interested in hearing no stories, old man. Say your peace and get out!"

185

Kaleb's eyes narrowed as he looked at the other man. "How old do you think I am?" he asked quietly.

"What the hell do it matter how old you are?"

"Just been a thinkin' on it, I figure how you might be nearly my age."

Jeb snorted as he looked at Kaleb's gray beard, badly wrinkled face and scarred head.

"You ain't gonna believe me none, but four year back my hair tweren't gray . . . it were the color of corn. Yes siree, my woman liked my yeller hair, used to run her fingers through it . . ." His voice drifted away at the memory of Mary's fascination with his hair, so different from her silky black locks.

After his third winter as a longhunter, Kaleb Smith knew he had found the kind of life he'd searched for. Unlike some men who quit after the first lonely winter of solitude, Kaleb relished every day of isolation.

Raised on a farm in the Carolinas, the third of fifteen children, Kaleb had never known a moment for quiet thoughts, or had the place to indulge them. Seventeen people in a two room cabin did not allow for privacy and every minute of every day was spent in providing for their existence.

Leaving home at sixteen, Kaleb tried several occupations. After five years of slowly drifting westward he joined up with an old hunter and spent his first winter running trap lines. That spring, with his share from the sale of the furs, he bought supplies and went out on his own.

His first winter alone he ran into a small tribe of Delaware wintering not far from the abandoned cabin he had found and claimed as his own. From the time he saw the woman, barely more than a girl, he knew she was the missing thing that would make his life complete. It took two years and a winter's worth of furs in gifts to make her his wife.

Kaleb learned a working knowledge of the Delaware language, but her name was almost impossible for him to pronounce. He renamed his sweet, gentle wife. Mary.

Eager to please her golden haired husband, Mary gave to Kaleb a gentleness he had never known. Her smallest smile gave him joy, her tender touch brought exquisite pleasure, her soft voice was a velvet whispered sigh caressing his senses.

Among the first of the many things Kaleb taught her of the white man's ways was how to kiss. An enthusiastic pupil, it was a lesson she learned quickly and practiced frequently . . . with his willing cooperation. More than once her lips, soft and tender against his, invited him to delay his plans for the day. He never refused her invitation.

Mary sent him off on each journey with the taste of her lips on his. When he returned, she greeted him in the same way. She never tired of the white man's way of showing affection. Usually she thought the Indian way of doing things was better, but she decided a kiss was something greatly missing from the Indian life.

She was gentle and eager to please, but she was stubborn too. When she thought she was in the right she would plant her feet firmly, raise her chin determinedly and not back down. Her black eyes would flash and she'd speak her own language so quickly Kaleb would have trouble following. He enjoyed these confrontations as much, if not more, than any other and on more than one occasion he had been guilty of instigating them.

Mary was his woman, his friend, his lover . . . his heart. And he had two short years with her.

Winter was coming and Kaleb journeyed to the nearest outpost one last time before the deep snow made the trip impossible. The round trip took ten days and was one he made two or three times a year. Mary usually travelled with him, but this year she was late in preparing for winter and decided to stay home. Kaleb felt no undue concern about leaving her alone. It was the way of the wilderness.

He kissed her goodbye and pushed his canoe away from shore. Looking back just before he rounded a bend in the river Kaleb saw her wave—it was over a year before he saw her again.

Kaleb shook his head, almost surprised to find himself in the cave. He seldom allowed his memories to run free rein anymore, but he felt Jeb deserved to know exactly why he was going to die.

"It took me a year to find her," Kaleb said, the gentleness leaving his eyes as they turned to a chilling sky blue. "And it took her another year to die.

"She died slow, one day at a time. Her smile, her gentleness and her pride was gone by the time I got her away from that Frenchie you sold her to." He didn't add that he'd left the man with a lead slug between his eyes.

"She wouldn't even let me touch her to help her into my canoe." His hands tightened on the rifle. "Said she was dirt, a whore. She'd been raised to believe it were wrong to be with any man but her husband.

"The year it took her to die she'd talk sometime. It took a while but I pieced it together, the things you and that crazy brother of yours did to her. It nigh on to kilt me when I learnt she'd been carryin' my babe

188

and when you found it out you beat her until she lost it.

"And you never stopped beatin' her. She was covered in scars. Your bastard brother even cut off one of her tits to make that pouch he carries his carvings in.

"My gentle, sweet Mary were an old woman when she died. You broke her spirit and there tweren't nothin' left for her to live for."

Jeb remembered the young Indian woman they had taken that first year after Zeke had killed the white girl they had planned to sell.

"She tweren't nothin' but an Injun whore!" he screamed.

"*She was my wife!*" Kaleb snarled. "If'n I'da found you right away affer my Mary died I'da killed you slow, make it last for days, but now I just want it done.

"You're gonna die. For what you did to my Mary and the other women you took. You'da done it again to that little gal I took to the Bear if'en I hadn't been there to stop it."

"Old man you can't do this to me!"

"Who's gonna stop me?" he asked softly. "You know, you never did tell me how old you think I am. Mayhap I'm a little older you.

"Come summer, if'en I live that long, I'll be thirty-four."

Kaleb's rifle no longer pointed at Jeb's head. The heavy weight of it had pulled it down, but Kaleb's finger was firm on the trigger. Jeb saw his chance and reached frantically for his own rifle. It was the move Kaleb had waited for. He let Jeb reach the weapon, pull it into his grasp and turn to aim.

Kaleb's finger tightened on the trigger.

* * *

Kaleb walked away from the cave, the falling snow whispering softly past his face. For the first time in years Mary's memory played gently through his mind. He again saw her shy smile and felt her velvet voice.

His Indian wife thanked him for his revenge.

Chapter Eleven

As Linsey slid quietly off the foot of the bed, Bear opened his eyes and stretched. He folded his hands behind his head and stared at the ceiling. Contentment wove around him with the delicacy of a golden web, spun magically from whispered words and tender caresses.

The blizzard that began the night they'd first made love had lasted for three days, followed almost immediately by another one and yet another several days later. Winter at its worst became a time of discovery for the snowbound lovers. They learned each other as only two people alone can, speaking of their pasts, their likes and dislikes, family and friends.

And they loved.

Bear muffled a groan of pleasure at the memory. After her initial shyness was overcome, Linsey had become a passionate and adventurous lover.

Turning his head, he watched her as she crossed the room. She wore one of his flannel shirts, the hem coming down to her knees and the sleeves rolled back several times to free her hands. His eyes narrowed as he thought of the beauty that shirt covered. Her body was perfect, and he never tired of touching, tasting, or caressing it. He could feel the hardness of her nipple in his mouth and her silky legs wrapped around him. His desire grew as she bent toward the fire, and his groan was almost audible at her unknowing display. He briefly considered telling her to forget breakfast and come back to bed.

Linsey moved gracefully around the room, confidently preparing their breakfast, unaware of his burning gaze. Sweeping away the cold ashes, she found the glowing embers she knew would be underneath and slowly added kindling. Building a fire seemed natural now, and she bore scarce resemblance to the helpless girl he had found in his cabin.

When the fire was burning brightly, she gathered the ingredients for the biscuits Bear had recently taught her to make. She set the Dutch oven in the glowing coals for it to warm while she carefully measured, mixed, rolled and cut.

Bear watched through lowered lids and fought to dampen his rising passion. He grinned at the bottom lip caught firmly between her teeth as she concentrated on her chore. Her hair hung down her back, a scarlet flame seeming to float around her. She left it loose at night because he loved to tangle his hands in it, and most mornings he willingly helped comb it free of snarls. Usually the first thing she did upon leaving their bed was to coil her hair into a rope and knot it through itself so that there would be no danger of it dangling in the fire. It was a measure of her concentration on her new task that she had not done so today.

Hating to give away the fact that he was awake, Bear opened his mouth to remind her just as her flour-covered hands went to her hair. She quickly knotted it, unaware of the coating of white she left behind.

Linsey moved the Dutch oven from the fire, put her biscuits inside and replaced the lid. She returned it to its place and carefully shoveled hot coals onto it.

A satisfied smile crossed her lips as she made coffee and began frying thin slices of venison. Her stomach growled noisily as the odors filled the cabin, and she looked toward the bed to see if they had awakened Bear.

"How can he still be asleep?" she muttered to herself, nibbling on a crisp piece of meat.

Determined to wake him, Linsey began banging pans and rattling dishes. When the meat was done, she moved it to a plate and made gravy from the drippings. Removing the lid from the Dutch oven, she blew away the ashes that had fallen in and found that the biscuits were golden brown, only slightly darker on the bottom.

The meat was crisp, the biscuits perfect, the gravy thick and the coffee dark brown. She was starving! *He* was still asleep!

Bear knew when she began making noises that he was supposed to wake, but he enjoyed watching her too much to cooperate. He knew that he would never tire of seeing her move unconsciously around the cabin, doing the chores a wife does for her husband.

He closed his eyes at the thought. Wife! How he longed to make her his wife, to spend the rest of his life with her. She was adapting amazingly well to the wilderness, no longer jumping at every strange noise or getting upset when it was necessary for him to leave her alone all day while he checked his traps.

But how could he ask her to stay with him in the wilderness when all he could offer was a floorless, one-room cabin, an uncertain future and constant danger? In a land of few white women, word of her vibrant beauty would quickly pass along. Men would travel for miles just to see her, and not all of them would come with honorable intentions. He could protect her when he was here, but how about the many times he would be away?

During their long talks, Bear had not been surprised to learn that her father had been wealthy, and he knew there was a mansion and a place in society waiting for her in Philadelphia.

He could offer love and the promise to cherish her for a lifetime, but would that be enough? If she stayed, would she someday remember all that she had given up and long for it?

He couldn't ask her to stay, but God, how was he going to let her go?

Abruptly, Bear swung his legs over the side of the bed and sat up. He rested his elbows on his thighs and stared at the floor . . . the dirt floor.

" 'Bout time you woke up, sleepy head," Linsey called softly. "I'm starving, and if you don't get over here, I'm going to eat without you."

Bear raised his head and stared at her, his eyes narrowed, his face expressionless. How could she be so cheerful when his heart was being torn from his body?

"Ah oh, somebody woke up on the wrong side of the bed," she teased. "Come eat, grouch, and see if it doesn't make you feel better."

He stood, and the fur slid from his body. Her look turned sensuously hungry as she stared at his hardened shaft. "Looks like you want something other than food." She raised glowing eyes to his. "Maybe something special for dessert?"

Bear turned his back, stepped into his pants and laced them closed. Grabbing his shirt, he pulled it over his head as he walked toward the table.

"I have to check my traps today." He sat down and

reached for the plate she was holding out to him. "I may not make it back tonight."

Linsey hid the shudder she felt run through her. Twice Bear had not made it back home before dark, and she had spent long, lonely hours sitting in a chair, staring at the door, willing him to come home. Every noise became magnified in her imagination as time seemed to stand still. When she'd finally heard him calling to be let in, she had been clumsy in her haste to remove the guard bar from the door. Her eyes drank in the very sight of him, and she folded her arms over her waist to stop herself from wrapping them around his neck and never letting go.

Linsey played with the food on her plate, pushing it from one side to the other, the taste suddenly turning her stomach. She stood and scraped the plate into a waste pot.

"Thought you were starving?" Bear asked, watching her closely.

"Guess I wasn't as hungry as I thought." Linsey shrugged, trying to act natural.

He tried to eat, but the food seemed to lodge in his throat. His free hand, resting on the table beside the plate, knotted into a tight fist. He had to put some space between them, to have time to try to ease the anguish that was tearing him apart. Finishing his coffee, Bear pushed away from the table.

He prepared to leave as Linsey cleaned the table, washing the plates and utensils and putting them neatly back into their place. She carefully kept her eyes turned from his, knowing he'd read her fear, and tried to tell herself she'd kept him away from his traps long enough. Spring would come, and he would not have the furs to sell. He was a trapper, and he couldn't do his job if he had to worry about her.

195

Bear put on his hat and coat, shouldered his pack and pulled his gloves on. At the door, he reached for his rifle and cradled it in his arms.

"I may be gone for a couple of days," he said gruffly, still facing the door.

"All right." Linsey stood facing the fire, her back to his.

"Keep the door barred."

"Yes."

"Stay inside. It's too cold for you to be out long, and I don't want to have to worry about you falling into another drift."

"Be safe," she whispered.

Bear reached for the rope latching the door.

Linsey heard it open; a sob clogged her throat.

Had he looked, Bear would have seen the loneliness and fear etched on her face, but all he was capable of seeing was the specter of spring.

Had she looked, Linsey would have seen the desolation carving his features to stone, but all she knew was that he was leaving her, and she didn't want him to go.

Leaning the rifle against the wall, Bear turned and held his arms out to Linsey, who spun around and flew into them. Their lips met in a kiss almost savage in its intensity, tongues dueling for supremacy, bodies as close as Bear's heavy coat would allow. Linsey wrapped her arms around his neck, and he lifted her off her feet, one strong arm around her shoulders, the other under her bottom. When the need for air forced them to separate, she buried her face in his neck, while he rested his cheek on her hair.

There was no need for words as they clung together. Finally, slowly, Bear lowered her feet to the ground and gently pulled her arms down to her sides. With a feather-light touch, he caressed her cheek, then turned abruptly, grabbed his rifle and walked out the door.

Linsey watched until he was out of sight, waiting for him to turn for a final wave. He kept walking . . . and never looked back.

This would be her life if she stayed in the wilderness. She would watch him walk away and leave her alone, sometimes for days at a time. Linsey briefly thought of the friends she would probably never see again, the parties and galas she would not attend, the shops and libraries she could not visit.

She turned to the one-room cabin with its dirt floor. Contentment filled her as never before. Yes, she thought, she would miss her friends, the parties, the shops. But she could live happily without them.

She knew she'd only be existing if she left the wilderness. She had found her home, her life. Bear.

From the angle of the glaring winter sun, Bear knew it was mid-afternoon. He had not stopped since he'd left the cabin, and had put many miles between himself and Linsey. His mind had been blank except for his visions of her. More than once he almost turned around and retraced his steps, but he convinced himself that he needed this time away—time to decide what he was going to do when spring arrived and she asked again to be taken home.

"Ho the trail!"

Bear was startled out of his thoughts by the bellowing yell around the bend. He realized it was another traveler using the trail who knew it was better to announce your presence than to find yourself facing an unfriendly rifle.

"Ho!" Bear bellowed back as an acknowledgment.

Even though he had not seen him since the winter before, Bear instantly recognized the man.

"Keeping your hair?" Bear asked.

"What there is left of hit!" Kaleb Smith replied with a chuckle.

"They could start on your face next."

Kaleb stroked the beard that hung down to the middle of his chest. "Yep. Least ways they'd get somethin'!"

Bear was anxious to move on, but Kaleb motioned that he wanted to talk. Bear knew Kaleb was a man of few words, and with the temperature well below freezing, it would be far from comfortable to spend much time standing around. However, when Kaleb invited himself to walk along with him, Bear reluctantly agreed.

"I was on my way to your cabin. Had me a powerful need to check on that little gal I left there."

"Why did you leave her with me?" Bear could almost hate Kaleb for causing the problems he faced.

"I had things to do and needed someplace safe for 'er; knowed ya'd take care of 'er." It had been a long time since he'd felt anything for another person, and Kaleb had been surprised by his feelings of concern for the girl. He had thought his gentler feelings had been buried with Mary.

"I tweren't wrong to leave 'er with ya, were I?" Kaleb needed to assure himself that he had not been wrong in his judgement of the Bear, that Linsey was safe and happy. If he found out differently, Kaleb had decided to offer to take her home when the snows melted.

Bear stopped walking and stared down at the older man. The look on his face would have made a lesser man step back. Kaleb held his ground.

"She is . . . fine."

Kaleb saw Bear's expression and easily read it. He smothered a chuckle and turned his glittering gaze to the distance. "Figgered ya'd be lonely, winterin' by yourself after havin' me fer com'any last year."

Bear answered with a grunt and starting walking again.

"Yes siree, there ain't nothin' like a spunky little ole gal to warm a cabin in winter." Kaleb liked the sense of satisfaction he felt. Bear's expression would have been intimidating to another man, but he saw the fleeting look in Bear's eyes. Yep, Kaleb decided silently, come spring he doubted the little gal'd be going anywhere.

They walked quietly for a few minutes before he began to tell Bear the other reason he was coming to search him out, to warn him about Zeke. Kaleb had searched for him, but with snow covering any tracks, it had been useless. Zeke could be holed up somewhere or buried in a snowdrift. But until he was found, Kaleb would not rest.

Before he could finish his tale, Bear had turned and begun retracing his steps. He lengthened his pace until it was just short of a run. From experience he knew that he could maintain the mile-eating stride for hours without tiring. He had to get back to Linsey. He had left her without protection, and a haunting premonition shadowed each of his steps.

Kaleb stayed with Bear for a short way, then let the younger man go on alone. He would get to the cabin . . . just not as quickly.

Linsey poured the last kettle of warm water into the tub and sighed with relief. Quickly removing Bear's shirt, she stepped in and knelt down. When she'd casually commented that she was tired of sponge baths, Bear had brought in a big barrel. He'd worked for days to cut it in half and smooth the rough edges. She had to sit with her knees folded beneath her or bent almost under her chin, but it felt incredibly good after weeks without a real bath.

She had already washed her hair, disgusted with herself when she discovered the flour in it. With it clean and almost dry, she pulled it on top of her head and fastened it with some wooden pins Bear had carved for her.

Bear had told her how he took baths nightly during the summer in the rapidly flowing creek out back of the cabin, where even on the hottest days the water was cool. Linsey thought the idea intriguing; she'd never bathed outside before, and it would certainly be easier than melting the endless buckets of snow to fill the tub. It had taken her all morning to heat enough water to wash her hair, and then she had started the process all over again to take a bath. Linsey grimaced, an entire day spent on nothing but getting clean!

As she thought of her many trips outside, Linsey looked toward the door. It was firmly closed, but she had forgotten to replace the heavy bar. The warm water lapped around her stomach, and it seemed too much effort to climb out of the tub. Deciding to leave the door until she was finished, she applied a generous amount of the flowery soap to her shoulders, liking the fragrance it left on her skin. She would have to ask Morning Moon how it was made. Maybe in the spring. . . .

At the thought of spring, Linsey's hands slowed their movements, dropping to her knees. In the spring, Bear would take her back to Philadelphia. She would not need to know how to make soap or anything else for that matter. There were more than enough servants to see to her needs and several establishments in which to buy pretty, molded soaps from Europe.

She would never see Morning Moon's new baby or listen to Chattering Squirrel's confusing gab. Her eyes slowly filled with tears, and she knew that once he left her on her doorstep, she would never again see Bear.

She loved him. Linsey had never known a man could be so gentle.

He had told her of his past and of future plans. With considerable patience, he had taught her how to do the many things she did not know how to do. He had laughed with her, never at her, and seemed to understand her fears almost before she could express them.

He had taken her to the world of their own when they became lovers, understanding her shyness and giving her time to accept her own role in this glorious new thing he'd shown her.

Absently, Linsey rinsed the soap from her shoulders. How could she leave him to return to Philadelphia? Yet, how could she ask Bear to let her stay? He had a life of his own; perhaps he wouldn't want the inconvenience of providing for her. Never in his plans for the future had he mentioned a wife and family.

A tear fell to the water, making a barely discernible splash. Linsey closed her eyes as the pain of parting sent bitter chills of hopelessness through her.

Lost in her torment, she was startled as the door opened and a never to be forgotten voice grated harshly through the silence.

"Jebby?"

Standing framed in the door, Zeke's maniacal gaze wildly searched the room. The days spent alone in the wilderness had sent him teetering on the brink of insanity. He had survived the first two snow storms only because he had stumbled onto a deserted lean-to. He had waited there for Jeb to find him until hunger finally drove him out of the shelter. For the last few days, he had wandered mindlessly, crossing and recrossing his own trail, sleeping where he fell when darkness came, eating little, and at times forgetting why he was lost and for whom he searched, surviving beyond all reason.

Zeke had not realized that he had crossed the frozen river and was following the trail toward Bear's cabin. When he saw the structure sitting dark against the snow, his irrationality told him Jeb was inside.

His gaunt frame had never carried excess weight, but now Zeke was emaciated. His coat appeared too heavy to be supported by his scrawny body as he stumbled into the room, bringing with him an odor of decay.

"Jebby? Zeke's here, Jebby." His eyes moved around the room, finally coming to rest on the naked girl in the tub. His brow wrinkled as he tried to concentrate.

"Girlie?" His brow cleared, and he smiled. "Girlie! Zeke's purty girlie!"

His happiness at seeing someone he recognized was pitiful. He came toward her, skeletal fingers outstretched. Long icicles hung from his beard and hair. His hands and parts of his face were a ghostly white, showing signs of advanced frostbite.

As he reached for her, Linsey jumped up, more revolted than ever at the thought of being touched by him. She stepped out of the tub, backing away.

Zeke stopped, looking confused. "Where's Jebby, girlie?" he whined.

Linsey's mind whirled frantically. Zeke seemed almost harmless, pathetically lost and bewildered. He didn't even seem to see her nakedness. But what would happen once he finally realized Jeb was not here? During their trip into the wilderness, she had seen his moods fluctuate with a blink of the eye from one to another and then back again. She slowly edged toward the table and the knife lying there, never taking her gaze away from Zeke.

"Where's Jebby? Zeke's been tryin' ta find him." He lurched toward her, his feet dragging as if they were too heavy for him to move.

Linsey stopped. Zeke had gotten between her and the table. In order to get to the knife, she would have to get closer to him. Revulsion trembled through her.

"Jeb isn't here right now, Zeke." Her eyes moved to the open door. "He . . . ah, he went to gather some firewood. He said you should go help him." If she could get him outside, she could bar the door.

"Firewood?" Zeke's eyes brightened.

Linsey held her breath when his gaze moved to the fireplace and the stack of wood Bear always kept there so that she would not have to venture outside.

"He needs your help." Her voice grew stronger with determination.

"Outside? Jebby's outside?"

"Getting firewood. You had better go help; you remember how angry he can get when you don't do what he's told you to do." It was an outright lie, since Linsey couldn't remember ever seeing Jeb angry with his brother.

"Firewood. . . ." Zeke turned and stumbled toward the door.

Linsey grabbed the knife from the table and edged nearer to the door. Zeke had stopped just inside, searching for signs of his brother.

"Jebby?" he called loudly. "Where you at, Jebby?"

"Just a little farther, just a little farther," she mumbled to herself. Her heart thumping until it seemed in danger of leaving her chest, Linsey waited for him to get far enough so that she could slam the door closed.

"Girlie, Zeke don't see Jebby." Zeke turned to her, and the knife caught his attention.

Linsey saw the transformation from bewilderment to anger but could hardly believe how quickly it happened. One second he was asking about his brother in a whiny voice; the next he had moved and grabbed the arm holding the knife.

"Jebby ain't here," he snarled.

"He's getting firewood, Zeke. He'll be angry if you don't go help him." Linsey held desperately to the knife.

"Whatcha done to Jebby, girlie?" His free hand grabbed her shoulder and shook her until her hair fell down around her hips.

It did not seem possible that there could be so much strength left in his gaunt body as his grasp tightened on her wrist until her hand went numb and the knife dropped harmlessly to the floor. Linsey twisted, kicking out with her bare feet, but her blows caused her more pain than they did him. Zeke savagely twisted her arm behind her back, pulling her tightly against him.

"You're lyin'! Where's Jebby?" he snarled, his fetid breath making her gag.

He jerked on her arm, and Linsey screamed as pain traveled like wildfire from her elbow to her shoulder. Darkness swam before her eyes as he grabbed her hair and pulled her head back violently, threatening to snap her neck.

Without warning, a shrill war cry splintered through the room. Zeke abruptly released her and turned to face his new adversary as Linsey backed away. Before them stood the fierce warrior ready for battle, in one hand a feathered tomahawk, in the other a wicked knife, his face contorted almost beyond recognition. Linsey knew him as a loving father, tender husband, gentle friend. This was the thing of her nightmares. Terror held her captive, her fear of him greater than any she had ever felt for Zeke.

Wolf noted the look on her face as he quickly scanned her body for signs of injury, but his attention was solely for the man who dared to touch his brother's woman.

"You die!" Wolf snarled.

Linsey watched the tomahawk descend. She heard the slashing of flesh, the crunch of bone. Zeke's scream was abruptly stilled as the blood gushed freely to the floor. Like a boneless rag doll, he crumbled to the dirt, twitched once and then was still.

Linsey's emerald gaze moved rapidly between Zeke and Wolf. Trembling hands covered her mouth as vomit burned the back of her tongue. The edge of the table cut into her bare thighs as she tried to back farther away.

"He is dead, Summer Eyes," Wolf said quietly, confused by the horror still so evident on her face. "He can no longer hurt you."

Thinking her fear was from the bloody body, Wolf grabbed a blanket and threw it over Zeke. Noticing the blood on his own chest, he walked to the tub of bathwater and used the rag to wash it away. He turned toward Linsey and saw that her skin was blue from the cold and she shivered violently. Taking a fur from the bed, he slowly approached her.

"Summer Eyes." His voice was soft, soothing. "He is dead. He will never again touch you, my sister."

His voice was familiar, he was again the man she had

known only as a friend, but over and over she saw the fierce warrior. She knew, with the quickness of a breath, he could become that savage. This was a facade, a mask hiding his true nature.

Wolf approached her as if she were a wild creature, ready to spring away at any moment. She was shaking so hard her teeth were chattering, and he knew it was as much from terror as from the cold that filled the room.

Linsey demanded her body to move, to run, but her legs refused to do more than support her weight. With each step, Wolf moved closer until her mind became blank of all thought except for terror.

Wolf's movements were slow as he approached her. Wrapping the fur around her trembling body, he pulled her into his arms. She was stiff and unyielding as he pushed her head against his bare chest.

"It is over, Summer Eyes. It is over," he repeated softly. Pulling her hair from beneath the fur, his fingers threaded through the silken strands, startled by the softness so unlike his own coarse hair. When he felt her relax slightly, Wolf bent and picked her up. Carrying her to the bed, he detoured to the door, kicking it closed with his foot.

Sitting down, he held her on his lap. Starting to feel the cold himself, Wolf grabbed a blanket and threw it around his own shoulders, then wrapped his arms around Linsey, cradling her closely.

His voice was soothing, his touch gentle as he stroked her hair. With her face buried in his neck, Linsey could smell the clean fragrance of his skin and recognized the flowery scent of the soap. Her pounding heart slowly returned to normal, and her trembling ceased except for an occasional shudder. She repeatedly told herself that this was Wolf, the man Bear considered his brother. He would not harm her; in fact, he had saved her from the insanity of Zeke.

He held her very much as she had once seen him hold his young daughter, Spring Flower. She had been amazed at his tenderness with the child, seeming content to cradle her and willing to let her sleep in his arms. Until then Linsey had never given thought to the fact that an Indian father would love his children as much as any white father or that he would freely show that love. Now he was holding Linsey in the same way, and the thought of sleep was very inviting as a sudden exhaustion claimed her.

She closed her eyes, but the vision of Zeke was all too clear. With a shudder she opened them, happier to stare at the copper skin against her cheek.

"It is done, Summer Eyes," Wolf whispered, feeling her shiver. There was no way he could wipe the memory from her mind, and he wondered if she would believe that sometimes he could still vividly see the face of the first man he had killed in battle.

The vision had haunted him until, feeling unmanly, he had spoken to his father. His father had calmly assured him that Wolf would be a better leader for remembering the faces of those he had killed in battle. With their faces as a reminder, Wolf would become a chief who never killed without reason, who would search first for peace not war.

"My feet are cold." Linsey broke the silence that had settled around them, wiggling her bare toes. She felt and heard the chuckle that vibrated through his chest.

"The rest of you was freezing, and you did not know of it, Summer Eyes," Wolf replied. His big hand covered her feet, and Linsey giggled as he tickled her arch.

"Ah, your feet will not suffer overmuch; they still

207

feel!" He pulled a fur over them, tucking it in and rubbing to help warm them.

"Don't you ever get cold?" Linsey suddenly remembered that twice he had entered the cabin bare chested while snow lay on the ground.

Wolf shifted her slightly, his hand resuming the soothing comfort of stroking her hair. "When one faces a battle, Summer Eyes, a coat gets in the way. It is better to suffer a little cold air on the skin and have the freedom to move than to be warm while you feel the blade of a knife slide between your ribs."

Linsey nodded. "Bear once told me to forget modesty in a battle." She sat up, a satisfied light entering her eyes. "I did! When Zeke came, I was in the tub, and I forgot all about it when I was trying to get the knife!"

Wolf smiled, his eyes sparkling. "You will become a worthy warrior, my sister. Most men would forget to fight if you came to them naked. You would have no trouble winning all your battles while your opponent stared at your beauty!"

Linsey blushed vividly and buried her burning face in his shoulder. Wolf chuckled, shaking his head over her strange modesty about nudity. To the Indian an unclothed body was natural, nothing to be concerned about. This was the first time that he realized it was something hidden by the whites.

As Linsey relaxed again, he thought of Morning Moon, who waited for him at home, her stomach growing with his child. He had chosen her for his wife among many maidens, and she gave him peace and contentment. He loved his wife and was happy that his brother would again know the love of a woman—this woman. Summer Eyes was his sister, the woman of his brother, and he would always honor her as such. But his respect and admiration were for her, for what she was and what she would become.

The terror and tension drifted away leaving her limp, eyes closed. She wandered in that nether world between being awake and asleep. Safe . . . in the arms of a fierce warrior.

Wolf heard the sound of the crunching snow shortly before Bear reached the door.

"Linsey, let me in!"

"Let yourself in, brother," Wolf called. He felt the woman in his arms stir, and he soothed her back to sleep with the touch of his hand in her hair.

"What the hell!" Bear saw the covered mound in the middle of the room and Linsey on Wolf's lap. He quickly surmised what had happened, and a savage expression equal to any Wolf could ever show crossed his face. He snarled deep in his chest and clenched his fists, the muscle in his jaw jumping fiercely.

"She is all right?" Bear tried to keep his voice low so that he wouldn't wake Linsey.

"Now."

"Did he hurt her?" A world of meaning passed between them.

"No, my brother. She fought him, and I came in before he could do her harm."

"I owe you."

"She is the woman of my brother; she is my sister," Wolf replied seriously. "I would do no less for her than you would do for me."

Bear bent and picked up Zeke's body. He was gone for a short time, returning just as Kaleb entered the cabin carrying a coat and fringed buckskin shirt.

"Looks like these might be yours," Kaleb said, holding out the coat and shirt as he surveyed the room and found the pool of blood that had soaked into the dirt floor. "Guess we're a might bit late."

Wolf recognized the man who had shared Bear's cabin the winter before. "You sound sorry, Kaleb. Were you looking for a fight?"

"Nope, just glad hits over. Is the little gal all right?"

At Wolf's nod, Kaleb threw the coat and shirt on the table and sat down. Bear soon removed all signs of the fight from the cabin, his thoughts twisting and turning in his mind. He was relieved Wolf had arrived in time to prevent Zeke from hurting Linsey, but he almost wished Zeke back to life so that he could kill him. He watched Wolf caressing Linsey's hair, and a tiny green monster rode his shoulder. Fighting back his feelings of jealousy, Bear reminded himself that Wolf was simply soothing her. The man had saved her life, and his holding her on his lap was totally innocent.

Trying to control himself, Bear walked to the bed. Wolf stood and handed his precious burden into willing arms.

At the movement, Linsey opened her eyes and saw the familiar face.

"Bear," she whispered with a sigh, wrapping her arms around his neck until he was in danger of being choked to death.

The fur around her started to slip, and he quickly realized that she was nude. Trying to grab the fur, maintain his hold on her and loosen her death grip on his neck, Bear was unaware of the enjoyment of his friends.

The two men watched him, grins spreading across their faces as he was successful only at maintaining his hold and a length of slender, feminine back was exposed to their appreciating gazes.

"Come, my friend," Wolf invited as he pulled on his

shirt. "We will leave Summer Eyes in the care of my brother."

"Er ya sure he can handle 'er alone?" Kaleb asked solemnly as they watched Bear fighting with the fur that was following the pull of gravity.

Wolf shrugged and pulled on his coat. "There are times when each man must face the dangers of life alone."

Chuckling, they left, closing the door behind them. Bear had not heard their teasing words and was barely conscious of their departure. He sat on the bed and slowly rocked Linsey, trying to comfort himself as much as her.

It was a torment he was not sure he could survive. He closed his eyes, his cheek against the softness of her hair. Losing her was a foe he had no weapons with which to fight and a battle he knew he could never win.

Chapter Twelve

Linsey contentedly dug through the huge chest kept at the foot of the bed, the events of the day before forgotten. Not wanting to intrude on Bear's privacy, she had forced herself to leave it unexplored. Curiosity finally got the upper hand, and she tried to sound casual as she asked him about its contents. Bear saw the inquisitiveness sparkling childlike in her eyes and with a grin told her to find out.

Feeling as if she was prying, Linsey carefully removed first one thing and then another, until interest overcame caution and she happily jumbled through the various items. At the bottom she could see a large wrapped bundle and grunted from the effort of lifting the heavy package out of the chest.

"Flannel!" There were several bolts of the soft, sturdy fabric with matching threads, needles and pins. "Why didn't you tell me you had this? I could have used it to make the gown for the baby."

Looking up from the hide he was cleaning, Bear shrugged. "It's been years since I've gone through that chest. I'm not sure anymore exactly what's in it. I guess I just forgot about the cloth."

Just like a man, Linsey decided as she set the fabrics aside and began replacing the other items in the chest. Now that she knew he didn't mind, she would investigate them more thoroughly another day.

She closed the lid and carried the material to the table. She discovered there was enough fabric for several shirts, which he desperately needed. In some of his old ones the cloth was so thin she could see her hand through it, and in others the weave was tearing apart. She had repaired them when possible, but most were fit only for the rag bag.

Sewing was something Linsey not only enjoyed but was good at. She put the flannel on her shelf and sat down with one of his old shirts. Using the point of her knife, she carefully picked at the seams. With it as a pattern, she could quickly make him several new shirts.

"I have decided that when I must be gone from the cabin you will go to the village."

"What?" Linsey looked up, startled out of her concentration by his abruptness.

"It's not safe for you to be here alone; so I'll take you to the village when I leave, and you can visit with Morning Moon."

All day long, Bear had seemed to almost haunt the cabin. Linsey had been expecting something like this, but now that it was out in the open, she wasn't sure how to handle it.

"What if I don't happen to want to spend the day with her?"

"You'll have no choice."

This wasn't going the way he had planned. After loving Linsey with a passion that bordered on desperation, Bear had lain awake most of the night, with her safely enfolded in his embrace, his thoughts in a turmoil. The day had seemed endless as he'd searched for a solution, and this had seemed the only reasonable one. He'd been sure she would agree. He was no longer so sure.

"Just like that"—Linsey snapped her fingers—"you decide what I will or won't do and I don't have a say in the matter?"

"You'll be safe there."

"I'll be safe here!" She looked down at the shirt in her lap and ripped a few more threads free.

"The next time someone like Zeke breaks in, you may not be so lucky!"

"There is no one else like Zeke," she muttered to herself.

Bear heard her but chose to ignore the comment. "I thought you'd gotten over your irrational fear of the Indians and that you liked Morning Moon."

"It wasn't irrational and I do like her!" Linsey stood and paced the small confines of the cabin. "I just don't happen to want to spend all day, every day, with her! There are too many things that need to be done here. Do the wives of other hunters spend their time being watched over?"

"I don't particularly care what other hunters do." It was the only way he could think of to protect her, and she was going to agree if he had to throw her over his shoulder and carry her to the village!

Linsey knew she had to win this argument. If Bear wouldn't let her stay alone, he'd never agree to letting her stay once spring arrived. And she knew she wanted to stay; she wanted it more than she'd ever wanted anything in her life. He had to see that she could survive in his wilderness.

"I'm not going to the village," she said firmly. "I've never been watched over, and I'm not going to start now."

"This is not the city with fifty people within shouting

distance. If Wolf hadn't happened along, God alone knows what Zeke would have done to you. I can't take that chance." Bear tried to make his voice sound reasonable. "You'll be safe with Morning Moon, and if I can't make it back at night, I won't have to worry about you."

Linsey sat on the edge of the bed and began unlacing the leggings. He could take her to the village, but he couldn't make her stay, she decided as she kicked off the moccasins, removed the leggings and reached for the hem of her dress. This discussion was getting them nowhere, and she refused to continue it. Time would show him that she was safe alone in the cabin.

Bear's breath caught in his throat as she pulled the dress up over her head. The shadows from the fire danced over her creamy skin, and he watched her nipples pucker from the chill in the room. All thoughts of tomorrow fled as he became a willing captive of her wild beauty. He put aside the hide he'd been working on and slowly approached the bed.

She unknotted her hair and let it fall in a cascade of russet fire around her shoulders. Grabbing the flannel shirt she'd claimed as her own, Linsey started to slip it on when she realized he was standing in front of her. He took the shirt from her hands and threw it to the foot of the bed.

"You don't need that," he murmured in a velvet whisper.

"It keeps me warm."

"I'll keep you warm."

Bear sat on the bed and pulled her between his thighs. Her breasts were level with his mouth, and he eagerly sought one of the puckered peaks. He teased it with his lips and tongue until she buried her hands in his hair and pulled his head against her. Her knees grew weak, and her legs began to tremble as he supported her weight with his hands cupped around the fullness of her bottom.

Linsey unlaced the thong of his shirt, running her fingers over his muscular chest and shoulders. With a groan, he released her long enough to pull it over his head and toss it away. He nuzzled the soft skin beneath her breast, his tongue making ever decreasing circles around the globe until he reached his goal. Linsey was unaware of holding her breath until she released it with a shudder as his lips closed warmly over her nipple.

Bear gave her other breast the same treatment while Linsey gently rubbed her stomach against the thick hair on his chest. Growling deeply, he moved his mouth lower, sampling the firm skin covering her ribs, the crevice of her waist and the swell of her hips. His hand followed the enticing slope of her bottom, his fingers finding the moist warmth between her thighs. When his mouth reached unchartered territory, Linsey grabbed handfuls of hair, pulling his head away.

"What are you doing?" she asked, startled by the invasion of his tongue. Her eyes were as wide as saucers, clearly showing her unease with this new caress.

His eyes were burning with desire as they searched hers. "There are so many things yet to discover and learn," he whispered huskily. Placing a kiss low on her stomach, Bear stood and easily picked her up. "When you are ready, I will show you other ways for us to please each other, for now this is enough."

He placed her in the center of the bed and quickly finished undressing. Carefully parting her thighs with his knees, Bear lowered his body to hers until they were one.

His weight was familiar as he filled her with his burning velvet shaft. Thoughts of yesterday and tomorrow faded like the light in the sky at dusk. Just as the sun would rise to chase away the dark, so would their dilemma wait for their return to reality. Only now mattered as they journeyed to the world they knew awaited their return—a world that only two who love can share.

"Linsey!"

The bellowing roar outside the cabin door startled her so much that she jabbed the needle deep into her finger. Ruby-red blood beaded on the tip, and she stuck the offended finger into her mouth.

"Open the damn door right now!"

"He's not happy," she mumbled to herself as she placed her sewing on the table and stood.

"Did you hear me?" A rattling of the door told of his impatience. "Dammit woman, answer me!"

A heavy pounding on the door tested the strength of the bar across it, and Linsey considered not letting him in until his temper cooled somewhat. But the longer she delayed, the angrier he seemed to grow, and his curses came clearly through the thick wood.

She had known that he would discover her deception sooner or later, but she had hoped for later! With a resigned shrug, Linsey lifted the heavy bar free and jumped back as the door was thrown open.

Anyone with an ounce of common sense would have run in terror from the expression contorting his face. Linsey briefly wondered when her common sense had deserted her, for she felt no fear. Someone had to win this standoff, and she was determined it would be her.

"You're back early today." Linsey turned casually and walked back to her chair. She sat down and picked up her sewing.

Bear stalked toward her, his hands knotted into tight fists. "You owe me an explanation."

"Why?" Linsey found it hard to maintain her casual pose. She knew he would not harm her; but only a fool baits a wounded animal, and standing over her with nostrils flared and a muscle jumping violently in his jaw, he much resembled his namesake.

"Woman! Don't play with me!"

"That's not what you said last night," she mumbled softly, her eyes sparkling.

Bear gritted his teeth and brought his hand down on the table with a bone-rattling slam. "What are you doing here?"

"Sewing?"

"Linsey . . . !"

She tilted her head slightly to the side and looked at him with a gentle smile. "I think that's the first time you've ever used my name."

"Stop avoiding the question! Why aren't you at the village?"

"Would you believe me if I said I got homesick?"

His eyes narrowed.

"No, huh? How about Morning Moon got tired of my company and asked me to leave?"

"When did you come home?"

"A little earlier today than I did yesterday. I must have stayed fifteen minutes this morning; yesterday it was closer to an hour."

"The day before yesterday?"

Her brow wrinkled as she considered the question. "It must have been mid-morning before I got home. I ran into Kaleb, and we talked for a while. You didn't tell me he had been invited to winter with the tribe."

"You've been at the village every evening when I've gotten there."

218

She smiled sweetly. "You almost caught me yesterday! I'd just gotten back and sat down to play with Chattering Squirrel when you arrived."

His voice lowered until it was deadly soft. "For three days you've gone to the village with me in the morning, then come back home a short time later. In the afternoon, before you think I'll get back, you return to the village?"

"Well, not really."

"Not really?"

"Actually, it's been four days."

"Linsey," he spoke through clenched teeth, "I've only taken you there for four days."

"I think I like it better when you call me Autumn Fire or Angel. The way you're saying my name makes it sound like a curse."

She didn't understand what he said next because he spoke in Shawnee, but she decided she was glad she knew so little of the language. His voice was harsh, the words snarled as he dropped his pack and removed his coat. Linsey folded her hands in her lap and looked the picture of innocence.

Bear fought to control his raging anger. He'd been frantic when he'd arrived at the village and Linsey had not been there. Wolf's face had been serious, but his eyes had sparkled with amusement when he'd informed Bear that she'd left early that morning and had not returned yet. The trip to the cabin had seemed endless as he pictured her hurt or lost. Finding her quietly sewing had only made his temper soar.

"Tomorrow you will stay at the village," he ordered.

"No."

"No?" His look was incredulous. He'd seen grown men back down when his temper had flared. Now this little bit of femininity was sitting as calmly as if they were discussing the weather, occasionally looking at him as if he were a child throwing a temper tantrum!

"No! Before Zeke broke in, you didn't worry about leaving me here. Nothing has changed. I refuse to continue going to the village every day."

"You refuse! Linsey, I'm not giving you a choice!"

"I dinna ask for a choice, mon! You canna make me go."

His eyes narrowed. "Would you like to place a wager on it?"

"You and whose tribe?"

"Woman, you will do as I say!" he roared.

"This is America. My father died from wounds he received fighting in a war that helped make this land and its people independent of a monarchy. If you want to be a king and rule your subjects, go back to France, but don't stand here and try to rule me!"

"I'll throw you over my shoulder and carry you like a sack of flour!" he threatened.

Linsey stood and placed her hands on her hips. "Aye, ya might get me there, but ya canna make me stay!"

"I'll put a guard on the door!"

"Won't that make you look just a little silly to your friends?"

"Hell with the way it looks! I don't care what they think. All I care about is your safety, and if guarding you is the only way I can do it, then so be it!"

Linsey had the grace to feel a little shame. His only concern was protecting her. Somehow she had to show him that she didn't need that kind of protection.

"Luc, when you got here, were you able to break down the door?" she asked quietly.

"What the hell does that have to do with anything?"

"Answer my question. Were you?"

"No."

She approached him and placed her hands on his arms. "Few men are as strong as you. If you couldn't break in, do you honestly think anyone else could?"

Her reasoning was sound; he could feel himself sinking but couldn't give up the battle quite yet. "Zeke got in!"

"That's because I foolishly left the bar off the door. If I hadn't been in such a hurry to take a bath, I would have replaced it, and nothing would have happened."

"But it did!" Her soft emerald gaze pleading with him, he found it difficult to continue insisting that she do something against her will. "I only want you to be safe, *mon ange.*"

"As much as I like Morning Moon, I don't want to spend every day, all day, with her."

"I can't protect you when I'm not here, and I can't be here all the time."

"I promise to bar the door when you leave and not remove it again until you return."

Bear folded her in his arms, his head resting on the top of her head. He'd lost. How could he refuse her? He shuddered when he thought of what could have happened when Zeke broke in. The possibilities had played around and around in his mind until he thought he'd go mad.

As if reading his thoughts, Linsey quietly soothed him. "It won't happen again. I won't let in anyone I don't know and trust." She moved back slightly until she could look into his eyes. "I want to stay here. This is my home."

The phrase echoed through his mind as he again pulled her against him. *This is my home.*

For the next few days, Bear left the cabin without comment but giving her a look that spoke volumes. He would wait outside the door until he heard the bar drop into place. Several hours later Wolf would come by, stay for a short visit and then leave. Finally Wolf's visits ceased. Linsey was left to enjoy the solitude while she waited for evening and the return of the man she loved.

Chapter Thirteen

"Enter, my sister," Morning Moon called, hearing her friend outside.

Linsey raised the hide and walked into the warm lodge. As usual, Chattering Squirrel squealed and ran to her with arms spread wide. Linsey lifted the toddler and kissed the soft, copper creases of his chubby neck.

"You're getting too big for me to pick up," she said, tickling his ribs and grinning as he giggled merrily.

"Me big boy!" he said proudly.

"You sure are. Pretty soon you'll be as big as your daddy."

Linsey carefully set him on his feet and turned to greet Spring Flower, who raised red and watery eyes to her, smiling shyly.

"What are you making?" Even as she spoke with the child, Linsey's eyes narrowed in concern. Spring Flower sneezed several times, followed by a hard, dry cough, rubbing the back of her hand over her runny nose.

Her English vocabulary was more limited than her mother's, and she wrinkled her smooth brow as she concentrated on the correct words, fingering the colorful carved beads she was stringing together on a thong. "Beads for baby chew."

"They are beautiful, Spring Flower." Linsey admired the beads. "I'm sure your new brother or sister will appreciate them when new teeth start coming in."

"The baby will be brother." Spring Flower seemed so certain, Linsey did not have the heart to point out that the baby could just as easily be a girl.

Finally Linsey turned to Morning Moon. "I always seem to greet you last."

"You honor me by showing affection for my children," Morning Moon replied softly. "I did not expect you today, Lin Zee."

She removed her coat and sat down on a mat on the floor. "I need to ask you a couple of questions, if that is all right?"

Morning Moon spoke softly in Shawnee to Spring Flower, and Linsey watched as the child set her beads neatly aside and picked up Chattering Squirrel. She balanced him on her slender hip and quietly left the lodge, but Linsey heard her racking cough marking her passage down the road.

"I didn't mean for you to send the children away. Spring Flower shouldn't be outside; the child is sick!"

Morning Moon shrugged. "It is only a cough that sometimes comes with spring. Several people also share it; it is of no concern, Lin Zee. They go visit their grandmother, who will fix her a soothing drink and fuss over her."

Hugely pregnant, Morning Moon moved gracefully around the room. She poured liquid into two cups but had to hand them to Linsey before she could sit down.

A sneeze caught her unaware, and she grabbed at the huge mound of her belly. "Baby come soon," she said, lowering herself to a mat.

Linsey tasted the liquid and found that it was the juice of some kind of berry, lightly sweetened with maple syrup. "This is delicious. Perhaps you will show me how to make it?"

Morning Moon nodded, then waited patiently for Linsey's questions while Linsey searched for the way to ask them.

"I think I'm pregnant," she finally blurted.

"Yes," Morning Moon replied with a smile. "Bear very much . . . ah, warrior. It no surprise!"

"My breasts are swollen, and my stomach's not flat anymore."

"You lose morning food?" Morning Moon asked.

"I feel like I'm going to, even when I haven't eaten!" Linsey's grimace expressed her thoughts, and Morning Moon giggled, showing no sympathy.

"It will pass soon. You have woman's time?"

Linsey had had her monthly flow only once since leaving Philadelphia. She smiled as she remembered the embarrassment she had suffered when it had been necessary to ask Bear for some rags.

"Not since the first snow."

Morning Moon patted her swollen stomach. "Our sons will be brothers. They will grow together and learn much from each other."

A few months earlier Linsey would have been horrified at the thought of her child playing with an Indian child, now the idea delighted her. But not nearly as much as the knowledge that she carried Bear's child.

She did not stay long. It was obvious that Morning Moon was catching her daughter's cold as her nose and eyes began to water. Suggesting that she take advantage of her children's absence and get some rest, Linsey thanked her for the confirmation of her pregnancy. Now she was anxious to be alone to savor the idea.

At the top of the hill overlooking the peaceful village, Linsey leaned against a rock to catch her breath. The coat that had provided necessary warmth earlier now seemed too heavy, and she let it gap open. The happy shouts of children at play floated on the breeze as the sun shone brightly on her face. Where the snow had melted, patches of rich, black earth made a geometrical pattern on the ground.

The days blended one to the other, and it was easy to lose track of the date, but she didn't need a calendar to know that spring was almost here. The snow disappeared a little more each day, and though the nights remained cold, the days were almost warm.

She placed her hands protectively on her abdomen and felt its gentle slope. His child rested warm and safe in her body, and sometime late in summer she would present Bear with a cub. She wondered briefly why he had not noticed the changes in her. After a winter together, he knew her body better than she did.

Turning away from the scene below, she began the journey back to the cabin. Bear had been gone for three days, bringing in his traps and checking on the ice in the river. He had wanted her to stay with the Shawnee, but Linsey convinced him she would be safe alone. It had been lonely, and she'd never liked him being gone over night; but she'd survived and could barely wait for his return.

Overhead, a bird chirped loudly, the call cheerfully answered by another. From beneath them, the trees still appeared bare, but at the village, Linsey had looked at them from a distance and noticed a hint of green on the branches. Spring. She had dreaded its arrival; now it was here. She had to decide what to tell Bear about the baby. Would he still insist on taking her back once he knew? Or would he let her stay and then someday grow to feel trapped by both her and the baby?

He liked children. She had seen his reaction to both Chattering Squirrel and Spring Flower. He played with the other children in the village, at times getting so involved he seemed to forget he was the adult in the group. He gently teased Morning Moon about the new baby, delighting in his role as uncle to the child.

Linsey wanted to stand on the tallest mountain and shout to the world that she carried his child. She felt that her heart would burst with pride from the fact. But how would Bear react?

If the warmth of the sun and the hint of new leaves were not enough to proclaim the arrival of spring, the tiny buttercup-shaped flower she saw peeking through the snow seemed to shout the message. Linsey knelt and carefully brushed the snow away from the small petals, so vibrantly yellow against their backdrop of white. Standing, she took two steps away before returning and carefully picking the flower. It had survived against all odds, and so would she.

Long after dark, just when Linsey decided she would spend another night alone, Bear arrived. She greeted him as she always did, by throwing herself into his arms and kissing him passionately.

"I like the way you say hello, *mon ange*. It almost makes going away worth it." Bear hugged her tightly, then carefully set her aside so that he could remove his pack and coat.

"Are you hungry?"

"I am starving." His voice lowered, and his eyes swept her body. "For food but mostly for you!"

"Well don't starve yet. It'll take a few minutes for

me to warm something. You can have food now so that you'll have the strength to have me later!" She moved to the fire that was already banked for the night. When it was burning brightly, she placed a pot of water and another containing left-over stew on the bar and pushed it over the flames.

The familiar sounds as Bear moved around the cabin were reassuring, and Linsey hungrily drank in the sight of him. When the food was ready, she spooned it onto a plate and sat across from him while he ate.

"Did you get all your traps?"

He shook his head and drank some coffee. "One was missing. I hate to think of a wounded animal forced to try to exist with it connected to its foot. There were signs that it gnawed through the leather to get free."

"Why don't you use steel traps?"

"Too much trouble. They rust badly and need constant attention. Besides which they can damage the furs, and then an animal has died for nothing." He grew silent for a moment. "I am thinking this will be my last winter trapping."

"Why?" Her heart jumped to her throat as she awaited his answer.

"My father was a farmer. It was a life I always enjoyed, planting the ground and watching it grow. We trapped occasionally for food, but it was only when we came here that we started trapping seriously.

"Because of the snow, you haven't seen the field I've worked to clear. I think I will plant it this spring and see what happens." He shrugged. "If it doesn't grow, I can always go back to trapping."

She had feared he would tell her that he was tired of this area and was planning to move on . . . which meant he would take her to Philadelphia first. But he was talking of making this site into a permanent home, and her hopes soared.

He talked of his plans until he'd finished eating, then leaned back in the chair with a contented sigh. His eyes narrowed as he closely watched her face at his next statement.

"The ice has broken up on the river. If the weather stays warm, it will be clear in a couple of weeks."

Linsey looked down at her hands folded in her lap and searched for something to say. He was waiting for a response, but she did not know what he wanted to hear. That she was happy she'd soon be going home? It would be a lie. This was her home, and while she knew there were things that needed to be resolved in Philadelphia, she did not care if she never saw the city again.

Bear waited impatiently for a response. Would she ask when he could take her home or would she ask to stay?

A voice from outside startled them. Bear rose and walked to the door, opening it to find Wolf, his face sheathed in worry. The two men spoke briefly in Shawnee before Bear turned and grabbed his coat.

"What's wrong?" Linsey asked as Bear closed his coat and reached for his rifle.

"I'm not sure," he replied, cradling the long rifle in his arms. "I'm going to the village. I don't know if I'll make it back tonight or not." He bent, his mouth meeting hers in a rushed kiss. "Bar the door."

"Bear, can't I go too?"

He stood at the door, and Linsey could see an impatient Wolf waiting for him. "No. I don't know what's going on. You go to bed, and I'll try to make it back before morning."

He closed the door and was gone. Linsey slowly fitted

the heavy bar in place and returned to the table. As she washed his plate and again banked the fire for the night, her thoughts were in a whirl. What could be wrong at the village? Everything had seemed normal when she was there earlier. True, her mind had not been on the activities around her, but still she would have sensed something wrong.

She undressed, climbing nude into the bed. Any kind of clothing was a waste of time when Bear was around; . . . he quickly dispensed with it! She yawned and snuggled under the fur. The baby demanded that she sleep more than usual, and she fell asleep, waiting for Bear to return.

Linsey was almost startled to open her eyes and discover that morning had come and Bear had not returned. Throwing back the fur, she hastily pulled on her flannel shirt and walked to the fire. As she knelt to add kindling, she wondered what had kept Bear away all night. When she stood, the room whirled away from her, and she had to clutch the table until everything righted itself. The feeling quickly passed but left behind the nausea that was becoming familiar each morning.

Linsey spent part of the morning trying to find ways to stay occupied, but her thoughts turned constantly to the village. She looked at the shirt she was sewing and tossed it on the table. There was no reason she couldn't go and find out what was happening.

Following the now familiar trail, Linsey discovered that the day was warmer than yesterday, and she quickly regretted her choice of the heavy coat. She considered returning to the cabin for her wool cape but decided against it. The village was not much farther anyway.

The scene that greeted her at the entrance of the

village could only be described as chaos. People ran from lodge to lodge, and the sounds of moans floated on the warm breeze. Most strangely of all, Linsey could hear the cries of babies and young children. The Shawnee rarely allowed their children to cry, and with so many people sharing living quarters, there was almost always someone to console them.

Linsey saw several people she knew, but no one stopped to talk with her as she walked to Wolf's lodge.

"Morning Moon?" she called from the door.

The flap was raised, and Morning Moon, looking exhausted, stood in the doorway. "You should not be here, Lin Zee," she said, her voice thick, her eyes swollen and watering badly.

"What's going on? Where's Bear?"

"I do not know the answer to your questions." At the sound of a moan behind her, Morning Moon motioned for Linsey to enter as she hurried to the sleeping platform.

Linsey's eyes quickly adjusted to the gloom, and she recognized the form of Spring Flower huddled beneath several blankets. Chattering Squirrel ran to her, but his happy squeal was absent. His huge dark eyes asked for reassurance, and Linsey picked up the child, nuzzling his soft cheek as she watched Morning Moon try to sooth Spring Flower's restlessness.

Readjusting the toddler to her hip, Linsey crossed the room. "Morning Moon, what's wrong with Spring Flower?"

"I do not know, Lin Zee," the Indian woman replied with a tired sigh. A hard, dry cough rattled through her, and she had to grab the sleeping platform for support until it passed.

"You should be in bed!" Linsey cried with alarm.

The Shawnee woman shook her head. "I must tend my child."

"Where is Wolf?"

"Again, I do not know. He and Bear left early to check on others of the village."

Linsey grabbed a blanket and drew it around Chattering Squirrel's square body. "Let's go find your daddy," she murmured to the child. "He needs to know your mama is sick."

Without another word to Morning Moon, Linsey left. She walked down the roads, realizing that something was drastically wrong. The usual visiting back and forth between lodges was missing, as were the happy sounds of children at play. The few people she passed hurried about their business, stopping only when the racking cough forced them to grab something for support. From nearly every lodge, she could hear the same cough and the fussy cry of infants. In some, the sounds of groans accompanied the coughs, telling her that many adults were also affected.

Her alarm grew as she searched for Wolf and Bear, asking anyone she saw if they knew their whereabouts. She clutched Chattering Squirrel to her, relieved by his clear eyes and normal color. His unusual quietness told her that in the way of small children, he knew something was wrong.

She finally saw Bear, with Wolf and Kaleb, when they came out of a lodge some distance down the road. She hurried with Chattering Squirrel bouncing on her hip, trying to catch them before they moved on.

"Bear!"

The three men turned, and she saw their identical expressions of exhaustion, concern and bewilderment. Bear's face grew stern as she approached.

"You shouldn't be here," he said harshly.

"When you didn't come home, I got worried," she explained quickly. "What's going on around here?" She looked at the three worried faces, waiting impatiently for one of them to answer.

"We do not know, Summer Eyes," Wolf replied. Chattering Squirrel lifted his arms to his father, and Wolf took the child from her. He gently caressed the silken head that rested beneath his chin.

"Spring Flower is so sick, and Morning Moon is too weak to tend her; but she refuses to lie down."

"I know." Wolf turned and began walking toward his own lodge; his broad shoulders seemed to slump, as if he carried the weight of the world.

"Bear? . . . Kaleb?" She searched their faces for answers.

Kaleb shook his head and rubbed his hand over his creased forehead. "We jist don't know, little gal. I've seen som'in like this in the whites but never so bad. I jist don't know if'n hits the same thin' or not."

"What?"

"Measles."

"Measles?" Linsey shook her head in amazement. "Children have measles, but rarely are they as sick as this! Why, I had the measles, and I can remember running a fever for a few days; but once the spots broke out I felt fine. In fact I gave Betsy quite a bad time because she wouldn't let me out of bed!"

"Hit jist ain't the same with the Injuns, gal. This is a white man's sickness, and they cain't seem to fight hit off like we do."

"Bear?" She turned pleading eyes to him.

He placed his arms around her and pulled her against his chest. "I don't know, Autumn Fire. Since I got here last night, seven people have died."

"Seven!"

"Four children, two old people and a young warrior." His voice was thick with hopelessness. "Nearly every lodge has someone sick in it; children, old people, strong warriors, it travels to all of them."

"Spring Flower and Morning Moon! They can't die! They can't!" She trembled, leaning against Bear, praying for him to deny the obvious.

Bear caressed the soft skin of her cheek, finding comfort for himself in the action. "We'll do what we can. But it seems so damn useless."

"When did it start? How did the measles come to the village?" Linsey felt Bear stiffen, his arms tightening painfully around her at her question.

"Small Dog!" He said the name as a curse.

"Small Dog? But he left the village months ago."

"I should have killed him! Then he couldn't have caused so much grief." When he realized he was nearly crushing Linsey, Bear eased his hold but kept her in his arms.

"Small Dog returned almost two weeks ago. He came in the night and hid in the lodge of his mother. When Wolf found out the next morning, he went there ready to force Small Dog to leave, but he was too late. Small Dog was delirious and died by early afternoon.

"Four days ago the next person died, Small Dog's mother. Her fever started that morning, and she was dead by that afternoon; but since she was fairly old, everyone just thought it was her time to die. Several people were showing signs of a cold: watery eyes, runny nose, sneezes. Two babies died two days later and five people yesterday, seven last night."

"Fifteen people in four days?" Linsey asked in a horrified whisper.

"There will be more before it's over."

"Oh, dear God, what can we do?"

"Whatever we do, hit won't be 'nough. Thar's gonna be a lot a dyin' afore hits done." Kaleb turned away, walking slowly back toward Wolf's lodge.

"You will go back to the cabin," Bear ordered in a harsh voice.

"No."

"Linsey, there will be no argument. You'll go back and wait for me. I'll send word when I can, and you'll be safe there."

"No, Luc, I won't go." She had no intention of arguing with him. "I've had the measles; so there's no chance of me catching it, and there are things here that I can do."

A look of fierce anger crossed his face, and Linsey rushed on before he could release it at her. "These people have become my friends. If I can do anything that might save only one life, it will be a way of repaying them for a disease that was brought to them by my people. I could no more leave now than I could willingly stick my hand in a fire."

Her eyes pleaded for him to understand, but her squared shoulders and raised chin spoke of her determination. Bear saw that she would stay and do what she could; his anger was a wasted use of energy.

"You must promise me that you'll rest when you get tired."

"I will."

Bear lowered his head, his warm lips meeting hers. He searched for some of her strength in that kiss. These people were her friends, but for years they had been his family. One of the old people that had died during the night had been his mother-in-law, Wolf's mother. Now her husband was showing signs of the disease, and Bear feared for the old man's life.

He raised his head, and with his arm across her

235

shoulders, they began walking toward Wolf's lodge. With each step, as the sounds of suffering shadowed their path, his heart a lead weight in his chest, Bear wondered where it would end. And when it was finished, would there be anyone left to wail the death cries to help the departed spirits find Manitou.

They entered the lodge and found Morning Moon bending over Spring Flower, trying to encourage the delirious child to drink. Morning Moon's hand trembled so badly that the liquid in the cup spilled onto the blankets covering her daughter.

"I will tend her while you rest." Linsey took the cup from Morning Moon, her fingers brushing over the dry, hot skin of the copper hand. An icy chill of dread circled Linsey's heart as she led Morning Moon to her sleeping shelf and helped her to lie down.

"Lin Zee?" Morning Moon whispered.

Linsey leaned down so that she could hear the soft voice of her friend. "Care for my children."

She placed a blanket over the Indian woman, tucking it carefully around her shivering body. "As I would care for my own," Linsey promised.

With an exhausted sigh, Morning Moon closed her dark, troubled eyes. Her hand outside the blanket caressed her swollen stomach for a few seconds, then slowly stopped, and from her light breathing, Linsey knew she slept.

Turning, Linsey found Bear holding Spring Flower upright against his own body, urging the child to drink. She must have heard his whispered Shawnee words, for she did try but choked when the cool liquid reached her closed throat.

Bear looked up, his gaze pleading with Linsey's. "What do I do?" His massively large hand soothed back

236

Spring Flower's silky black hair. "She's so sick, and I feel so helpless."

"Can you get me several buckets of water?"

He nodded, laid the child down and covered her carefully. "There's a branch of the river at the far end of the village. It'll only take a few minutes."

Before he could leave, Wolf entered the lodge, still carrying Chattering Squirrel. At first Linsey feared his red, swollen eyes indicated he was also ill, but she quickly realized it was a sign of his grief and exhaustion.

Linsey motioned Bear from the lodge and turned to the fierce warrior she had come to like and respect. Taking the toddler from his arms and placing him on a mat with a piece of dried meat to chew, she turned to Wolf.

"You must rest."

"My people need me."

"Yes, they do. But what good will you be for them if you're too tired to even think much less act?" Without a thought for her actions, Linsey took his hand and led him toward a bed. "Sleep for a little while. I will wake you if you are needed."

Almost against his will, Wolf lay down, his gaze staring at the thatched roof overhead. "And when I wake, Summer Eyes, how many more of my people will have left on their journey to Manitou?"

Their gazes met and held, both reflecting their worry and sense of hopelessness. "Sleep," Linsey whispered, tears pooling in her emerald eyes. "Escape the horror for a time in dreams of happier moments."

"A warrior does not run from an enemy, Summer Eyes. He fights until the battle is done."

"This battle will not be over quickly, Wolf. You will have more strength to fight after you've rested."

Linsey checked on Morning Moon, who slept restlessly, her skin dry and hot. Turning back to Spring Flower, Linsey found the child muttering, her fever having risen to the point that touching her was unnecessary; the heat seemed to radiate from around her.

"How'd ya git him ta sleep?"

Startled, Linsey turned to find Kaleb in the entrance. His gaze rested on Wolf, who slept deeply.

"Told him if he didn't lie down he'd fall down, and then he'd be a help to no one."

"He ain't slept none since the first young'un died three day ago." Kaleb walked over to Spring Flower and smoothed back her hair, his touch surprisingly gentle. "Whatcha awantin' me ta do, gal?"

Linsey suspected he'd had as little sleep as Wolf, but his tiredness was hidden in the folds of his face.

"Kaleb, do you know anything about children?"

"Only what I learnt helpin' my ma raise me and fourteen others."

If she hadn't been so worried, Linsey would have smiled. He certainly knew more than she did! "I'm concerned for Chattering Squirrel. He doesn't seem to be sick yet, and I was wondering if we got him away from here maybe it would protect him."

"Hit might. Ain't no way a knowin' lessen we gives hit a try."

"Would you take him to the cabin and stay with him until this is over?"

Kaleb ran his hand over his face. "Ya don't think I'd be a sight more help if'n I stayed here?"

"Oh, Kaleb." Linsey sighed and placed her hand on his arm. "I just don't know. Spring Flower is already so sick, and I'm worried about Morning Moon. I don't think I could stand it if Chattering Squirrel got sick, too."

"Hit might be too late already," he warned softly, patting her hand. He'd been right about her; she was spunky and full of spirit. But her concern for the Indians showed how caring she was. Later, when all of this was over, Kaleb decided he'd congratulate himself on finding the perfect mate for the Bear. For now, he'd do what he could to help relieve her worry.

"We've got to try," she insisted.

With a nod of understanding, Kaleb approached the strangely quiet toddler. "Come on, young'un, lets you and me go find us some trouble."

"Trewble?"

"Yep. Bet we ken cause more trouble than a whole tribe of Iroquois." Kaleb took the tiny hand in his own and led the docile child to the door, where he turned to Linsey. "Ya know where I'll be if'n ya want me, gal. Don't worry about this 'un. I'll keep him busy."

"Thank you, Kaleb," she whispered as she watched the old man and the little boy walk hand-in-hand down the long road.

Bear returned with the water, and Linsey began sponging Spring Flower. Her small body seemed to absorb the cool water when she placed a damp cloth on it. The heat quickly warmed the rags, making Linsey move constantly to replace them.

Bear checked on Morning Moon and Wolf, then silently left the lodge. He would help where he could, offering suggestions to those who asked, giving support to those who needed it.

Wolf woke after a couple of hours, his face still haggard but some of the extreme exhaustion gone from his eyes. He found his wife asleep and feverish and his young daughter critically ill. He nodded his approval when Linsey explained about Kaleb taking Chattering Squirrel away, his dark eyes thanking her for her care.

As evening drew nearer, Spring Flower's temperature rose, her small body trembling so violently that the blankets would not stay in place. Linsey kept a fire burning, and between her efforts and the heat in the lodge, her brow grew damp from perspiration.

Her worry grew for Morning Moon when she did not waken from her sleep. She began to wonder if the birth pains had begun since Morning Moon's flailing arms seemed to clutch at her stomach and she moaned frequently.

Placing a cool cloth over the Indian woman's fevered brow, Linsey sighed and stretched, turning once more to the child. Spring Flower lay quietly, her breathing so shallow her chest barely moved. Replacing the rag on her forehead with a cool one, Linsey gently stroked the flushed childish cheek. She seemed to be resting easier than she had all day, her skin not so dangerously hot.

Linsey never knew how long she stood there, staring down at the peaceful face before she admitted the truth to herself.

"Oh, God, . . . no," she whispered softly, hopelessly, tears slipping down the slopes of her cheeks. "I'm sorry. I'm so sorry."

As quietly as she had lived, Spring Flower's spirit departed on its journey in search of Manitou.

"You promised me you would rest," Bear reminded Linsey as he helped her up from the floor. He had entered the lodge and found her asleep, her head resting against the sleeping shelf.

"I know, but—"

"No buts, Linsey," he said sternly, guiding her to an empty shelf.

"I couldn't save Spring Flower, but I've got to with Morning Moon."

"I know, *mon ange*." He sat down beside her and smoothed the curls of flame from her damp forehead. "You've done so much and you're so tired. Sleep for a short while. I'll watch over her until you wake."

"You've had less sleep than I've had," she reminded him needlessly.

"I'll sleep when you're awake again."

"Promise you'll call me if—" Linsey couldn't finish the sentence, not wanting to admit even to herself what could happen.

"I'll call," he whispered, pulling a blanket over her. "Morning Moon will need you in the morning. Sleep for now, my love."

My love . . . my love. . . . The words echoed through her mind as sleep quickly claimed her, wrapping her in the blessed arms of oblivion.

Chapter Fourteen

Linsey thought she had barely closed her eyes when she felt Bear's hand on her shoulder gently shaking her. She was startled to discover that it was morning; she had slept through the night.

"Morning Moon?"

"The same." His eyes searched her face. "I was beginning to worry about you. You slept so deeply you didn't stir all night."

She swung her legs over the edge of the bed, then waited for the world to stop spinning. She watched Wolf tenderly care for his wife, his hands surprisingly gentle for a man who could be so fierce. Hoping Bear would think she was slow to waken, Linsey cautiously stood and walked across the room.

"Summer Eyes." Wolf acknowledged her when he saw her standing beside him.

Linsey touched Morning Moon's flushed cheek, quickly withdrawing her fingers from the burning skin. Wolf's hand rested on the mound of his unborn child.

"The child moves," he said quietly.

"You and Bear need to eat and get some rest," Linsey urged. "I'll tend Morning Moon."

"You must eat," Bear ordered.

As usual in the morning, even the thought of food made her stomach turn. "I will in a while." She tried to sound firm. "Let me see if I can make her more comfortable first."

As Linsey sponged the Indian woman, the sounds of the two men eating were almost more than she could bear. Fearing she would shortly lose the contents of her stomach, she placed a fresh cloth on the fevered brow then turned and walked to the open doorway where she stared, disbelieving, at the day.

It should have been dark and gloomy; but the sun shone brightly on her face, and the spring breeze hinted of summer. In the distance the tops of the trees were a pale green, and patches of grass dotted the ground. Most of the last snow had melted, and the first flowers of spring gave the earth vibrant color.

It was the kind of day that made a person glad to be alive. And it cruelly mocked those of the village who mourned the loss of family and friends.

Bear walked up beside her and drew her into his arms. She rested her head against his chest, receiving comfort from the firm beat of his heart.

"How many?" she asked.

He did not need clarification of her question. "Twenty-three yesterday, nineteen last night, eleven already this morning."

"Oh, sweet Lord," she gasped, tremors running through her. "Fifty-eight people! My God, how many more before it's over?"

"I don't know, sweet." His voice held a harshness of total despair. "I just don't know."

"The measles! A childhood disease! When was the last time you heard of a white person dying of measles?" Linsey turned to face him, wanting to put her back to the day that promised nothing but more grief.

"What have we done to these people? We've chased them from the land they've lived on for centuries; we've brought diseases they can't fight against; we've called them savages without even trying to understand them. Is it any wonder they hate us?"

Bear's face softened, and he teased her gently. "Is this the woman who was terrified by just the thought of Indians?"

"I was a fool," she said with a sigh. "I've learned so much from them; they've shown me nothing but kindness. I can't believe how ignorant I was!"

"They are not perfect, sweet. But neither are they the savage most people seem to believe. Maybe some people sleep easier at night if they think they've taken the lands and lives of someone they consider to be less than human. Maybe that is the only way they can justify their actions to themselves."

They shared a quiet moment, holding each other tightly, searching for the strength that would be necessary to withstand another day, finding it in the unspoken bond of their love. With the sun warm on their faces and death all around, Linsey and Bear found a momentary peaceful solitude in each other's arms.

Reluctantly pulling away, Linsey lightly caressed his face. "I must go back to Morning Moon."

Bear nodded. "I'll bring you some fresh water and then make my rounds again. I wish I could say I was doing some good, but about all I do is make myself as useful as possible."

Bear left for the river branch, and Wolf went to check on his father, fearing the old man would not survive the day. Not one lodge in the village was free from the disease, and most had already suffered at least one death in their families.

Linsey worked diligently, sponging Morning Moon's burning body. Remembering the experience with Bear, she asked Wolf to help her undress his wife so that she could place the cool, damp rags on her. The baby kicked frequently, causing waves of movement beneath the tightly stretched skin of her swollen abdomen, reassuring Linsey that it still lived.

Wolf left the lodge, returning whenever he could to relieve Linsey of some of the care of Morning Moon. The first time he did, she decided to go outside and get some fresh air, but the sounds of illness and grieving were so disheartening that she quickly retraced her steps to the lodge and didn't venture farther than the door after that.

By mid-afternoon the death toll had climbed to over one hundred, including Wolf's father, a sister-in-law and two nephews. The Indian warrior hid his grief behind a face that could have been carved of granite as he again took a turn at sponging his wife. Linsey could offer no words of solace, laying her hand on his shoulder as tears rolled down her cheeks. So far Wolf showed no signs of the illness, and Linsey prayed he would remain immune.

Most of the time, she stayed in the lodge by herself, diligent in her care of Morning Moon. No other members of the tribe visited to check on the woman's progress—none had the time—they were too busy caring for their own ill and dying families.

"Lin Zee?"

Placing a cloth over the engorged breasts, Linsey was startled by the weak voice calling to her.

"Morning Moon?" The Indian woman had been delirious all day, muttering frequently. This was the first time she'd been conscious.

"Spring Flower?"

"She's resting." Linsey could not bring herself to tell her friend that her child was dead; time enough for the truth later.

"Squirrel?"

Linsey smiled into the glazed eyes. "Kaleb took him to the cabin so that he wouldn't get sick. They were going to see how much trouble they could get into."

"My baby?" Her hand tried to move to the mound of her child but fell short of its goal.

"Your baby moves around all the time. He's doing fine."

"Wolf?"

Linsey laid another cloth on her fevered brow. "Wolf is tired, worried and sad, but healthy. He should be back soon. I know he'll be so glad you're awake."

Morning Moon closed her eyes, and Linsey continued the routine she'd established earlier for changing the rags, talking softly all the while. She spoke of the flowers in bloom and the leaves on the trees. She drew a slight smile from Morning Moon when she told of ordering Wolf around as if he were a cranky child badly in need of sleep. She described the sight of Kaleb and Chattering Squirrel walking hand-in-hand down the road, Squirrel's tiny legs pumping furiously to keep up with the old man.

She didn't speak of the ravages of the disease destroying the village or the ever climbing number of deaths or how it looked as if it would never end. And Morning Moon did not ask.

Linsey saw Wolf at the door and was relieved he'd returned before Morning Moon had gone back to sleep. She rose stiffly from the floor and walked over to him.

"She's awake . . . I think," she said in a hushed whisper. "I didn't tell her about Spring Flower or anyone else." She turned pleading emerald eyes to him. "She doesn't need to know now."

Wolf nodded agreement and moved toward his wife. Linsey watched as he knelt by her side, lightly touching her cheek. Morning Moon's eyes opened, and in the fevered gaze, Linsey read the love she felt for her husband. His hand went to her abdomen as he spoke softly in Shawnee.

Giving them the privacy they deserved, Linsey walked outside the lodge, breathing deeply of the early evening air. She desperately needed Bear to hold her, to reassure her that this nightmare would end. He was somewhere in the village, but she couldn't find the willpower to go in search of him. Her walk earlier still clung to her memories, and she knew she'd forever hear the sounds of anguish in her dreams.

Night fell, the death toll mounted and Linsey tried to fool herself into believing that Morning Moon was cooler. Exhausted, she slept when Bear returned to the lodge and insisted she needed to rest. She woke before daylight, the whisper of voices penetrating her fogged mind.

"What's wrong now?" Linsey sat on the edge of the bed and looked at the two men who stood near the door on the far side of the room.

Seeing that she was awake, Wolf left the lodge and Bear approached her, his eyes searching hers, finding them clear but still showing signs of exhaustion.

"You shouldn't be awake yet."

"Well, I am." Linsey felt dizzy and nauseated, not at all in the mood to be pleasant. "What's wrong."

"Morning Moon has gone into labor. Her water broke a short while ago."

"Oh, God," Linsey moaned, burying her face in her hands. "Why now? The baby's waited this long; why can't he wait another week?"

"Babies choose their own time, which is rarely for the convenience of others," Bear replied, sharing her discouragement. He sat down and pulled her into his arms. He didn't need to tell her that there was every chance neither Morning Moon nor the baby would survive.

"Bear, I don't know anything about delivering a baby! What do we do?"

"Wolf has gone for the old Grandmother."

Linsey looked up, shocked. Not knowing exactly who had died, she figured the very old and very young would be the first to do so. "She's alive?"

"It makes no sense. The disease does not discriminate; it kills the old and the young, the healthy and the weak. Somehow, Grandmother has missed catching it and is working like a slave to help others."

Wolf returned, the Grandmother following on his heels. Linsey had thought the elderly woman looked old before; now she appeared barely strong enough to support her meager weight. Her heavily wrinkled skin stretched tautly over her fragile bones; blue veins pulsated vividly beneath the pale copper flesh. Sparse gray hair hung in stringy strands around her face, and she walked with a shuffling slide.

But her dark eyes were bright and clear, glittering with intelligence as her timeworn hands moved quickly and deftly over Morning Moon.

She talked with Wolf for several minutes, then turned her attentions toward Linsey. Forcing herself not to flinch as the knarled hands touched her face, Linsey knew the Grandmother was asking questions and wondered what reply Bear was giving. With a satisfied nod and a toothless smirk that might have been a grin, she slapped Bear firmly on the back and walked out of the lodge.

"What was that all about?" Linsey asked in bewilderment. "Where did she go?"

Bear's eyes narrowed, and he looked at her for long minutes before answering. "She says it will be hours yet before Morning Moon has her child. She says others need her now, but she'll return when the baby is ready."

"She can't just leave!"

"Maybe she can't, but she did," he replied, running his finger through his thick hair.

"What do we do for Morning Moon?"

"Just what we've been doing. The Grandmother will be back later in the day to check on her again."

The nightmare seemed to have no end, Linsey thought as she sighed deeply and stood up. She had started to move away from the bed when Bear stopped her.

"Linsey?"

"Yes?" She turned and noticed his puzzled expression.

"She asked . . . she said . . . uh, is it possible. . . ."

His bewildered hesitation was so unlike him that Linsey grew curious. "Who said what, Bear?"

"Oh, never mind, we'll discuss it later." Bear stood, grabbed the water containers and walked out of the lodge.

His confusion played through her mind until concern for Morning Moon washed away any other thought.

Later, Linsey would remember the day as the longest of her life.

Morning Moon moaned, the pain of labor reaching through her delirium. Linsey placed the cool damp rag

249

on her brow, then straightened, rubbing at her lower back to ease the annoying pain that had been bothering her for hours.

Wolf and Bear had come and gone frequently during the day, giving her news of any development in the village. When the death toll climbed to over two hundred by mid-afternoon, Linsey had quit asking.

Morning Moon opened her eyes, her gaze unfocused. She had been lucid only once that morning but had been too weak to speak. The Grandmother returned twice to check on the progress of her labor, but since she spoke no English, Linsey did not know how it was going.

"Are you all right, Summer Eyes?"

Linsey turned, startled by Wolf's question. "Just tired, like everyone else."

"You rest, I will tend her for a while."

"Wolf, you've had no rest for two days," Linsey could not shake her fear that he, too, would get the measles.

"I have gone longer without sleep, Summer Eyes." He turned toward his wife, his eyes closing briefly. "When it is over, we will all have too much time to rest . . . and remember."

Linsey stretched out on the shelf, the pain in her back easing immediately. She did not sleep but lay there staring at the thatched roof and listening to the quiet sounds of Wolf caring for his wife. Tears filled her eyes, slowly flowing down her face. She cried silently for what had been and what would be.

When her tears dried and she knew sleep was impossible, Linsey prepared a meal from the supplies in the lodge. She set the kettle to the side of the fire so that anyone wanting to eat could do so whenever they were ready. To her, food had never looked or smelled so revolting.

When the Grandmother reappeared, Linsey was glad Wolf was there to ask questions; she didn't think she could stand not knowing again. The old woman placed her hands on Morning Moon's belly, a frown crossing her face. She spoke with Wolf, shaking her head sadly.

"What's going on?" Linsey asked, hurrying across the room.

"Grandmother says that the labor has stopped. Morning Moon is too weak to birth the baby."

Instinctively, Linsey touched the swollen abdomen. "Is there nothing we can do?"

Wolf carried on a brief conversation with the old woman, then turned to Linsey. "Grandmother says it may do some good if we rub Morning Moon's stomach. She has seen it work before, but sometimes nothing helps."

Beneath her hand, the baby kicked as if telling Linsey it wanted help to be born. "Have her show me how," she said with determination. "You will have to continue with the sponge baths."

The old woman took both of Linsey's hands, placing one on each side of Morning Moon's stomach. Pushing firmly, she slid them down and around, until they met at the base. Each time the movement was repeated, Linsey's hands were placed slightly higher on the sides of the swollen mound. When they reached the top, she started working her way back down. She was instructed to slowly slide her hands from the top of Morning Moon's abdomen to the bottom of her pelvis but never in reverse. Over and over Linsey's hands moved along the tight burning skin, pressing firmly, evenly.

When the old woman was satisfied that Linsey was doing the massage correctly, she told her, through

Wolf, what to look for that would tell her the labor had begun again. Wolf did not repeat the Grandmother's words that she thought it to be a useless waste of time. He knew Linsey would try to save the unborn child in spite of all obstacles.

The afternoon turned slowly to evening. Linsey and Wolf worked well as a team. When she tired, Wolf insisted that he take a turn. They traded places, Wolf massaging, Linsey sponging.

When Linsey thought she'd surely drop from fatigue, Bear returned and understood the situation at a glance.

"Show me what to do."

Bear was startled by the heat beneath his fingers when they first touched Morning Moon's body. He almost withdrew his hands in shock as the baby kicked.

"It moved!" he said in amazement.

Tired beyond exhaustion, worried beyond hope, Linsey and Wolf looked at each other and suddenly grinned.

"What did you expect?" Linsey asked. "That poor baby is all scrunched up in there and wants out!"

"Oh." Bear looked sheepish. Despite the growth of hair that nearly formed a beard, Linsey thought she saw a blush creep up his cheeks.

The light moment was over as quickly as it had come. Linsey rested while the two men worked, returning shortly to relieve Wolf, who rested, then returned to relieve Bear. Through the darkness of the long night, they shared the loving chore of saving Morning Moon and her child.

The inky darkness of the never-ending night slowly turned to shadows with the rising of the sun. The Grandmother returned, her knowing eyes seeing the fatigue on the three faces as they stood back and watched hopefully while she examined Morning Moon.

The words were Shawnee, but the tone might as well have been English; Linsey knew clearly what the old woman said.

"It has done nothing, Summer Eyes," Wolf translated, confirming her fear. "Grandmother says that Morning Moon's body is not opening for the child."

"There must be something else! We can't give up now!"

Intent on their conversation, they were not prepared for the sudden movement from the bed. Three pairs of eyes clouded with horror as Morning Moon suddenly stiffened then thrashed wildly; her eyes opened wide before rolling up into her head. The Grandmother nodded grimly, her shoulders slumping with defeat. The convulsion lasted for a fraction of a minute but seemed to go on for hours as they stood helplessly back.

It ceased as suddenly as it had begun. Morning Moon relaxed, her body going limp. She opened her eyes, her gaze locking with Wolf's. Only because of the total quiet in the lodge were they able to hear her whispered words. As her eyes closed, Morning Moon released a deep sigh and was still.

"My husband," Linsey whispered. It was one of the few Shawnee words she recognized.

Wolf reacted first, moving to her side and laying his hand on her chest. His eyes closed, devastation aging his face far beyond his years.

"She is dead."

His words seemed to echo around the lodge. Linsey put her hands to her mouth, fighting back the urge to scream as the pain of loss racked her body with agony.

"No," she moaned. "Please, God . . . no. . . ."

Bear wrapped his arms around her, holding her tightly. They watched the mound of her stomach move

253

and roll. The new life extinguished before it could begin as the infant fought its last battle.

"The baby! Oh, dear God, the baby!"

"I know, *mon ange*." Bear's voice carried the desolation of the helpless.

With no words to anyone, the Grandmother moved to the side of the bed. Her knowing hands rested on the swollen abdomen, feeling the position of the baby. She snarled a command to Wolf, who responded in a daze by handing her the knife he carried strapped to his thigh.

Once more confirming the location of the baby, the Grandmother placed the knife at the top of Morning Moon's abdomen. With a swift movement, she slit open the stretched skin.

Linsey's eyes widened in panic at the actions, but the old woman ignored her startled scream; time was more important than a white woman's squeamishness. She cut through the uterus, exposing the membrane containing the child. Piercing through the sack, the Grandmother lifted the baby from Morning Moon's body. Laying it on the edge of the shelf, she quickly tied off the cord and cut it.

The child was still, its dark, wet skin tinted blue. Supporting the baby's head, the old woman cleared its mouth and firmly slapped its behind.

Linsey held her breath, her fingernails digging unheeded into Bear's arms.

In a world filled with dying and dead, one little body filled new lungs with air. Its voice, feeble at first, quickly gathered strength. Tiny eyes opened to squint in the light of a new day, small arms and legs waving as cool air rushed over its skin.

"You have a son." The Grandmother turned, handing the child to his father.

Wolf gently held his son, rubbing his cheek against the soft, wet one, then handed the baby to Linsey. She wrapped him in a soft blanket, carefully wiping him clean, the job made difficult because of the tears clouding her vision.

The Grandmother pulled a fur over Morning Moon, whispered quietly to Wolf then shuffled out of the lodge. Wolf knelt and tenderly gathered his wife in his arms, resting his cheek on the head against his chest. In a voice breaking with emotion, he chanted the death song of his people as he rocked her back and forth, stroking the thick black hair that flowed over his arm.

Linsey held the baby against her breasts, turning her back on Wolf so that he could have privacy in his grief. His song flowed around her, and she closed her eyes against the haunting sound, tears washing her face with silver.

Bear picked her up and carried her to a shelf. He held her tightly, the baby cradled between them.

"A life was taken, another spared," he whispered, his voice husky with grief.

"Oh, Bear." Linsey's voice was filled with agony. "Why Morning Moon? She was so good, so gentle and sweet. Why did she have to die?"

"I don't know, *mon ange.*"

Linsey stroked the thick black hair covering the perfectly round head, lightly touching the baby's downy soft cheek. "She loved her children so much and was so excited about this baby."

"I think she would be happy to know he lived."

Linsey shivered, vividly remembering the manner of his birth. "It seemed to brutal. At first I didn't know what the Grandmother was doing, and I was horrified. Then, when I realized she was trying to save the baby, all I could do was pray she wouldn't be too late."

"I admit that I, too, shared your horror," Bear confessed without shame. "The Grandmother had the courage and wisdom to save the babe when others would have stood back and watched it die. His life will be special; he has already survived when perhaps he shouldn't have."

Linsey looked down at the child who slept contentedly in her arms. His tiny face was wrinkled like an old man's, but it showed the high cheekbones, square jaw and aquiline nose he had inherited from his father. His full, well-shaped lips and arched brows were Morning Moon's, and Linsey knew when he smiled anyone who had known her would be reminded of his gentle mother.

Wolf finished his song, caressed his wife for a final time and laid her gently on the bed. He pulled the fur over her head, stood and crossed the room to Linsey. Taking the baby from her arms, he carried the child outside and held him up to the morning sun. Repeating words older than memory, he thanked Manitou for blessing him with a son, promising to teach him of life, helping him to grow into a brave warrior.

Returning to the lodge, he again placed the child in Linsey's arms.

"What is his name?" she asked.

"I do not know, Summer Eyes," he replied, shaking his head. "It is usual for the mother or grandmother to give a baby his first name. Later his name will change many times, and they will be of his choosing."

Linsey still sat on Bear's lap and Wolf knelt down in front of them. "I ask you, woman of my brother, to name my son."

"I don't know what to name a Shawnee baby," she whispered, bewildered by the thought.

"There is time; let the name come to you. You will

know when it is the right one." Wolf stood, walking to the center of the room. Linsey saw that his limp was more noticeable than usual, as if he were too tired to try to hide it. "I must ask something else of you, my sister. I ask that you take my son away from here. Take him to the cabin with his brother and watch over them until the sickness has left the village.

"Protect my sons for me, Summer Eyes, so that they may live to know tomorrow."

Linsey nodded, her eyes reflecting the pain she suffered. How much greater was his pain, she wondered. He had lost a wife and child, a mother and father, sister and nephews. Friends he had known all his life lay dead from this white man's disease.

"I will love them and watch over them until you come."

"Thank you, my sister." His gaze met hers, and Linsey almost flinched from the deeply etched agony she saw there.

Linsey laid the baby on the sleeping shelf and gathered the things Morning Moon had prepared for the arrival of her son. The Grandmother returned, carrying several strange items. She told Linsey, through Bear, how to feed the baby, using something that looked suspiciously like a cow udder. Linsey decided she didn't want to know exactly what it was. All that mattered was that it worked!

Bear carried the blanket filled with the necessary items while Linsey cradled the baby. The sun had cleared the horizon, chasing away the shadows of dawn. The morning breeze was cold, still chilled from the long night, but already the warming rays were promising a day of exceptional beauty. As they walked down the long row of lodges, the sounds of sorrow accompanied their steps. Guilt rode her shoulders for the relief she felt upon leaving the village.

Linsey looked up at the azure sky and saw a hawk floating gracefully on the wind. His wings were wide spread, gliding in effortless circles far above them, carefree of the tragedy below, determinedly searching for his next meal or perhaps simply enjoying the gift of flight. She envied the great bird his freedom from the tortures of losing a friend or loved one.

When they reached the hill overlooking the village, they stopped and looked down on the peaceful scene. It was difficult to believe the horror hidden there.

"When will it stop?" she whispered.

"I didn't tell you earlier—there just wasn't any time—but I think a few of the people are surviving. Once the rash breaks out, the fever goes down and quickly disappears. So far only three or four have lived that long, and they're still pretty weak; but they may make it."

"Thank God."

He touched her arm and motioned for her to go on. Walking side-by-side under the quiet trees, Linsey tried not to question why Morning Moon couldn't have been one of those survivors.

"I'll make sure you and the children are settled, then I'll go back," Bear said as they approached the cabin. "I don't know how long it will be before I return, but I'll ask Kaleb to stay."

Linsey nodded, knowing beforehand that he would return. She would never have left if it had not been for the children and Wolf's plea that she protect them.

"That's not necessary. We will be all right without Kaleb."

"Please? Kaleb is for me. I need to know he's here

with you, or I'll spend all my time wondering if you're all right."

The cabin was a welcome sight, beckoning to them from its clearing. Smoke poured lazily from the chimney and a robin perched on the pitched roof squawked at them. It looked so blessedly normal, offering peace from the tragedy they suffered. It was home.

"Kaleb!" Bear knew better than to enter even his own cabin without warning the old man inside.

Kaleb opened the door, Chattering Squirrel clutching tightly to his fringed pant leg. "Din't look fer ya back so soon." His eyes lowered to the bundle in Linsey's arms.

"I brought Linsey and the babe here," Bear replied, reaching down to pick up Chattering Squirrel. "The babe is his brother."

"Morning Moon?"

Bear shook his head as he followed Linsey inside. Chattering Squirrel buried his face in Bear's neck, peeking shyly at Linsey and the bundle in her arms. She sat down at the table and placed the baby on her lap.

"Come meet your new brother," she invited softly. "He's very tiny, and I'll need you to help me take care of him."

Bear placed Squirrel on his feet and gave him a gentle shove toward her. She folded back the heavy blanket, exposing the tiny baby.

"Bro'er?" Chattering Squirrel asked, hesitant to approach too closely.

"Brother," Linsey repeated clearly. "Come here, sweetheart." She held out her free hand.

Chattering Squirrel moved closer, step by slow step, his dark eyes huge with curiosity. He placed his chubby hand in hers. When she pulled him nearer, Linsey wrapped her arm around him, kissing his head and hugging him tightly.

"Me bro'er?" With one finger he touched the baby's foot, snapping his hand back when the infant moved. When he realized what he'd done, Chattering Squirrel touched the baby again, giggling merrily when the tiny foot kicked.

The sound of the childish giggle captured the three adults; their eyes met. In the tragedy of death, a child was born; his brother greeted him with sparkling eyes filled with mischief.

They shared the thought that nothing ends; it only begins again with the young.

Chapter Fifteen

The open shutter allowed the late afternoon breeze to drift into the cabin. The songs of the birds filled the air with joyful noise as they darted busily from tree to tree, preparing their nest for the eggs that would soon be laid.

Nearly lost in the center of the huge bed, the still-unnamed baby slept with knees folded beneath his chest and bottom in the air, undisturbed by the frequent giggles from his older brother.

Linsey and the children had been by themselves since Kaleb had left at sunrise the morning before. He'd been very mysterious about his mission, saying only that he would be back in two days but she wasn't to be concerned if it took him longer.

The boys kept her busy, giving her little opportunity for a moment to herself. It seemed to her that when Chattering Squirrel slept, the baby was awake, and when the baby slept, Chattering Squirrel was awake. Her respect for mothers with several children grew daily as she discovered that for each problem solved two more sprung up. Linsey had never guessed being a mother was such hard work! Morning Moon had made it appear so easy!

On the rare occasions when both children slept, Linsey's thoughts turned to Bear. She missed him, Lord how she missed him! When the nightmares disturbed her sleep and she woke, knowing the nightmares were real and would not go away with the rising of the sun, Linsey longed to reach for Bear. She wanted him to hold her against his massive body and kiss away the horror that would always be a part of her.

He had not returned since leaving them at the cabin five days earlier. Kaleb had visited the village once, returning with the news that the death toll was still climbing but several of the people looked like they might live.

"Whas 'at?" Chattering Squirrel asked, his alert gaze turning to the open window.

Linsey looked up from the corn bread batter she was mixing and listened to the chiming of a bell followed by a baaing bleat. "I'm not sure, but it sounds like it's coming this way."

Squirrel hurried to the door on chubby legs, stretching to reach the rope that was well above his head.

"Out?" He turned dark, pleading eyes toward Linsey, then tried the new word she had taught him. "Preeze?"

"You think that word and those big eyes will get you anything you want, don't you?"

Chattering Squirrel batted his long lashes, his head held at an angle. "Preeze? Me out?"

"You're probably right." Muttering to herself, she wiped the cornmeal from her hands and walked to the door. "Who could resist you when you turn on the charm?"

She ruffled his thick hair and pulled open the door.

Chattering Squirrel darted outside, skidding to a halt when he saw Kaleb coming up the trail followed by a strange creature tied with a rope.

"Whas 'at?!" His eyes were huge, and he darted behind Linsey, peeking from the safety of her legs.

"Kaleb, a goat! Where ever did you find it?"

"Howdy, gal. You 'an the babes all right?"

"We're fine, Kaleb. Now tell me, where did you get the goat?"

Kaleb tied the animal to a tree, lowered his pack and reached for Chattering Squirrel. He tickled the plump belly, and Squirrel giggled but kept his eyes on the goat.

"Thar's a family what settled down aways. Met 'em last fall and 'membered they had several goats. Thought that young'un in thar would soon need some'in more ta eat than that sugar tit, so I paid 'em a little visit. This here nanny is real fresh; dropped a set of twins three or fours weeks back."

"You bought a goat?"

"Naw, onct I told 'em 'bout the babe's ma a'dying they let me borry hit. Gotta bottle with a nipple in my pack. The missus said hit'd be easier fer ya ta feed the babe with hit." He looked at Linsey, fighting to hide a smile. "Ever milked a goat?"

"No . . ." she replied hesitantly.

" 'Bout time ya larned, gal."

"I was afraid you were going to say that!"

"Whas 'at?" Chattering Squirrel asked, getting Kaleb's attention by pulling firmly on his beard.

"That thar's a goat, boy." Kaleb carried the child over to the animal. When he saw Linsey's leary expression, he stopped to reassure her. "This nanny is used ta young'uns. The folks had at least six with 'nother on hits way 'bout any time."

263

"At least six? Don't you know for sure?"

"Gal, with that many young'uns runnin' 'round, hits plumb hard not ta count the same one more'n once!"

Linsey shook her head with amusement and watched as Kaleb patiently introduced Chattering Squirrel to the animal. Squirrel hesitantly reached out to rub the long nose, and the goat nibbled on his fingers.

"Bite! Me hurt!" Squirrel held his grubby hand in front of Kaleb's face to show him the imaginary injury.

"She ain't gonna bite ya, boy. She's just a'tastin' ya a little."

"No bite, goat," Chattering Squirrel turned to the animal, scolding it. "Bad, bite hurts!"

"Where'd he hear that?" Kaleb asked Linsey.

"He sampled his little brother this morning," she replied with a shrug. "Are you sure the goat won't hurt him?"

"All goats like ta take a little taste now en then, but hit don't hurt none. Feels kinda like a tickle." Kaleb set the toddler on his feet and walked toward her. "I'll milk her fer tonight, tomorry we'll teach ya how hits done."

"You milk; I'll fix dinner." Linsey turned toward the door. "We'll discuss milking arrangements later!"

They laughed at the baby's first taste of the milk. Startled by the new flavor, dark eyes opened wide; he smacked his lips several times, then searched hungrily for the nipple. He made his dissatisfaction well known each time Linsey stopped the feeding in order to burp him.

After his late meal, she placed him on the bed against the wall where he would be safe. Chattering Squirrel slept peacefully in the center of the bed, undisturbed by the noise his brother had made.

Linsey walked back to the table where Kaleb sat contentedly watching her care for the baby. She placed a hand on his shoulder and gave a slight squeeze.

"Thank you, Kaleb."

"Tweren't nothin' ta thank me fer, gal," he responded gruffly.

"Yes it is. You've stayed with me and the boys so that Bear could return to the village with peace of mind. You spent two days walking to get the goat and made sure Squirrel wasn't frightened by it. I think there's a lot to thank you for."

"Hit gives me pleasure ta watch you and the young'uns, gal." He rubbed his hand over his face. "Hits been a mighty long time since I remembered thar's good things in life. Sometimes a man 'members only the bad and gets ta thinkin' thar ain't no good left."

Linsey poured him the last of the coffee, then sat down across from him. "Sometimes it's hard for anyone to remember the good. Then something happens, and we wonder why we thought the world such a terrible place to live."

Kaleb thought of Mary and realized her image wasn't as clear as it had always been. It was hazy around the edges, as if he were looking through a fog, but it was a peaceful feeling.

"Ya've had a long day, gal, en that babe's gonna be wantin' more a that milk afore long. Ya'd better be a'findin' sleep whilst ya can."

"Good night, Kaleb," she replied, moving toward the bed. He would sleep on the far side of the cabin, on the floor, as he'd done every night.

Linsey slid onto the edge of the bed, pulling the blankets around her shoulders. Chattering Squirrel wiggled until his warm body was snuggled against hers. Stroking his soft hair, she closed her eyes. As she drifted to sleep, her last thoughts were of Bear, wondering if he missed her half as much as she missed him.

Kaleb sat at the table long into the night, watching the glowing fire and listening to the silence. Occasional sounds from the bed reminded him that he wasn't alone. It felt good to have the responsibilities of Linsey and the children. It had been a long time since someone had needed him.

He thought of the terrified girl he'd rescued several months earlier. She had matured quickly, becoming a woman any man would be proud to claim as his mate. She was confident in her abilities but had maintained her femininity rather than hardening from her experiences.

That she adored the Bear was as obvious as a full moon at midnight. Kaleb wondered what would happen now that spring had come. He knew Bear would insist on taking her back to the city. It was something Kaleb himself would do. He also knew Linsey would demand to stay. He had no doubt that she would use every weapon in her feminine arsenal. It would take a strong man to win the coming battle, for he would fight not only Linsey but himself. And Kaleb didn't think Bear was strong enough to win. It was obvious to anyone who looked that the mighty Bear loved the woman with a passion far surpassing even his tremendous strength.

Two head-strong people were about to lock horns, and Kaleb smiled in the darkness. If he had any money, he knew whom he'd place his bet on. He wondered how long it would take for Bear to discover he'd met his match.

* * *

In less than three weeks, the death toll at the Shawnee village climbed to over six hundred men, women and children. Within a month, eight more would be added to that total—eight who had survived the measles only to die from complications of the disease rather than the disease itself. A tribe claiming just over seven hundred members now numbered less than one hundred. It was not the first time a white man's disease had annihilated the Indians . . . nor would it be the last.

Bear returned eleven days after taking Linsey and the babe to the safety of the cabin. Haggard, exhausted, he walked quietly to the open door, stopping at the sight that greeted his weary eyes. Linsey sat at the table, the baby cradled in her arms. She talked softly to the tiny child as she held the bottle to his mouth.

Bear felt a justifiable envy for the baby, wanting to be cradled in Linsey's arms, needing to be held and reassured. The contentment radiating from inside the cabin was such a drastic difference from the total destruction he'd just left, it was difficult for him to accept.

Linsey looked up and was startled to find Bear at the door. She set down the bottle, swung the baby up to her shoulder and stood. Wanting to run and throw herself in his arms, she tried to refrain, but the look on her face told him everything he needed to know.

"You're home." It sounded so silly saying something so obvious.

"I'm home." He pulled her into his arms. "I'm home."

He held her tightly against him, careful not to crush

267

the baby. For long days and even longer nights, he'd dreamed of holding her again, telling her all the things he needed to tell her. He had learned, as never before, how fragile life was, and he wanted to protect her by taking her back to the city. But he'd also discovered that he'd never be happy without her.

Bear fought an inner battle; should he protect her or should he selfishly keep her with him and pray for the best?

The baby let them know he did not appreciate his meal being interrupted, and Linsey reluctantly pulled away from Bear and returned to the table.

"It's over?"

"Yes." Bear entered the cabin, feeling its strangeness after being away so long.

"Wolf?" she asked in a whisper.

"Discouraged, weary beyond words, but healthy."

"Thank God."

Bear sat down across from her while she finished feeding the baby. Linsey laid the infant on the bed, then turned to Bear. She could feel his depression from across the room. His shoulders slumped; his arms hung limply to his side. She hurried to him, slowly massaging his shoulders.

"The Grandmother?" Linsey was still in awe of the old woman and had worried that she would become ill. At her age, there was little doubt that she could survive the disease.

Bear remembered the last few days and shook his head with amazement. "That old woman is tireless. When Wolf and I would stand around in a daze of exhaustion, she was there forcing us to eat or telling us what needed to be done next. She looks like a slight breeze would blow her away, but I swear she never rested."

He reached up and grabbed Linsey's hand, pulling her to his lap. "I tried to get her to rest once, and she told me not to worry about her. Said it wasn't her time to go yet and she'd get plenty of rest when it was. Her people needed her; how could she let them down?"

Linsey's touch was tender, offering comfort as no words could ever do. She stroked his face, pulling lightly on his full, dark beard. His eyes were closed, but she had seen his horror reflected in them.

"How many are going to live?" she questioned softly.

"Too few . . . God, too few. There were no deaths last night or all day today, but there's a toddler and its baby sister who probably won't last through the night.

"There's fourteen, maybe fifteen, who survived the measles, but two are blind, and four or five others are coughing up blood."

"So they survived, but for what?" Her voice was bitter at the cruel fate that let the few survive only to suffer further.

"I don't know, *mon ange*, I just don't know."

They sat quietly for several minutes, just holding each other, finding comfort from light touches, gentle caresses.

"You need to rest."

Bear nodded in agreement, but was too weary to make the necessary motions of walking to the bed.

"Where's Kaleb and Squirrel?"

"Out back somewhere, building a pen for the goat."

"Goat?"

Linsey smiled and explained how the goat had arrived. Bear chuckled softly, as she had intended for him to, when she told him of her experiences at milking, exaggerating only slightly.

"When Kaleb does it, the milk just flows out, but I swear that goat turns off the pump when I try it!"

"What would your city friends say if they saw you milking a goat?"

"I don't care!" Linsey climbed off his lap and held out her hand. "Bed! If you're a good boy and take a nice long nap, I'll show you my great lack of expertise at goat milking later this evening."

"You've been around the children too long," he said, standing slowly. "You're starting to sound like a mother!"

She took his hand and led him to the bed. Bear was so weary he stumbled as he crossed the room, and Linsey suspected it would be tomorrow evening before he woke.

He saw the baby on the far side of the bed and grew concerned. "What if I roll on him?"

"You won't." Linsey rolled several furs into a large bolster and placed it near the infant. "There, that should take care of it, but if it doesn't, believe me that little guy has very strong lungs and will let you know if you're squashing him."

She turned back to Bear and discovered he had stripped. Her gaze roved over him, drinking in the sight of his well-muscled body. Her eyes narrowed at ribs showing under his flesh and his concave stomach. He had lost weight during the siege at the village.

Linsey started to ask him if he'd rather eat first, but Bear sat on the edge of the bed, lay back and stretched. His eyes closed, and before she could pull a blanket over him, he was asleep.

Linsey stood and stared down at him, needing the visual reassurance that he was really home. She dreaded turning her back, afraid he would disappear. There were so many things they had not discussed, among them was when Wolf wanted his children returned. She knew the boys had to go back to their father, but she would miss them desperately and hoped to delay the inevitable as long as possible.

Smoothing Bear's hair from his forehead, Linsey finally forced herself to move away. She would begin the evening meal before searching out Kaleb and telling him of Bear's return.

Bear opened his eyes and found himself alone in the cabin. The silence was broken only by the rustle of new leaves in the spring breeze. Stretching, he bit back a moan at the aches and pains running riot through his body. He sat on the edge of the bed, wondering where everyone had gone. Hunger gnawing at his belly, he stood, pulled on his pants and searched for something to eat.

Linsey had left a pot of stew hanging near the fire, which Bear nearly finished before he felt satisfied. He quickly dressed and went in search of Linsey, Kaleb and the boys.

The sun was lowering, which surprised him. He felt like he'd slept longer than a couple of hours. Breathing deeply of the fresh air, Bear knew he could no longer doubt that spring had arrived.

Time to take Linsey home, he thought to himself. The decision was made instantly, easily. He could not submit her to the constant dangers that awaited in the wilderness. It would be easier to live alone, knowing she was alive in far off Philadelphia, than to live if she should die in the wilderness.

Now all he had to do was tell her of his decision.

The sounds of voices floating on the breeze drew him to the back of the cabin. Linsey, Kaleb and Chattering Squirrel were near a fenced pen that Kaleb had built during Bear's absence. The baby in his cradleboard hung from one of the corner fence posts. The goat was being held by Kaleb as Linsey knelt at its side. From the gleeful chuckles he heard, Bear knew she was trying to milk it, perhaps with little success but with a lot of amusement.

Suddenly, feeling left out of their fun, Bear approached. Linsey looked up, and it nearly took his breath away. The sun shone on her hair, making it burn with reddish flames, and her sparkling eyes were a truer green than the leaves on the trees above her head.

Linsey stared at him with equal intensity. She saw that the exhaustion had left his face and his shoulders no longer drooped but were held back in his usual proud stance. His eyes were clear and bright, if still slightly haunted. His smile warmed her heart.

With her attention on Bear, she forgot about the goat she'd been attempting to milk. Impatient with her clumsy fingers, the goat kicked out. It hit the bucket, spilling the small amount of milk she had worked so hard to obtain.

"No, goat!" Linsey's attention instantly reverted to the animal and the milk being slowly absorbed by the thirsty ground.

Chattering Squirrel clapped his hands, and Kaleb chortled beneath his breath.

"I don't think it's funny!" she said, the exasperation filling her voice belied by the smile tugging at her lips.

"Having troubles?" Bear asked when he reached them.

"Now that you're here, sleepy head, you milk the stupid animal!" Linsey stood, motioning for Bear to take her place.

Bear knelt beside the goat, ignoring Linsey's smug

smile. "Since when does sleeping two or three hours qualify a person as a sleepy head?"

"Two or three hours?" Linsey and Kaleb exchanged a grin. "You've been asleep since yesterday afternoon!"

"Guess I was a little tired." He petted the animal as they chuckled at his understatement, straightened the bucket and began to milk.

Linsey's smile was wiped away when it quickly became evident that he could milk the goat with the same expertise Kaleb displayed.

"How come I'm the only one who can't do it?" she moaned.

"Little gal, I think you're fergittin' we's both farm boys," Kaleb offered as consolation. "I learnt how ta milk a cow afore I could walk," he exaggerated.

"Since you're so good at it, and it's obvious Bear's equally as talented, I'll leave you to it!" She grabbed the baby off the fence post and, ruffling Bear's hair as she passed him, headed back toward the cabin. "Come on, Squirrel, let's go make supper!"

Chattering Squirrel followed joyfully. Cooking supper was one of his favorite pastimes. Linsey gave him taste samples and let him play with the various pots and pans. He liked the different sounds they produced when he banged them with a wooden spoon.

The men watched Linsey walk away, then turned back to the goat. The milking was quickly dispensed with and the bucket moved out of harm's way.

"Where'd you get the goat?" Bear asked.

"Folks settled a couple days south a here. Got a passel a young'uns with 'nother on the way." Kaleb shook his head as he thought of the young couple and their children. "Spent the winter in a lean-to half as big as your cabin. Ain't got but a couple a trees down to start

273

thar house. Lessen he works good, they's gonna spend next winter in the lean-to."

Bear's eyes narrowed. "They good folks?"

"Seem ta be. The missus ain't no older than your little gal, but them kids was clean as a whistle. The man was quiet-like, but likable."

"There's several good building sites not far from here. Think they'd be interested in moving up this way?"

"How about the Shawnee? They's friends of yours, so they don't mind ya bein' here. How they gonna like more neighbors?"

Bear sighed deeply and looked toward the woods. "Wolf talks of moving west. There's few of the tribe left, and they say the village has bad spirits."

Kaleb did not respond; nothing needed to be said. He knew how close Bear and Wolf were. The separation would not be easy for either man.

"How about you, Kaleb? Would you be interested in staying around?"

"Now that ya mention hit, thar's a purty little spot 'bout a mile from here. Overlooks the creek. Been a'thinkin' hit'd make a nice spot fer a cabin."

"Talk to the other people," Bear said with a nod of satisfaction that the other man chose to stay. "Don't want a crowd around here, and we might have to start staking land claims. Be better to know who your neighbors are than to wake up to total strangers some morning. If we work at it, we should be able to get both cabins up this summer."

Kaleb turned his gaze to Bear. "What about the little gal?"

"I'm taking her back as soon as Wolf comes for his sons."

* * *

Chattering Squirrel watched with utter fascination as Bear shaved off his beard. Linsey watched with the same fascination while feeding the baby his morning bottle. Both of his spectators smiled and giggled at his facial contortions, and Bear admitted to himself that he was enjoying their attentions. It reminded him of his own childhood, watching his father shave and wondering why he never cut himself with the sharp razor.

Kaleb had left before sunrise, mysteriously disappearing while Linsey and the children still slept. Bear would only say that Kaleb would be back when he wanted to come back. Linsey felt she owed him so much and had the feeling he'd left only because he knew she and Bear could have no privacy with him and the children in the cabin.

It was true she wanted to be alone with Bear, but not at the cost of hurting Kaleb.

The door was closed against the early morning chill, and as Bear was washing the shaving soap from his face, they heard Wolf.

With all his giggles and smiles, there had been something missing in Chattering Squirrel during his stay. When she saw his face light up at the sound of his father's voice, Linsey knew what it was. He was happy with Linsey but would only be truly content with his father. She selfishly hoped Wolf had only come to visit with his sons but knew it was time for them to go home.

Chattering Squirrel danced impatiently at the door, waiting for Bear. When it was opened, he threw himself at his father, his chubby arms going around Wolf's neck squeezing tightly.

Linsey was almost shocked by the change in Wolf's

appearance. He was gaunt, his flesh pulled tightly over his bones. There was no longer any softening in his face, his features hauntingly stark. His eyes reflected the tragedy of his loss, their piercing clarity almost frightening. But he stood proudly, with shoulders back and square chin raised. He was now chief of his people, and their lives depended on him. He carried the added responsibility with a dignity far beyond his years.

"I have come for my sons."

Linsey's heart sank to her toes. "Come in, Wolf," she called quietly. "If you can wait, the baby is just about finished with his morning bottle."

Bear and Wolf talked while she burped the baby. She laid him on the bed and gathered up his things while the men walked out back to get the goat. Doing as Kaleb had instructed her, she carefully tied the infant in the beaded cradleboard made by his mother.

"You be a good boy," she whispered through her tears as she tightened the last thong. "Your daddy needs you so badly. You and your brother are the only family he has left."

The baby's sparkling eyes looked at her as if he were trying to understand her words. Opening his mouth, he wiggled and squirmed, trying to coo.

When she heard the men return, Linsey kissed his velvet cheek and carried him to the door. Squirrel importantly led the goat, his little hand tightly clutching the rope while the docile animal followed behind him.

Blinking away her tears, Linsey handed the baby to his father, then knelt to hug Chattering Squirrel. Bear carried the children's things out of the cabin and handed them to Wolf.

"My sister," Wolf spoke quietly, waiting for Linsey to stand. "You have given my son a name?"

She nodded. "But I don't know if you'll approve or not. Morning Moon once told me that Shawnee names have a meaning, but I knew few Shawnee names. One of the English names I did know was Nathan, which means 'Gift of God.' "

She hesitated, waiting for Wolf to respond. When he didn't, she continued. "He was born at sunrise, so for that but mostly for his mother I added Morning. A hawk circled above us that morning we left the village. He seemed to be guarding us and flew away once we reached the cabin. He looked so strong and free, so I chose Hawk."

"Nathan Morning Hawk." Wolf said his son's name in a strong, quiet voice. "Gift of God, taken from his mother at sunrise. The hawk is a mighty hunter with much grace and strength. It is a good name, my sister. I will tell him its meaning often, and perhaps he will decide not to change it."

He strapped the baby to his back, picked up the bundled blanket and turned toward the trail. Chattering Squirrel followed behind, loudly scolding the goat, which stopped frequently to nibble on the tender new grass.

Bear wrapped his arms around Linsey as they watched the family walk away. When they were out of sight, she buried her face in his shirt.

"I'll miss them so much!"

"I know, sweet, but right now Wolf needs the security of his sons. It won't be easy for any of them, but with him as their chief, they will survive and rebuild their lives."

He turned and led her away from the cabin, toward the creek in the back. It sparkled and bubbled in the morning sunlight, its rippling sounds soothing. He sat beneath a tree, his back against its huge trunk, and pulled her onto his lap. With his lips buried in her hair and her head against his chest, he began to talk quietly.

"It's time for you to go back to Philadelphia."

Chapter Sixteen

Linsey pulled away from Bear's hold and jumped up, walking to the edge of the creek. "Do you ever catch any fish here?"

"You're changing the subject, *mon ange*," Bear said quietly.

"I can't wait for it to get warm enough to bathe in; I'm so tired of lugging water to the cabin for a bath. It certainly was easier when there was snow on the ground and all I had to do was carry it in and melt it." She knelt and let her fingers drift in the rapidly flowing water. "It's icy!"

"Spring run-off usually is." Bear stood and walked up behind her. "You won't be here when it warms up. By then you'll be taking baths in your bedroom with maids carrying the water for you."

Linsey turned and walked away from him. "I don't want to talk about it."

"We have to, sweet." His eyes followed the course of a leaf as it floated on the glittery surface of the water. Bear turned toward Linsey, drinking in the sight of her shapely back. Her head was bent, but her shoulders were held rigidly straight.

"Early next week we'll leave for Philadelphia. We'll stop at Big Jim's trading post so that I can sell my furs, then head east."

"Have a nice trip."

"It won't be an easy trip, but we'll make it—"

"*You'll* make it! I'm not going."

Bear ignored her interruption. "It will probably take close to a month if we walk, but we may be able to catch a boat."

Linsey turned, her chin raised determinedly. "Bear, I am not going back to Philadelphia. There is nothing back there for me."

"There is nothing here," he said softly.

"You're here!"

"Non, mon ange," he replied, shaking his head. "I am not for you. I am a rough man with little education. I speak French only because it was my father's language. I do not know the social niceties, nor do I want to learn them."

"What do I care for society or education!" she stormed, her eyes turning the dark shade of shadowed leaves. "I have been to a private woman's school, but I can't speak French or Shawnee!"

"You need a man who will love you and give you the protection the city can provide."

Linsey's eyes narrowed, and her voice softened to a whisper. "Can you stand there and tell me you don't love me, Luc LeClerc?"

Bear's eyes rose to above her head, and he had to clear his throat before he could speak. "I have never said that I loved you."

"Haven't you?" Linsey moved closer to him until he could feel her warm breath at the opening of his shirt. She let her hands rest against his chest, lightly stroking him through the cloth. "Look at me and tell me you're taking me back because you don't love me."

Bear looked down at her. He saw her vibrant red hair and high forehead, her upturned nose with its powdering of freckles and her stubborn jaw. He saw the pleading in her eyes and closed his heart against it.

"I am taking you back because I love you."

"That doesn't make a whole lot of sense," she whispered softly. "I didn't know I could love someone the way I love you. I want to spend my life with you, wake up beside you every morning, sleep in your arms every night."

He pulled her against him and felt every supple line of her body meshing and blending with the hard contours of his own. His heart seemed a lead weight as he thought of the rest of his life without her.

"You must go back, my love."

"Why? Give me one good reason, and I'll go without further question."

"You are not safe here."

Linsey smiled softly, rubbing her cheek against his chest. "I don't know any place on earth where I'd be safer than I am right now."

"Linsey." He held her away from him and looked deeply into her eyes. "Think of the things that have happened since you've been here. First you were kidnapped."

"If you'll remember correctly, I was kidnapped in the city you seem to think is so safe!"

"Then sold!" he continued, ignoring her interruption.

"How lucky for us Kaleb bought me. . . ."

"You almost froze to death."

"Bet I can light a fire as fast as you can . . . besides, it's nearly summer, and you won't have to worry about me freezing anymore."

"Zeke broke in, and God alone knows what would have happened if Wolf hadn't been there in time."

"Don't have to worry about Zeke anymore; Wolf took care of him." Her eyes twinkled, knowing she was matching him disagreement for disagreement.

"The measles . . ."

"No danger, had them years ago."

"Small Dog—"

"Measles got him. . . ."

Bear started to feel irritated. She was taking the dangers too lightly. "You'll go back because I want you to go back!"

"Do you love me?" she asked softly.

"Yes!" he replied through gritted teeth.

"Then I stay."

"You go!"

Linsey pushed against his chest, knocking him off balance. She placed her hands on her hips and narrowed her gaze.

"Ach, mon, have ye lost your mind?" she asked.

"I can't protect you here. There are too many things that could happen to you that I would be powerless to prevent."

"Do you think the city safer? I could walk out in front of a carriage or trip on the cobbled streets and break my neck. Do you have any idea how many diseases travel through the city during the winter and spring? I could catch one and die of it! If you want me safe from everything, you'd have to put me in an ivory tower and never let me out!"

He could not argue against the rationality of her statements. Nonetheless, the decision had been made, and he would not change his mind.

"We will leave next week."

Linsey swore at him in hotly flowing Gaelic, turned on her heels and stamped toward the cabin. Bear watched until she rounded the corner of the structure, the slamming of the door confirming her safe arrival. Lowering himself to the ground, he leaned against a tree, one leg bent and a heavy forearm resting on his knee, the other hand lying palm up on his thigh. Lost to the soothing sounds of the creek, Bear sighed deeply and closed his eyes.

When he'd read the pleading in her eyes, he had wanted to take her in his arms and make passionate love to her here at the edge of the creek. That was something he could never again do. His body ached at the thought of touching hers, joining with her. It would not be easy to deny himself, or her, the special joy that came to them when they became one. But if he made love to her, he wasn't sure he'd be able to take her back.

He loved her with a depth that surprised him. But how could he make her understand that his love gave him the strength to send her away?

He wished the argument was over, but he knew better. His Autumn Fire would not give in so easily. Now she was angry. Soon her temper would cool, and she would begin to plot and plan. He groaned at the thought of the devious methods she would use to make him change his mind. Somehow he had to stand strong, resist her at every turn.

Bear did not even attempt to fool himself into thinking it would be easy.

It was midday before Bear returned to the cabin. Without a word, Linsey placed a meal on the table, sitting across from him and calmly eating.

Bear watched her with narrowed eyes, waiting—for what, he didn't know—but he knew the battle was far from over. When they were finished, she cleaned the table, quickly dispensing with the dishes. He silently admired her efficiency, remembering her awkwardness months earlier when she attempted to do the slightest chore.

Grabbing two buckets, Linsey walked to the door, ignoring him when he asked where she was headed. She returned, the buckets filled with water, and emptied them into a kettle. Moving it over the fire to heat, Linsey picked up the buckets and left the cabin again.

On her third trip from the creek, Bear could stand it no longer. When she poured the water into the tub she used for bathing, he grabbed the empty buckets and left.

Linsey smiled to herself. It wasn't fair, what she had planned, but she didn't have time to be fair. Arguing would obviously get her nowhere, and she didn't want to use the baby as one of her arguments for staying. Her smile disappeared, and she placed her hand on her slightly swollen abdomen. If nothing else worked, she would tell him of the baby, but she didn't like the idea. With a sigh of determination, she poured the kettle of boiling water into the tub and waited for him to return.

She was sitting in a chair looking meek, hands folded in her lap, when he carried in the water. He added it to the tub and turned away, retracing his steps to the creek.

When he again returned from the creek, Bear stopped dead still in the doorway. Linsey had stripped and was sitting in the tub, her knees folded beneath her. Her hair was pulled carelessly to the top of her head, long strands hanging in enticing curls on her shoulders.

The water came to the tops of her thighs, waving invitingly around the curls of her femininity. Her soft, pale skin was silvered as she cupped her hands and let water cascade down her chest. Bear watched as it flowed from the tips of her puckered nipples. Her breasts bobbed with each of her movements, and he barely stifled a groan as she ran her hands down her body.

"Oh, you're back," she said nonchalantly. "Would you mind pouring it into the kettle to warm?"

"Is this enough?" he asked through gritted teeth as he added the buckets of water to the kettle.

Linsey bit her lower lip and pretended to consider the amount of water. "Maybe one more trip? Just a little more."

Bear turned to leave, thinking a little more was a whole lot more than he could stand.

"Could you hand me the soap, please?" She smiled sweetly, her hand casually drifting over the slope of her breast. She watched his eyes follow her hand, and she wondered if he had any idea how hungrily he looked at her.

"Where is it?" He had to get out of here! Another minute and it would be too late. As badly as he wanted to make love to her, he knew he couldn't. He could never let her go if he did.

Linsey leaned back against the edge of the tub, raised her arm until her nipples seemed to point directly at him and pointed to the soap, which was conveniently just out of reach.

Bear handed her the soap, grabbed the buckets and left. His return trip took considerably longer than previous trips, and the water was beginning to cool when he again entered the cabin.

"Oh, good, could you check and see if the water is warmed yet?" Linsey asked beguilingly. "This is getting pretty cold."

Bear set down the buckets and checked the kettle over the fire. He'd stayed away, fighting to get himself under control. He told himself that this was only the first stage in her battle to get him to change his mind; he had to be strong. He'd gone so far as to believe everything he'd told himself . . . until he'd walked back into the cabin.

"Do you want me to pour it in?"

"Please?"

He emptied the kettle into the tub, careful not to pour it directly onto her skin. Linsey sighed as the warmth flowed around her, closing her eyes and leaning back against the edge of the tub. She listened to Bear move around the room, and as his steps neared the door, she spoke.

"Bear, would you wash my back."

"Don't do this to me, Linsey!" he snarled, hands clenching into white-knuckled fists.

"Do what?" she asked innocently. "All I'm doing is taking a bath." She splashed the water over her shoulders. "You wash my back, and then I'll wash yours."

"It won't work! You will go back to Philadelphia!" He walked out of the cabin, slamming the door behind him.

Bear realized he needed a bath . . . desperately. Pulling his shirt off over his head, he dropped it on the path. Stopping long enough to unlace his leggings, he removed them and his moccasins, leaving them where they landed. Barely missing a step, he took off his pants and walked into the freezing water of the creek.

Bear returned to the cabin just as dusk was turning to dark and found the table set, dinner waiting only for his return. Linsey greeted him as if nothing different had happened all day, talking conversationally during the meal, casually ignoring his grunted replies.

After the meal, Linsey sat quietly sewing while he prowled restlessly around the room. Nothing held his attention, and he watched her from the corner of his eyes, waiting for her next move. He couldn't help but wonder if the wait was worse than her action. He was to discover that it wasn't.

"Bear, would you mind trying on this shirt?" Linsey held up a bright plaid flannel shirt she'd been working on for days. It hadn't been easy with the boys to care for, but with them gone, she had quickly finished it.

He narrowed his eyes. Something wasn't right. She had made him several shirts but had checked the fit on only the first one. Why, suddenly, did she need to see how this one fit?

"Oh, never mind," Linsey replied with disgust when she saw his look. "I had to use the end of the bolt of material, and I was afraid I cut the sleeves too short. If it doesn't fit when you put it on, it will be no one's fault but your own!"

Rather sheepishly, he began to remove his shirt. He was acting childishly, being suspicious over her slightest request. Bare chested, he approached her, reaching for the shirt she had thrown onto the table. He slid his arms into the sleeves and flinched when he felt her hands on his chest.

"Don't!"

"Don't what? I was only helping with the buttons." Linsey folded her arms and took a step back. "Do it yourself then!"

"I'm sorry, Autumn Fire," he replied softly. "It's only that . . . ah, well I mean. . . ."

"Just finish with the buttons and turn around," Linsey said with a sigh.

Standing with his back to her, Bear did not see the narrowing of her eyes or the slight smile that crossed her lips.

Linsey placed her hands on his shoulders, satisfied with the fit of the shirt . . . and the tightening of his muscles beneath her fingers. Instructing him to lift his arms out to his sides, she lightly ran her hand from under his arm to the bottom of the shirt at his hip, delighting in his nearly silent groan as she followed the hem across his tight buttocks.

"Looks good," she mumbled, pulling on the hem as long as possible. "Turn around. Let's see how it looks from the front."

Linsey carefully controlled her expression when she saw the muscle jumping in his jaw and his tightly clenched teeth. Her hands moved to his shoulders, and she heard his breath catch as she slowly smoothed the shirt over his chest. Again she had him hold his arms out to his sides, making a great show of checking the fit.

He flinched visibly when she took his hand and put it beneath her arm so that it rested against her breast. Linsey fiddled with his sleeve, pulling, stretching, straightening, insuring that each of her moves pushed her breast against his hand.

As she dropped his arm, Bear's sigh of relief was choked off when she positioned his other hand in the same manner. Her hardened nipple burned into his palm, rubbing very gently with each of her movements. It was torture of the most subtle kind.

"Are you about finished?" His voice grated harshly in the silence as he fought to control the hardening of his body. It was a battle he was closer to losing each time she took a breath and her breast filled his hand.

"Men!" Linsey said, shaking her head. "You're so impatient! I realize you don't like trying on this shirt, but I promise I'll finish as quickly as possible."

She stepped away and let his arm fall. She had him move his arms in several different directions and made a show of studying how the shirt pulled. With his arms over his head, Linsey tugged at the hem, muttering about the length, letting her fingers appear to accidentally slip. They slid down the front of his pants, gently caressing the rigid bulge they encountered.

"Enough!" Bear roared, pulling away from her.

"Well, I guess it fits," she sighed. "I really was worried about it, particularly after spending so much time on it."

"I appreciate your work," Bear said, his fingers clumsy as he attempted to undo the buttons.

"You really sound it," she replied sarcastically.

"I guess I'm just tired." He knew he sounded ungrateful, but another minute of her innocent touches and he would have thrown her onto the bed, and nothing would have stopped him from making love to her.

"I'm kind of tired, too. Let's go to bed." Linsey walked across the room, sat on the edge of the bed and began removing her leather shoes.

She rarely wore her dress and shoes, preferring the comfort of the Shawnee clothing, but after her bath, she decided it would suit her purposes better. When the shoes were untied, she kicked them off. Extending first one leg and then the other, she slowly rolled down her carefully mended stockings. Reaching beneath her skirt, she pulled off her drawers. From the corners of her eyes, she saw that Bear had unbuttoned the shirt and it hung halfway down his shoulders. His eyes were riveted to her hands, following her every move.

As her fingers moved to the buttons down the front of the dress, Bear began to wonder why he had decided not to make love to her again.

With painful slowness, first one button and then another came free. He decided it was a stupid decision—Linsey unworked the last button and slid one shoulder from the gown—a ridiculously stupid decision, he admitted to himself.

When her other creamy shoulder appeared and the dress slid to the ground, he knew he'd never made a dumber decision in his life.

The top of Linsey's lacy cotton chemise was just above the slope of her breasts. The bottom rode at the very top of her thighs. Bear found himself hoping she'd raise her shoulders, very slightly. He nearly choked when she did and he caught a peek at tight red curls.

When they disappeared beneath the lace again, his eyes moved once more to her hands. Her nimble fingers opened the first two flat, white buttons. Bear let his shirt slide off his shoulders, unaware of it landing on the dirt floor.

Two more buttons and Linsey's breasts bobbed before his eyes, only their rosy peaks hidden beneath the soft cotton. Bear hastily tore at the thongs lacing his moccasins.

He grew impatient when she moved her hands from her chemise, but as she raised her arms to release her hair, he lowered his eyes, once again feasting like a starving man on the fiery curls between her thighs.

When the curls disappeared, he groaned aloud, unaware of the sound drifting across the room. Linsey hid a smile, continuing to appear innocent of his growing passions.

Bear's gaze traveled up her body, and he wondered when she had let down her hair. It hung over her shoulders, veiling her flesh. His eyes snapped back to her hands as she worked another button free, and he saw the inviting crevice of her navel. Bear's hands went to the buttons on his pants. He stepped out of them before she could finish her last button.

"Woman!"

Linsey raised her eyes, and he watched as her expression turned from studied innocence to total seduction. She let her gaze drift slowly over his body, and it felt like a caress when it reached the level of his throbbing hardness. Slowly her eyes returned to his face, and she lightly licked her lips.

She tossed her head, and her hair flipped behind her

shoulder, exposing one cotton-covered breast while seductively covering the other. With a slight shrug, the chemise seemed to drift from her shoulder, hanging for the length of a heart beat on the tip of her breast before sliding down. Linsey reached for the other side, effectively shielding her naked breast from his gaze with her arm.

Bear felt sweat bead his upper lip as he waited for her to free her other breast. An eternity passed before she slid the other strap down her arm. The lacy article of clothing clung to her hips, and Bear swallowed hard as he tried to pierce the hazy veil of red effectively hiding her breast.

Linsey turned toward the bed, put her hands under her hair and flipped it so that it cascaded down her back. It rippled in a fiery waterfall as she wiggled and let the chemise slide down her long legs.

"Woman, are you trying to drive me out of my mind?" Bear's voice was a barely audible, husky whisper.

Linsey looked over her shoulder, her silken tresses successfully hiding her body from his view. She smiled softly, her eyes a beckoning emerald gaze.

"Why would I do that?"

"Because you're wicked!" He was unaware of moving toward her, his legs following a command of their own.

"Are you complaining?"

"Never!"

Bear reached for her, turning her into his arms and pulling her against his body. His mouth met hers in a kiss hot enough to set the world on fire as he slowly lowered her to the bed. He knelt between her welcoming thighs, his body ablaze with a passion too intense for the slow, gentle loving he'd always known with her.

"Woman, what am I going to do with you?"

"Love me."

He did.

Chapter Seventeen

Held captive by the glowing aftermath of their nearly violent loving, Linsey lay with her head on Bear's shoulder, listening as his pounding heart slowed to normal. His arms were wrapped protectively around her, and she knew she'd never feel as safe anywhere else on earth. This was where she longed to spend the rest of her life. And she would fight to stay there, using any available weapon.

"Don't take me back." She kissed the smooth skin beneath her cheek. "I don't think I could live without you."

"Mon ange." Bear's voice was thick with regret. "I must. You have been protected all your life. There are too many dangers waiting around every corner, and I can't assure you a happy future here."

Linsey sat up beside him, and he caught his breath at the beauty of her body as the firelight danced over it.

"Bear, no one knows the future. We can only take each day as it comes. With you, I would live my life to its fullest, and when problems arise we will handle them together."

He shook his head, his eyes pleading with her to try to understand. "If you were to die because of something that could never have happened in the city, how do you think I'd feel?"

Placing her hand against his cheek, Linsey bent and kissed him. "It would be my choice to stay; you would go on, knowing I had been happy. We will create memories that will stay with us forever. Don't make us spend the rest of our lives lonely for each other, perhaps growing bitter by the separation. I would rather have one year with you than fifty without you."

Bear closed his eyes feeling the loneliness he knew would be his when she was gone. The future loomed bleak, every new day as desolate as the last.

"I will move to your city," he finally said.

Linsey knew, without a doubt, that Bear would not survive living in a crowded city. He was a man of the wilderness, as free as the wind. He had to have the space of the forest, the challenges that went along with living on the frontier.

"No." She slowly shook her head. "You couldn't live in a place that has buildings instead of trees, people instead of animals. It would be easier for you to cut off your right hand than it would be for you to live in town."

Bear knew she was right, but he wondered if he'd ever again be content anyplace without her at his side.

Lifting his hand from his chest, Linsey placed a gentle kiss in his palm. Slowly she lowered it to the slope of her abdomen.

"I carry your child."

Silence as thick as storm clouds filled the room. It rolled and bounced around them as Bear closed his eyes while a pain sharper than any he'd ever known shredded his heart.

"I know," he whispered.

"You know?" Linsey's brow rose in amazement.

"The Grandmother told me."

"Are there no secrets from that woman?"

Bear let his hand drift over the rounded mound, treasuring the touch. He raised up and kissed her belly, then pulled her back into his arms. Side by side, legs entwined, they shared the knowledge of the life they had created.

"We will be married before we reach Philadelphia."

"What?" Linsey tried to sit up, but he held her firmly.

"I will give you and the child my name; then no one will frown at his illegitimacy."

"I will be a wife without a husband?"

"You'll have a husband," he replied.

"Sure, one I never see." Again she struggled to be free, and Bear let her go. She sat up and pulled a blanket around her shoulders.

"I will come each spring to see you and my son."

"Your son?" Linsey murmured a Gaelic curse. "The baby will be nearly a year old before you know if it is a son or daughter! Will you come each spring and leave me pregnant with another child that you can visit the next year?"

"No," Bear pulled his arm over his eyes, trying to evade the picture she was painting. "I will not touch you again."

"Oh, how nice!" Her voice thickened with sarcasm. "A husband I'll see every spring, who will not be my lover. A father whose own child will not know him. I don't need a husband like that!"

"My son needs my name."

"Why? Since the war, illegitimacy carries no stigma. It is the duty of every woman to produce children to populate this new nation." Linsey climbed off the bed and began pacing the room, the blanket flowing cape-like around her. "We will not be married. I'll not wed a man who will not be my husband."

"I will not argue this with you, woman." Bear sat up and leaned against the wall. "My son will have my name."

"We'll consider our time together as a handfast," she continued, ignoring him. "It is a time-honored tradition in Scotland. Sometimes it leads to marriage, sometimes not. I'm wealthy enough to support my child. He, or she, will want for nothing . . . except a father."

"Linsey!" Bear clenched his hands into tight fists.

"Who knows, I may find a man in Philadelphia that I want to marry. He will become the father to my child."

Pain tore through him with the swiftness of a breath as he thought of another man as her husband. The promised agony of their separation was nothing when compared to the torturous knowledge of another man touching her, holding her . . . loving her.

"You are destroying me," he said with a moan.

"What do you think you're doing to me?" she whispered. "I love you so much I feel like I'm dying from just the thought of being away from you."

Tears filled her eyes, making her voice quaver with anguish. "Please, Luc, don't send me away. I will die little by little without you."

"I must." His voice, too, was filled with agony. "For your own safety, I must take you back. I couldn't protect Snow in the center of a crowded village. How could I ever hope to protect you, here where there is nothing or no one for miles? I don't think I could survive losing you, Autumn Fire. Don't ask that of me."

Linsey walked to the table, sat down and placed her

head in her hands. Nothing was resolved. The long night passed in silence, except for the occasional sob escaping her control.

From the bed, Bear listened, his heart breaking. He wanted to comfort her, to seek her comfort. The tortures of the damned were their companions through the long, dark night.

Linsey walked around the small cabin, touching this and that, letting the memories tumble through her mind. Tomorrow they would begin the journey back to Philadelphia. Months ago it had been all she wanted, to go home to the only life she had known. But now this had become home, this floorless cabin deep in the woods. She had fallen in love not only with Luc Le-Clerc but with his wilderness.

She could hear Bear outside the opened door finishing his preparations for the trip. Their departure was several days earlier than he had originally planned, but neither of them could stand the wall of silence that had grown up between them. They shared the same cabin, the same bed, but when night came, Linsey curled up in a tight ball, her back to Bear. They spoke only when necessary, which was seldom. All the words had been said, all the arguments aired. To wait longer just caused the agony to grow.

Linsey touched the kettle she had used to melt endless buckets of snow and felt the tears slide silently down her cheeks. She had never cried so much in her life! She fought to hide the tears from Bear, but she knew he was aware of them. He would catch sight of her flushed face, and the telltale muscle in his jaw would start to jump.

He still insisted that they marry before reaching

Philadelphia. With a shrug, Linsey agreed. It seemed to mean so much to him, and she knew she'd never marry any other man. Nothing seemed to matter much to her now.

Startled from her thoughts by voices outside, she dried her tears and walked to the door. Wolf spoke quietly with Bear. The baby was in his arms; beside him stood Chattering Squirrel holding a rope tied to the goat.

Seeing her, Chattering Squirrel dropped the rope and ran across the clearing, throwing himself into her arms. Linsey hugged the toddler tightly, her green eyes again clouding with tears.

"Maman?" Squirrel pulled away, his face showing his bewilderment. "Maman here? Fower here?"

Linsey bit the inside of her lip, blinking fiercely. "No, sweetheart. Your maman and sister are not here," she whispered, trying to swallow the lump forming in her throat.

His dark eyes expressed his disappointment with heart-breaking eloquence. "Maman gone, no take me. Why maman go, no take me? Me good boy!"

Linsey raised her eyes to the men and found in their dark gazes the same torture she was feeling. How to explain to a two-year-old that his mother and sister were dead was far beyond her ability. She pulled Squirrel into her arms and tried to comfort the child as he repeatedly asked for his mother.

"My sister," Wolf said quietly, "I must ask a great thing of you. If you choose to say no, I will understand."

Linsey stood and carried Chattering Squirrel with her as she crossed to him. She handed the toddler to Bear, then turned to Wolf, waiting for him to continue.

"Many years ago, the Shawnee nation split. Half of

the people decided to leave this land that the white man wanted and journey west. The other half, including the people of my tribe, decided to stay and fight for the land of their birth. If we had gone, my tribe would still be strong, but because we stayed we have suffered as never before.

"I must lead my people over the great mother of all rivers, in hope of finding and joining with our own people. It will not be an easy journey. My people are weak, still sick. Whole families are gone; in some a child survived, in others an old person. In some several lived but suffer blindness or a cough that shows with blood.

"We are no longer strong and proud. Many will not live to see a new land, but all insist that we go. The spirits surrounding our village are no longer friendly. As their chief, I must lead them in a search for a new home.

"I ask, woman of my brother, that you care for my son until I may return for him." Wolf looked down at the child sleeping in his arms. When he lifted his eyes, Linsey almost flinched from the agony on his face. "There is no woman to see to his needs. I fear for his life should I try to take him with me.

"Summer Eyes, will you care for my son so that I may lead my people without having to be concerned for him. Will you keep him and protect him for me? It is not an easy thing I ask of you, my sister."

Linsey looked quickly at Bear and saw his almost imperceptible nod. "Wolf, it is a great honor to be asked to watch Nathan Morning Hawk. I will love him as my own child until you can return for him."

Wolf raised the baby to his shoulder and spoke softly to the sleeping infant. Closing his eyes for a brief moment, he gently rubbed his cheek against the soft one of his son's, then handed the baby to her.

"I shall return when my people are safe." He moved his gaze from the baby to Linsey.

"Squirrel?" she asked quietly, holding the infant against her breasts.

Wolf shook his head. "He would be safe here with you, but I am selfish, my sister. I know I should leave him also, for the journey will be filled with its own horrors; but I have lost so much." He turned his eyes to the child in Bear's arms. His voice lowered to a whisper. "I need him with me."

Bear hugged the toddler and set him on his feet. He turned to Wolf, his right hand reaching out. The two men clasped hands to forearms, their free hands to the other's shoulder. The parting was not easy; they had been brothers for many years, sharing a past and memories of family and friends now gone.

"May Manitou guide you to a home for your people where they will again be happy. Your son shall be my son until you again return to this land. I will guard him with my life," Bear said, his voice husky with emotion. "Go in peace, my brother."

"My heart stays here in the lands of my birth, and I shall return when my people are safe." His eyes darkened, his words spoken softly in Shawnee. "I am glad my brother, Bear Who Walks Alone, no longer walks alone. It fills my heart with joy that he has found a woman to share his days."

Linsey clutched the baby tightly as Wolf took Chattering Squirrel's hand and walked away. The tall man and the small boy spoke not a word as they left the clearing, nor did they turn as they walked out of sight. Linsey watched until they had disappeared, then moved slowly toward the cabin.

Tears made her vision swim, but she managed to keep them from flowing down her cheeks until she laid the baby on the massive bed and unwrapped the heavy blanket covering him. He was dressed in the shirt she had made and embroidered with her own hair. Around his neck hung a string of colorful beads, each carefully tied so that if one pulled free the others would not come off . . . made lovingly by a proud older sister he would never know.

Linsey sat on the edge of the bed and gathered the baby to her. With her cheek resting lightly on his soft hair, she cried for the friends she had found and lost so quickly. They had been Shawnee, as was the infant in her arms, members of a tribe of people she had considered savage only months earlier. But she had come to know and respect them, gladly calling them friend.

Hawk had been fed his evening bottle and now rested on the lap of the huge man. The baby clutched at the finger in his hand and fought to direct it to his mouth, with little success since Bear moved his hand away each time it was within reach of Hawk's goal. With determination, the baby tried again and again to get the finger into his mouth.

Linsey finished cleaning up from their evening meal while she listened to Bear talk softly to the baby, first in Shawnee, then in French and finally in English.

"Is that the way you confused Chattering Squirrel, talking in three languages all in the same sentence?" She dried her hands and walked to the table.

"This little guy looks exactly like Squirrel at this age." Bear looked up from the baby. "We need to talk."

302

"I know." It hadn't dawned on her that the baby would be the answer to her problems until long after Wolf had left. With Hawk to tend, she realized that Bear could not take her back to Philadelphia.

"Hey!" Bear felt a warm, wet pull on his finger and looked down. The baby had finally managed to get it in his mouth and sucked contentedly, his eyes already growing heavy with sleep.

"Bedtime, little warrior," Linsey said, dislodging Bear's finger and picking the baby up from his lap. She carried him to the bed and laid him on his stomach. Hawk wiggled and squirmed, getting his legs beneath him. With his bottom in the air, he sighed contentedly and drifted into sleep.

Bear stood in the doorway staring into the night. A full moon lit the dark, casting freckled shadows through the trees. A night bird called and was answered by its mate while a light breeze ruffled through the leaves, its coolness a reminder that winter was not far behind them.

Finally, Linsey could no longer put off going to him. She had won the fight to stay, but she did not think Bear would be any happier about it than he had been about her going.

"Look about you, *mon ange*. What do you see?" He didn't wait for an answer. "Trees, a wilderness where there is no one to depend on but yourself. In the wilderness a man and his woman become as one person. Each does his own job and sometimes his mate's job as well. They must share—their lives, their work, their minds—just to survive.

"Are you such a woman, my lovely Linsey?" He turned, framing her face with his hands. "Can you truly give up all that waits for you in Philadelphia for this small cabin in my wilderness where every day could be

303

your last? Can you bear your child with none to see to its birthing but me? Can you bravely watch me walk out the door never knowing if I'll return? Are you strong enough to watch your child die from an accident or disease that would not have happened in the city?"

In the darkness, her eyes burned with green fire.

"You are my woman; you carry my child beneath your heart. I can not promise you safety, security or even protection, but I will love you with a passion never before known by any other. I will have none but you as my wife, and for the rest of the days of my life I will cherish you."

Linsey reached up and cupped his cheek. How long ago it seemed since she had been so frightened by his appearance.

"I will be the woman you need me to be, Luc Le-Clerc. You will never know my fears until the time to fear is done. I will gladly bear every child you give me with none but you to guide it safely into the world. I will share my laughter and tears with you, for without you my life would be truly empty."

She wrapped her arms around his waist and rested her head against his chest. "When problems arise, we will solve them. Together we can do anything! Just never send me away, Bear. Let me spend my life beside you, through good and bad."

Bear wrapped his arms around her as he leaned back against the door frame. For the first time in his life, he was frightened by the unknown future.

"We take such a big chance, Autumn Fire."

"How boring life would be if everything was a certainty." She looked up to the stars twinkling so far overhead, then back to him. "As long as we have love, we can survive anything else the world throws at us."

"We have love. More than any others have ever known."

Bear leaned over, and their lips met in a kiss of sweet promise. He felt a weight lift from his shoulders, knowing he would not have to take her back to the city. Somehow, in some way, he would protect her from all harm, for if he lost her, he would surely lose himself.

"I could never have taken you back," he whispered.

"I would never have stayed." Her eyes twinkled brightly. "I would have followed behind you or found my way back here alone."

Long minutes of silence passed as they held each other closely. It was a comforting silence as they searched beyond the stars for their tomorrow.

"Will you be able to care for two babes at the same time?" Bear asked, finally breaking the quiet.

"Two?"

"Hawk will only be a few months old when our son is born."

"You are so positive this baby will be a boy!" Linsey responded with a smile. "What are you going to do if 'he' is a 'she'?"

"The Grandmother said it is a boy." Bear's dark eyes sparkled, and a leer crossed his face. "But if she is wrong, then we'll just have to keep having them until we get a boy."

A troubled thought crossed her mind. "Will a girl disappoint you so very badly?"

"*Non, mon ange.* A daughter who looks just like her mother will bring me the greatest joy. But I must have a son, my love," he whispered as his mouth lowered to hers. "I greatly fear with two like you I'd never stand a chance of winning an argument!" His breath teased against her lips; his eyes burned with a fever of growing passion.

"Do you think we'll argue?" Linsey asked as she moved her body slowly against his.

Bear threw back his head with a shout of laughter that disturbed the sleeping baby. He picked her up and carried her to the bed. With disgust he looked at the infant who wiggled and squirmed at the noise.

"Tomorrow I make a cradle!"

"Tonight?" Linsey asked, biting softly at the pulse throbbing in his heavily corded neck.

"Tonight . . ." Bear laid her gently on the edge of the bed. "Tonight we are very careful."

The noise that had interrupted his sleep had quieted to velvet whispers. Hawk closed his tiny eyes and drifted back to sleep, soothed by the gentle rocking of the bed beneath him.

Epilogue

Linsey looked out the opened door and watched the wind flutter through the colorful leaves. Mother Nature was again showing her power by painting the landscapes in glorious shades only she could create. The days were still comfortably warm, but as the sun left the sky, the temperature lowered until the night air was nippy.

Linsey found it difficult to believe that nearly a year had passed since she'd been kidnapped by Jeb and Zeke. At times her life in Philadelphia took on a dreamlike quality. She was content in her wilderness home, missing few of the luxuries she had been accustomed to having. The one item she hated doing without had arrived unexpectedly a week earlier.

Before summer had arrived, Kaleb had decided to travel to Philadelphia. He said it was because he'd never seen the city, but Linsey knew it was for her. Carrying messages to Linsey's lawyers and friends, he had taken care of necessary business for her and while there, at Bear's request, had ordered a bathtub. It had taken weeks for the tub to be shipped downriver, and Linsey was startled speechless when it arrived at the

307

cabin. Bear had been startled speechless by her display of gratitude.

There were now three cabins in the area, separated by the trees so that each afforded privacy for its occupants. Kaleb had returned from his mysterious journey a few days after the Shawnee had left. Following behind him were Josh and Sarah Willowby, their five children and numerous goats. In an incredibly short space of time, the three men had put up a two-room cabin, Sarah and Linsey had become friends and the children had made new trails with their numerous trips between cabins.

While Kaleb was gone to Philadelphia, Bear and Josh put up a small cabin for the old man, who was delighted by it at his return. Next summer Bear planned to add to their cabin and put down a floor. Linsey had convinced him that she could live with the dirt floor the rest of her life, if necessary. There were so many things that needed to be done, and flooring the cabin came far down on the list.

They now had neighbors in their wilderness, and Bear seemed more relaxed at the idea of leaving Linsey alone when he had to be away overnight. She smiled to herself, wondering what he'd say when he came in and discovered she'd spent this day, alone, in preparation for their baby's arrival.

A pain spread from the middle of her back to the center of her massively protruding stomach, causing it to harden like granite. Linsey grabbed a chair for support and held her breath until it passed. When she was able to move again, she lowered her ponderous body into a chair and looked down at the infant in the cradle.

Nearly five months of age, Hawk had just discovered his feet and was most content when chewing on his toes.

Unaware of the drama unfolding around him, he babbled happily to himself, squealing with delight when he managed to catch his elusive foot and carry it to his mouth.

"Oh, that was a good one," Linsey said to the infant, her voice breathless. "By this time tomorrow, he should be here." Her hand rested protectively on the swell of her stomach, and she looked longingly toward the empty cradle sitting across the room. Bear had made Hawk's cradle, but Kaleb had made the one for their baby. He had carried it into the cabin one evening before dinner. He'd worn a shy look on his puddled face when he'd presented it to Linsey, saying the grandfather should always be the one to make the cradle not the father.

Another pain, starting slowly in her back, forced Linsey to remain in the chair. When it passed, she stood and continued with her preparations. Bear would soon be home for the evening meal, and as was his custom, Kaleb would come with him. The meal was ready and waiting, but she had a feeling it might be eaten a little later than normal.

Bear was delighted that Sarah lived near them. He felt that having given birth to five children, Sarah was an expert. Little did he know that Linsey intended for no one to deliver her child but him. Kaleb would be the likely person sent to fetch Sarah, and Linsey had already spoken to him, asking him not to get her. This was a time she wanted to share only with Bear. When it was over, Sarah could be called, but not before.

Another pain was easing when she heard their voices outside.

"Think we'll get that crop in before we get a killing frost?" Bear asked.

"Jist don't know," Kaleb replied. "Hit might be

close. Signs point to a early winter this year. Been wrong afore, but I'm right more'n I'm wrong."

"We'll just have to keep an eye on it. Let it ripen as long as we can."

They entered the cabin, and Kaleb's keen eyes immediately detected Linsey's discomfort. His gaze searched hers, then a wicked grin split his face.

Bear greeted Linsey, then removed his shirt as he walked to the wash bucket. It was only when she gasped and grabbed the wall as another pain took hold that he realized something was wrong.

"Linsey?" He turned, water dripping from his chin to his chest. "What is it, *mon ange?*"

She could not speak until the pain began to ease, and even then her voice wavered. "I think your son has finally decided to join the world."

"The baby? It's time for the baby?" Bear felt a fissure of fear run up his spine.

"Well, not this minute, but I'd say sometime before morning."

Kaleb walked over to the cradle holding Hawk and reached down for the infant. "Come on, little warrior. This ain't no place fer us men ta be." He confidently cradled the baby in the crook of his arm and grabbed the bottle sitting on the edge of the table.

Hawk, recognizing the grizzled face, grinned his toothless smile and reached for Kaleb's long beard.

"Kaleb, go for Sarah," Bear ordered, little realizing that it was a command rather than a request.

"We'll do that, yes siree, we'll jist do that." Kaleb looked across the room at Linsey and winked. "Don't ya be a frettin' none about this young'un. I'll be a'tendin' him. You jist be sure en have us a new babe when we come a'callin' in the mornin'.

"Les go, mighty Hawk. Ole grandpa Kaleb'll tell ya

'bout the time them damn Iroquois lifted my hare. Why if'n hit waren't fer your uncle Bar, I'd still be . . ."

They heard his voice drift off as he walked away. Bear wondered how long it would take Sarah to come. Feeling helpless and more frightened than he could ever remember, he turned to Linsey.

"What do I do until Sarah arrives?" he asked.

Linsey smiled gently and thought about his reaction when he discovered she was not coming. "You could help me get undressed and into bed," she suggested.

Just as he reached for her, another pain began. Linsey clasped his hands, waiting for it to pass, and beads of sweat dotted Bear's brow before it was done. When she looked up at him and smiled, he swore fiercely in French and picked her up. At the edge of the bed, he lowered her feet to the floor and reached for the hem of her loose dress. Pulling it over her head and throwing it out of the way, Bear helped her to sit down. Piling several furs into a huge mound, he encouraged her to lean back into an upright position.

Bear couldn't help but notice her swollen breasts, the blue veins showing beneath the tightly stretched skin. His eyes lowered to her stomach, and as he watched, another contraction tightened it to rock hardness. Linsey squeezed his hand at the height of the pain, and he was amazed by her strength.

Grabbing a blanket, Bear shook it out and started to cover her, but she stopped him with a smile.

"I'm already hot and will probably get hotter. I don't want that scratchy thing on me."

"Do you want a shirt or something?" he asked anxiously.

"I thought you liked to see my body," she teased. "Last night down by the creek, you told me I was beautiful even swollen up like this."

311

"I did . . . you are . . . I mean—" Bear turned and walked to the door. "Where is that woman? She should be here by now."

"Sarah's not—" Linsey gritted her teeth as another pain racked through her. They had started early in the morning and were finally coming closer together. Sarah had told her what to expect, and so far everything was happening just as she had said.

"Sarah's not what?" Bear asked, agitation making his voice gruff.

"Coming!" The pain was at its peak, and Linsey almost screamed the word.

"Sarah's not coming?" He walked back to the bed, waiting impatiently for her to be able to respond.

Linsey let her breath out with a deep swoosh and tried to relax. "You will deliver our child," she said quietly.

"What?! Woman, have you lost your mind?"

"Not yet." Linsey's attempt at a smile quickly turned to bared teeth as another pain reached its peak.

"Kaleb went to get her!"

"No . . . I talked to him a few days ago and asked him not to send her here. This is such a special time, Luc. I don't want to share it with anyone but you. Please?"

He knelt by the bed and brought her hand up to his mouth. Lightly kissing her palm, Bear tasted the salty flavor of sweat. Her brow and upper lip were beaded, and as he watched, her belly tightened again.

"I can't, Autumn Fire."

Linsey felt his big hands shake as they held hers, and she knew he was truly frightened. He had faced a tribe of Iroquois to save Kaleb, his thirst for revenge had led him to fight a grizzly with nothing but a knife

312

and his bare hands, but the thought of delivering his child made him quiver with fear.

"It is too late, Bear."

"I can get to their cabin and back in only a few minutes."

"The pains are coming with almost no space between them."

"I don't know what to do!"

The pains were flowing together with no break. Through gritted teeth Linsey guided him. Bear stood beside the bed and between her open thighs saw the top of the dark, fuzzy head of his child, and for the first time in his life he wondered if he would pass out.

"I see it," he murmured. "*Mon Dieu*, I see it."

Linsey bent her knees and grabbed the back of her thighs with her hands. She panted as Sarah had instructed and kept her eyes glued to Bear's face where the wonder of the moment stamped multiple expressions of joy, amazement, fear and hope across his rugged features.

Biting her lip until she tasted blood, Linsey forced back a scream as the head pushed out of her body. Tears streamed down her face to join with the sweat pouring off her as the tiny body slipped free.

Reverently, Bear lifted the child still connected to her by the cord of life. He held it up so that she could see the life they had created. Tiny legs kicked as small arms batted the air and new lungs filled with life-giving air.

"You have given me a son, Autumn Fire," Bear whispered, tears filling his eyes to overflowing and streaming down his face. "A son . . ."

Linsey smiled and lay back, a feeling of utopia vying with exhaustion. Quietly she instructed him how to tie off and cut the cord. Bear laid the infant on her flat belly, his hands now sure as he finished with the birth.

Linsey stroked the damp head of her son; a feeling of pride and love filled her heart. His hair was dark, and she suspected when it was dry it would be thick and black. His face, wrinkled like an old man's, showed his father's wide brow and aquiline nose. He wiggled and kicked, screaming lustily his outrage at being removed from his warm, quiet world.

When the cord was safely cut and the afterbirth delivered, Linsey held her son against her breast, fascinated as he rutted around searching for her nipple. She jumped with surprise when his tiny mouth closed around it and he began to suckle fiercely.

"Being born must be hungry work." Bear chuckled at the baby's enthusiasm.

Linsey counted fingers and toes, examined ears, arms and legs while Bear gently ministered to her. When he was finished, he drew a light cover up to her breasts, then knelt down beside the bed.

"He's so tiny."

Linsey snorted. "You wouldn't have said that if you'd been in my position!"

The reality of the moment set in, and Bear's hands began to shake. They had been completely steady as he helped his son into the world, but now he felt weak with reaction.

"Was it bad, *mon ange*?"

Linsey turned her gaze from her son, and her eyes melted with love for her gentle giant. She lifted her free hand from the baby's leg and caressed Bear's cheek.

"No, my Bear. Holding your son in my arms and knowing he is our child wiped every bit of the pain from my mind."

He believed her; the expression in her eyes was joy. No hint of the pain she had suffered marred their clear emerald light.

"Thank you, Autumn Fire."

"For the baby?"

"Him, too. But I would have run for Sarah and have never known this incredible joy of sharing his birth with you."

"Since you like it so much, we'll have to do it again soon," Linsey teased.

With a groan, Bear leaned down and kissed her, then softly kissed his son. "Can we wait a few days? I don't think I'll stop shaking for a week or two."

The sound of their gentle murmurs and quiet words drifted on the crisp night air. A leaf twirled and twisted in the gentle breeze before it relinquished its hold on life and drifted to the ground below. One life had lived its short span of time on earth. The silence of night was broken by the tiny voice of a new life just beginning.

FIERY ROMANCE

CALIFORNIA CARESS   (2771, $3.75)
by Rebecca Sinclair

Hope Bennett was determined to save her brother's life. And if that meant paying notorious gunslinger Drake Frazier to take his place in a fight, she'd barter her last gold nugget. But Hope soon discovered she'd have to give the handsome rattlesnake more than riches if she wanted his help. His improper demands infuriated her; even as she luxuriated in the tantalizing heat of his embrace, she refused to yield to her desires.

ARIZONA CAPTIVE   (2718, $3.75)
by Laree Bryant

Logan Powers had always taken his role as a lady-killer very seriously and no woman was going to change that. Not even the breathtakingly beautiful Callie Nolan with her luxuriant black hair and startling blue eyes. Logan might have considered a lusty romp with her but it was apparent she was a lady, through and through. Hard as he tried, Logan couldn't resist wanting to take her warm slender body in his arms and hold her close to his heart forever.

DECEPTION'S EMBRACE   (2720, $3.75)
by Jeanne Hansen

Terrified heiress Katrina Montgomery fled Memphis with what little she could carry and headed west, hiding in a freight car. By the time she reached Kansas City, she was feeling almost safe . . . until the handsomest man she'd ever seen entered the car and swept her into his embrace. She didn't know who he was or why he refused to let her go, but when she gazed into his eyes, she somehow knew she could trust him with her life . . . and her heart.

Available wherever paperbacks are sold, or order direct from the Publisher. Send cover price plus 50¢ per copy for mailing and handling to Zebra Books, Dept. 3133, 475 Park Avenue South, New York, N.Y. 10016. Residents of New York, New Jersey and Pennsylvania must include sales tax. DO NOT SEND CASH.

YOU WON'T WANT TO READ
JUST ONE—KATHERINE STONE

ROOMMATES   (2156, $4.50)
No one could have prepared Carrie for the monumental
changes she would face when she met her new circle of
friends at Stanford University. Once their lives intertwined
and became woven into the tapestry of the times, they
would never be the same.

TWINS   (2646, $4.50)
Brook and Melanie Chandler were so different, it was hard
to believe they were sisters. One was a dark, serious, ambitious New York attorney; the other, a golden, glamourous,
sophisticated supermodel. But they were more than sisters—they were twins and more alike than even they knew
. . .

THE CARLTON CLUB   (2296, $4.50)
It was the place to see and be seen, the only place to be.
And for those who frequented the playground of the very
rich, it was a way of life. Mark, Kathleen, Leslie and
Janet—they worked together, played together, and loved
together, all behind exclusive gates of the *Carlton Club*.

*Available wherever paperbacks are sold, or order direct from the
Publisher. Send cover price plus 50¢ per copy for mailing and
handling to Zebra Books, Dept. 3133, 475 Park Avenue South,
New York, N.Y. 10016. Residents of New York, New Jersey and
Pennsylvania must include sales tax. DO NOT SEND CASH.*

Contemporary Fiction From
Robin St. Thomas

Fortune's Sisters   (2616, $3.95)

It was Pia's destiny to be a Hollywood star. She had complete self-confidence, breathtaking beauty, and the help of her domineering mother. But her younger sister Jeanne began to steal the spotlight meant for Pia, diverting attention away from the ruthlessly ambitious star. When her mother Mathilde started to return the advances of dashing director Wes Guest, Pia's jealousy surfaced. Her passion for Guest and desire to be the brightest star in Hollywood—pitted Pia against her own family—sister against sister, mother against daughter. Pia was determined to be the only survivor in the arenas of love and fame. But neither Mathilde nor Jeanne would surrender without a fight. . . .

Lover's Masquerade   (2886, $4.50)

New Orleans. A city of secrets, shrouded in mystery and magic. A city where dreams become obsessions and memories once again become reality. A city where even one trip, like a stop on Claudia Gage's book promotion tour, can lead to a perilous fall. For New Orleans is also the home of Armand Dantine, who knows the secrets that Claudia would conceal and the past she cannot remember. And he will stop at nothing to make her love him, and will not let her go again . . .

Taylor—made Romance From Zebra Books

WHISPERED KISSES (2912, $4.95/5.95)
Beautiful Texas heiress Laura Leigh Webster never imagined that her biggest worry on her African safari would be the handsome Jace Elliot, her tour guide. Laura's guardian, Lord Chadwick Hamilton, warns her of Jace's dangerous past; she simply cannot resist the lure of his strong arms and the passion of his *Whispered Kisses*.

KISS OF THE NIGHT WIND (2699, $4.50/$5.50)
Carrie Sue Strover thought she was leaving trouble behind her when she deserted her brother's outlaw gang to live her life as schoolmarm Carolyn Starns. On her journey, her stagecoach was attacked and she was rescued by handsome T.J. Rogue. T.J. plots to have Carrie lead him to her brother's cohorts who murdered his family. T.J., however, soon succumbs to the beautiful runaway's charms and loving caresses.

FORTUNE'S FLAMES (2944, $4.50/$5.50)
Impatient to begin her journey back home to New Orleans, beautiful Maren James was furious when Captain Hawk delayed the voyage by searching for stowaways. Impatience gave way to uncontrollable desire once the handsome captain searched *her* cabin. He was looking for illegal passengers; what he found was wild passion with a woman he knew was unlike all those he had known before!

PASSIONS WILD AND FREE (3017, $4.50/$5.50)
After seeing her family and home destroyed by the cruel and hateful Epson gang, Randee Hollis swore revenge. She knew she found the perfect man to help her—gunslinger Marsh Logan. Not only strong and brave, Marsh had the ebony hair and light blue eyes to make Randee forget her hate and seek the love and passion that only he could give her.

Available wherever paperbacks are sold, or order direct from the Publisher. Send cover price plus 50¢ per copy for mailing and handling to Zebra Books, Dept. 3133, 475 Park Avenue South, New York, N.Y. 10016. Residents of New York, New Jersey and Pennsylvania must include sales tax. DO NOT SEND CASH.